**It was like grabbing a live wire,
Bobbie thought as his lips closed over hers.**

And although common sense told her to run, she couldn't deny that death had been too recent a visitor in her life and his touch made her feel alive again.

His kiss sparked sensation all along her body, whipping up the need that had already been simmering between them. Shifting ever nearer, she laid her hand on his shoulder to center herself as her head swam from the force of the desire snaking through her body.

He was a wonderful kisser, skilled in the way he slipped his tongue in to play with hers and then teased her with a gentle bite of her lower lip.

She moaned at that, imagining his gifted mouth exploring her body. Wanting to discover other parts of him.

As she splayed her hand across his chest, the rapid beat of his heart drummed beneath her thumb before she moved to strum it across his hard nipple.

He groaned and the sound rumbled through her, creating an answering vibration between her legs. Making her want more.

"Touch me, Adam," she said, and was unprepared for his response.

———————————

"Utterly unique, original, and brilliant...Piñeiro is breaking the mold."
—Maggie Shayne, *New York Times* bestselling author,
on *Stronger than Sin*

"Second in this series and just as tightly written as the first. It stands alone. This is suspenseful and the passion is strong."   —*Romance Reviews Magazine*

SINS OF THE FLESH

"This has all the makings of a great paranormal romance—a beautiful heroine, a dark, sexy, and protective hero, and a compelling and relevant subplot."
     —*RT Book Reviews*

"Caridad Piñeiro never disappoints, and her new series looks to be a winner in every possible way. No author is better at crafting novels which explore the paranormal than Caridad Piñeiro. *Sins of the Flesh* expertly intertwines suspense and passion to create a spellbinding story of the paranormal."   —SingleTitles.com

"Page-turning action and sizzling love scenes as only Caridad Piñeiro can deliver!"
     —L. A. Banks, *New York Times* bestselling author

"Faster than the speed of light...an action-packed thriller that never takes a breath...Caridad Piñeiro provides another one of her super romantic suspense thrillers."
     —*Midwest Book Review*

"I can hardly wait for the next in this exciting new series to come out. This is as good as paranormal gets!"

—RomanceReviewsMag.com

"Captured my full attention with its too-human characters and its too-real plot. A fascinating, adrenaline-fueled read! I could not stop turning pages!"

—Debra Webb, national bestselling
author of *Everywhere She Turns*

"The beginning of what promises to be a fascinating series...If you're looking for a book that will grab your attention and keep it, get a copy of *Sins of the Flesh* today."

—RomRevToday.com

"The best romantic suspense I've read in years. It's truly her best book yet. Caridad has created a whole cast of characters who seem to live and breathe...Thankfully, *Sins of the Flesh* is first in a series."

—AmericanChronicle.com

"If you're feverish for a chilling scientific thriller with a sharp edge of romance, I prescribe *Sins of the Flesh* as a sexy, satisfying cure!"

—Jessica Anderson, award-winning
author of *Skykeepers*

ALSO BY CARIDAD PIÑEIRO

Sins of the Flesh
Stronger Than Sin

THE LOST

CARIDAD PIÑEIRO

FOREVER

NEW YORK   BOSTON

This book is a work of fiction. Names, characters, places, and incidents are the product of the author's imagination or are used fictitiously. Any resemblance to actual events, locales, or persons, living or dead, is coincidental.

Copyright © 2011 by Caridad Piñeiro Scordato
Excerpt from *The Claimed* copyright © 2011 by Caridad Piñeiro Scordato

Book design by Giorgetta Bell McRee

Forever
Hachette Book Group
237 Park Avenue
New York, NY 10017
Visit our website at www.HachetteBookGroup.com

Forever is an imprint of Grand Central Publishing.
The Forever name and logo is a trademark of Hachette Book Group, Inc.

The publisher is not responsible for websites (or their content) that are not owned by the publisher.

Printed in the United States of America

First Printing: August 2011

10 9 8 7 6 5 4 3 2 1

ATTENTION CORPORATIONS AND ORGANIZATIONS:
Most HACHETTE BOOK GROUP books are available at quantity discounts with bulk purchase for educational, business, or sales promotional use. For information, please call or write:

**Special Markets Department, Hachette Book Group
237 Park Avenue, New York, NY 10017
Telephone: 1-800-222-6747 Fax: 1-800-477-5925**

This book is dedicated to the brave men and women of the U.S. military and their families. Without you and the sacrifices you make, we could not enjoy the Liberty and Freedoms of this great Nation and for that we owe you an immense debt of gratitude.

THE LOST

PROLOGUE

El Paso, Texas, 1991

As darkness slowly fled from his eyes, the boy woke, his head aching and his body sore, as if he had been beaten. He looked around the room, but nothing in it seemed familiar. Nothing except the man slumped in the rocking chair beside him.

He remembered the man and some kind of accident, the boy thought, recalling the bodies, fire, and debris surrounding him the last time he had roused. He had been afraid, unsure of how he had gotten there in the midst of all the destruction. Wondering why he was alone because he was certain he had been with others.

A man and a woman. Close by. Holding his hand until...

An attack? he thought, not that he really remembered. He had a vague image of light so bright that it burned his eyes and face. Another memory suddenly came to him of flying through the air and hitting something hard. Possibly a wall.

Then he had been all alone until the man had come to save him.

A jingling sound intruded and the bed dipped as a big old beagle rested its paws on the edge of the mattress. The huffing sound of its breathing and the clang of the dog's tags as it shook its head woke the man.

Gingerly the man sat up, wincing from apparent stiffness. He scrubbed his face with his hands to wipe away the remnants of sleep. His dark eyes looked sad and tired, the boy thought. When the man realized that he was awake, he said, "How are you feeling?"

The boy shrugged and even that small movement brought discomfort as every muscle complained. "Hurts," he said, surprised by his own voice. He didn't remember what it sounded like. But then again, he didn't recall much of anything.

Except fear. Fear was the only real memory alive in his brain.

The man nodded and stood awkwardly, as if in pain himself. He gently urged the dog away from the bed with a soft nudge of his knee and a "Scat, Spottie." Then he faced him and said, "Why don't you lie back down while I get you some food..." His voice trailed off in question, but the boy didn't understand what he wanted.

"Your name, son. What's your name?"

The boy searched his brain, but couldn't find the answer to that simple question, much less any of the others ricocheting through his brain.

"I don't know."

With a resigned sigh, the man said, "Could be the shot you took to your head. It'll come back. Don't worry."

The boy lay down and as his head touched the pillow, he experienced tenderness at the back of his skull. He delicately rubbed his hand along the bump there, wondering how he had been hurt.

As soon as the man left the room, the beagle returned to the bed, but this time the dog scampered up right beside him. Almost as if sensing that he needed the comfort, the dog lay along his side and playfully butted his hand with the tip of its cold wet nose.

The dog's antics pulled a smile to his face. He stroked the dog's head, wondering if he'd had his own pet. There was something familiar about the dog's actions that cried out to him as the warmth of the animal's body seeped into his hand.

The boy welcomed the comforting warmth.

Unexpectedly the heat became even stronger, almost as if it had developed a life of its own. Beside him the dog whimpered, but the boy was too caught up in the surge of heat and vigor flowing through his body, driving away the assorted aches and pains.

With an almost tired groan, the dog's body relaxed and the beagle released a weary little breath. Was it sick? he wondered, but then heard a soft snore and realized the dog was asleep.

He jumped from the bed, but there was something weird as he landed on the floor. He could barely see past the dusty skirt along the bottom of the mattress and as he moved, the wood on the floor was cold on both his hands and feet. On his paws, he realized as he padded out of the room, the scent of the man alive in his nostrils as he tracked him to the kitchen.

The man was at the sink, beating eggs, and turned as the boy entered the room.

"What are you up to, Spottie? Excited about our guest?" Smiling, he came close, bent down, and rubbed his head.

The boy tried to speak, but only a low woof erupted from his mouth. Fear took hold and he barked again, hoping to reach the man and make him understand.

The man heard the almost urgent yaps and peered at him more closely. He narrowed his eyes to examine him and must have realized the dog was different now. Lurching upright, the man ran back to the bedroom, the boy following awkwardly on all fours.

The man jerked to a stop as he noted the beagle sprawled on the bed, its muscles twitching as it chased imaginary prey in its sleep. With a hesitant glance from the dog lying on the comforter to the one hopping excitedly beside him, the man pivoted on his heel, looking all around the room as he sought out the boy.

The boy let out another yowl and jumped up and down on his front paws, long nails clacking on the floor, wanting the man to understand that he was right there.

The man finally dropped to his knees and touched the boy's head. Trailed it down to cup the bottom of his long jowly jaw and urge his face upward. As the man's gaze connected with the deep emerald of the dog's eyes, the man's eyes widened in stunned surprise.

"Holy Mother of God," he whispered before scooping him up and holding him tight to his chest.

The boy let out a contented little mewl and wag of his tail at the comfort the embrace brought. The man would help him, the boy thought. And with his help, he would be home again soon.

CHAPTER
1

Twenty Years Later, Jersey Shore, New Jersey

Selina stood in the wash of the ocean, arms beckoning the sea breeze to sweep over her. The wind was like a living thing as she commanded it to circle around her and she fed from the power in its embrace. So different from the hot desert zephyrs to which she was accustomed. There was so much life from the wind's journey over the vast ocean shifting and swirling before her.

Selina could better understand now why this clan of Light Hunters had chosen to live here along the water. The ocean and all that flowed from it would be an excellent source to recharge their life energies. With such power nearby, they could avoid taking from the humans as they hid in plain sight amongst their possible prey.

Even as she absorbed the refreshing energy, Selina was aware of her husband's approach long before he slipped his arms around her waist and drew her against the lean body that she would never tire of exploring. From the first moment she had seen him nearly forty years ago, his power had called to her the way two sides of a magnet drew one other.

"You feel it, don't you?" Kellen said, but he wasn't referring to their bond. He, too, sensed the life force emanating from the nature all around them.

"It's hard not to sense such vitality. It makes me wonder why our ancestors chose the desert for our clan."

He shrugged and laid his chin against the top of her head. She was a tall woman, but Kellen was well over six feet and broad, nearly swallowing her up as he held her. There was comfort in that physical power, although Kellen understood she possessed the more powerful Hunter gift.

"They thought we would be safe there. Away from the humans and the Shadows," he replied, but there was a sadness in his tone that was impossible to miss. Their isolation in their desert commune had only made it easier for the Shadow Hunters to find them and attack. For nearly twenty years, Kellen had blamed himself for that fateful night and the loss of their son Kikin along with so many other members of their clan.

"We will find him this time. I know it." Selina turned in his arms and laid her hand along the side of his face. She glanced around the beachfront to make sure they were alone before allowing her power to join with his. As she did so, the energy created a shimmering glow wherever skin met skin. Their auras brightened and merged into an iridescent red-gold, and within her core the power awakened passion, dark and demanding.

"I want to believe that," Kellen said, dropping a kiss

at the edge of her brow before laying his forehead along hers. Beside her belly his desire was evident and growing stronger as their life forces melded with each other.

"Believe," she whispered against his lips, caught up in the exchange of energy, an exchange made even more potent by the love she had for him.

He groaned and tightened his hold until not an inch separated them and returned her kiss before promising, "I will not fail you."

Selina smiled, more hopeful than she had ever been that their search was finally over and their son Kikin would be with them soon. And when he was, the continued existence of both the Ocean and Desert clans of the Light Hunters would be guaranteed.

She knew that as surely as she knew the sun would rise each day to bless them with its power as it had for the many millennia that the Light Hunters had existed.

But for now, she wanted another kind of blessing, she thought as she took her husband's hand and led him home, awaiting the satisfaction that only joining with him could bring.

The energy poured off the collection of bodies and equipment occupying the vast expanse of the SolTerra facility. The force of it sang in the air, and as he closed his eyes and inhaled deeply, Adam Bruno experienced the rush as he absorbed that free-floating power into his body.

The strength of it surged along his nerve endings, making him almost light-headed from the vitality it created within his core. Lately the energy called to him more and more, almost demanding that he acknowledge his need for it.

Not that he had any choice but to do so. He could only ignore the energy for so long before a strange sense of emptiness developed within him. But replenishing the energy in his body had grown ever more difficult in the last few months, as his craving for it seemed to be growing exponentially. If he fed his need, the weight of the power would be heavy in his core and lead to pain that scratched at his brain like the noisy riff from a DJ mixing discordant tunes. At times the pain would be so great that he felt as if his brain might explode.

He had battled those moments with gradual discharges of power—a small pulse of light from his hand, like the flash of a camera—because releasing a full blast with his current potential could be dangerous, if not downright deadly. Because of that, Adam reined himself in, marshaling control and disconnecting from that cosmic outlet. Until he knew more about his abilities and how to use them, he could not give in to his growing hunger.

When he opened his eyes, he leaned forward with his hands on the metal railing, wondering if the people down below could sense the life forces wafting around them, oozing off their bodies and leaking from the arrays of solar panels and other alternate energy devices they were busy packing for his company.

SolTerra Systems. His baby. Maybe even his salvation if his collection of experts could somehow help him understand more about the nature of the energy. He hoped that with that knowledge he would be able to master his own unique powers—powers that were sometimes more curse than gift.

A footfall sounded behind him on the breezeway landing overlooking the warehouse floor.

Adam turned and encountered his father, Salvatore Bruno, the man who had adopted him nearly twenty years earlier.

His father took a step back, warning alive in his eyes.

Adam wondered why until he glanced over his father's shoulder and caught a glimpse of his own reflection in the glass doors of the breezeway. A bright silver and blue aura limned his body, but even more shocking was the intense neon green of his eyes. They were almost glowing in response to the energy he had absorbed just moments before. Contrary to what he had thought, the power was not under his dominion, making it very visible to any human in the vicinity. Closing his eyes and fisting his hands, he willed the energy back into his core, felt it skirt along his muscles and sinew to form a tight heavy ball in the center of his body.

When he opened his eyes, this time nothing but the reflection of a normal man greeted him.

Adam approached his father with a smile and held out his hand. An uneasy glance downward came before his father shook it, but as always the contact was brief. Uncertain. Maybe even a bit fearful, Adam thought, given the slight shudder in his father's body, until his father surprised him by clasping his shoulder for a longer hug.

"You cannot let others see you in that form," his father whispered close to Adam's ear, but didn't release him right away. The prolonged contact roused a vibration along each place where their bodies were in contact, as if the energy within Adam were searching for a way to escape, but encountering resistance in his dad's human body. When they broke apart, the sensation ended and a watery sheen glimmered in his father's eyes.

"Is something wrong? Are you sick?" Adam asked, concerned. His father hadn't been the same in the last couple of months. Ever since Salvatore had gone undercover for his latest assignment, there had been something different about him. Was it sadness or just weariness from the burden of responsibility? Adam wondered.

His father's smile surprisingly turned indulgent. "It's just that it's been a while since we've spent some time together, so I decided to come by and invite you out for your birthday."

"Birthday?" Adam said and tried to recall if he had made any plans for later in the week, although it really wasn't his birthday. Like everything about him—his name, his age, and what he was—his birthday was just another invention to try to make him seem like everyone else. But Adam was nothing like his father or any of the people around him.

"I thought you might want to have a nice dinner to celebrate turning twenty-six," his father offered, then thoughtfully added, "Unless you planned on going out with friends. Maybe even a girlfriend?"

A girlfriend? Adam thought cynically. He had women who warmed his bed on occasion, but Adam knew little about them. If there was one thing that he had discovered about his powers, it was that emotions totally messed up his control over them. That made involvement of any kind a risky proposition.

As for friends, he had business partners, but he wouldn't call them friends.

In short, he had no one who cared—other than his father—and maybe that was for the best, Adam thought. Relationships could only lead to complications that he could not risk.

"No friends, no girl, no plans," he responded, more curtly than he wanted.

Salvatore arched a brow and his mouth quirked into a sad smile. "Seriously, Adam. I understand, but don't you think it's time—"

Adam slashed his hand through the air, leaving behind a shimmering trail of light as anger ate into his restraint. Glancing around to make sure no one had seen, he shoved his hands into his pockets to keep from repeating his error.

"You can't understand, Dad. You can't for a moment imagine what it's like to be me," he said, his voice low and filled with anguish.

His father surprised him yet again by laying his hand on Adam's shoulder. "I can try, son. I hate seeing you alone and maybe, just maybe, there's a girl out there for you."

Adam snorted. "Really? You think there's someone—"

"There's a young CIA agent I know. Beautiful and smart. Trustworthy," his father said, surprising Adam yet again.

"Seems like you've been giving this a lot of thought. More thought than I have," he teased, although recently there had been a sense of discontent growing in Adam. He had attributed it to the ever more insistent call of the power, but maybe it was about something much more human than that. Maybe it was just about companionship and his lack thereof.

"I married when I was about your age. It didn't work out, but at first...It was worth it." The smile on his father's face confirmed just how fondly he recalled those early years with his ex-wife.

"I have been feeling a little different lately," he

confessed. After all, if he couldn't be honest with his father, who could he confide in?

"It's time you weren't so alone, Adam. Maybe you should start thinking about a wife. I'd even like some grandkids."

"Seriously, Dad," Adam rebuked, but his father just smiled and teased with a dip of his head, "You are getting up in years. Maybe I can introduce you to her."

"I'll think about it," he said with a chuckle and heartily clapped his dad on the shoulder, appreciating the heart-to-heart.

His father motioned toward the door of the breezeway with his hand and said, "I need to get back to work. How about I come by later tonight to firm things up?"

In his father's line of employment, long hours weren't unusual. In fact, it was almost weird to have him near and available, since normally his undercover work took him far from home, often for months at a shot.

"How are things at work?" Adam asked as he walked with his father across the breezeway connecting the Sol-Terra office building to the warehouse and laboratory facilities.

"Fascinating, but also depressing."

The admission shocked Adam. Although he and Salvatore were close, his CIA father rarely discussed the details of his cases. In all the time that Adam could remember, his father had never provided information about an assignment, much less shown any emotion about one. Which made Adam wonder why this case was so different.

"Depressing?" he speculated aloud, hoping to elicit more information.

A tired shrug barely lifted the fabric of the ill-fitting suit over his father's shoulders and was chased by a heavy, heartfelt sigh. "We lost another one."

Another death, Adam thought. As someone who lived with the specter of death every day . . .

"I'm sorry. Death is never easy, is it?" He gently grasped Salvatore's shoulder and squeezed it in condolence. As before, the hum of power beneath his hand as he touched his father tainted the heartfelt gesture.

"No, it isn't. I've got to run," Salvatore replied, growing uneasy. After another hesitant embrace, his father hurried from the SolTerra offices, leaving Adam in the gleaming granite and steel lobby of the building.

Alone except for the trio of security guards at the semicircular reception desk.

Alone being a state with which Adam was well familiar.

As he strolled to the elevators to return to his penthouse office, he wondered about his father's latest mission and why he was so emotionally involved with it. Maybe over a birthday dinner later in the week he could pry more information from his dad and discover what was affecting him so profoundly.

Adam headed to the elevator bank and up to his office. When he passed by the assorted cubicles filled with people at work, pride filled him, but couldn't eliminate the emptiness within him. Much as he had confessed to Salvatore, he felt different. There was a hole in his center that seemed to expand each day, much as the summons of the energy surrounding him grew harder to ignore.

At the door to his office, he forced a smile for his assistant. "Good morning, Sandy. I'm not to be disturbed," he advised and entered his office. Striding to his desk, he plopped into the state-of-the-art ergonomic chair and waved his hand over a button built into a panel underneath the stainless steel surface. Without physically touching the button, he sent a gentle surge of power to trip the switch, lowering the shades built into the exterior windows together with those along the interior glass wall of his office, closing him off from the world.

A world in which he really didn't belong.

With the natural daylight dimmed by the shades, the lights in his office automatically adjusted. Once again he sent a scintilla of his energy along the wires to power down the lights.

Steepling his hands on the arms of the chair, he brought them up to his mouth while he sat in the darkness, considering the exchange with his father. Salvatore had meant well, he knew. No father liked to see his child alone and Salvatore wasn't much different, even if Adam wasn't his flesh-and-blood son. But Adam couldn't envision getting involved with anyone, much less having a family. Not with the way he was. Not even with a beautiful, smart, trustworthy CIA agent his father felt might be right for him.

Within him the power grew heavy again in response to the emotion troubling him. If he didn't get the energy under control, its weight would continue to grow, creating that vicious static in his head. The first buzz of that noise was already setting up shop in his brain, and there was only one way to tire the beast so that he could contain it.

Raising his hands, he outstretched them and focused. Between them a pinpoint of light blossomed, and as Adam centered himself on that dot, it grew in size. Tendrils of energy slipped from his hands and danced around his wrists before they swam through the air toward that solitary point of light.

Solitary as he was, but not for long, Adam thought. Under his direction, the wisps of energy tangled and weaved together, nurturing that pinpoint until it formed a silver-blue orb about the size of a golf ball. Its light gleamed brightly and reflected off the polished surface of his desk, creating a halo of light.

Inside him the burden of the power lessened, providing a calming release. He pushed yet more power from inside him into the orb, experiencing a growing lightness of being as he discharged the energy he had gathered earlier.

The orb slowly blossomed in size from golf ball to softball. Adam imagined tossing it up and down and the ball bounced in the air accordingly.

Although he was capable of absorbing energy and creating these balls, it was little more than an amusement. He had no clue what he was supposed to do with such abilities. Until he understood that, what he could do was no better than a cheap parlor trick.

Frustrated, he ripped his hands away and the ball stretched flat as the energy clung to him, feeling almost tacky and elastic before something snapped. With a firework shower of light that dissipated some of the energy, the remaining power surged back into him.

The weight of it filled him, less than before, since he had expended some energy with his sideshow display, but still demanding. It was almost as if the power needed something from him. Something more than he could provide on his own.

If he had been a woman, he might have said it was some biological clock ticking, warning him that time was fleeting. But at twenty-five, almost twenty-six, his life had barely begun. Maybe, as his father had hinted, it was time for him to do more than just work, he thought. Maybe that was what was pulling at him so. Not the energy within and around him, but something easily explicable and certainly more human: loneliness.

With another zap, he flipped the switch and the shades along the exterior windows rose, allowing the bright spring sun to enter. Spring always contained the promise of so many new beginnings.

Hell, even the squirrels knew that spring was the time to mate and procreate. Adam smiled and thought, *Maybe it's time*.

CHAPTER
2

Salvatore sat in his car, staring at his cell phone. The heat increased within the small interior with each second that he delayed making the call.

He knew that once he did so, his son's life might not ever be the same. But then again, his son's life had never been just like everyone else's. From the moment Salvatore had found him in the desert, Adam's life had changed. When Salvatore had realized that the young boy possessed special powers, Adam's destiny had been determined and Salvatore's dream had been born.

Genesis, he thought. If he made this call he could finally get the wheels rolling on his project. To do so, however, meant betraying Adam, but that act had been set in stone long ago. It had never been a question of *if* Salvatore would be disloyal, just of when.

As he took a long last look at the SolTerra building, he noted that the shades on his son's fifth-floor office suite were closed tightly. He imagined what Adam might be doing inside. Was he playing with those weird balls of energy or just reading a report from one of his engineers? Probably the energy, he thought, recalling the state Adam had been in when Salvatore had arrived—all charged up with power.

Power that could be deadly to someone, which was why Salvatore must act now, before anyone got hurt.

Using the speed dial, he phoned the man who had come to him barely a month ago, claiming to know about his son and the unique abilities he possessed. Salvatore had been dubious at first, until the man had given him a little demonstration, a private light show disturbingly similar to Adam's, from the orbs of energy to the intense aura and glowing eyes. Then the man had teleported from one side of the room to the other. If Adam possessed that power, Salvatore had not yet witnessed it.

He had gone to meet the man—Alexander Sombrosa—in his New York office, or rather, office building, located on Sixth Avenue in the heart of the high-rent business area close to Central Park. Either the Sombrosa money was capable of buying a great deal of information or one of Sombrosa's people had used his powers to break into the CIA building and obtain copies of a number of Salvatore's CIA files, including a dummy file for Genesis. The real one was in Salvatore's home and contained the details of how he had planned to use Adam to create another race of individuals with Adam's incredible capabilities.

"Well?" was all that Alexander said as he answered the phone.

"I mentioned the possibility of meeting one of my agents to Adam."

"And how was that received?" Alexander asked, the cultured tone of his voice droll.

Annoyed by Alexander's seemingly cavalier attitude, Salvatore replied, "Neutral would be the best description."

Silence followed and Salvatore could picture the fine Mr. Sombrosa in his office, pacing high above the crowds in a suit that likely cost more than Salvatore made in a month. Sombrosa's plans were not so far removed from Salvatore's. Bring Adam back into the fold of his people and have him mate with one of their more powerful females to secure the continuation of their race.

Salvatore suspected Alexander was pondering his next move, as if he and Adam were nothing more than pawns on a chessboard. Salvatore wasn't a man who liked getting played. Deciding to take command, he said, "I'd rather not push right now. Adam can be stubborn."

"Just remember that time, while not critical, is of importance. The growth of Adam's power is logarithmic now as the Equinox approaches. He will need our help to master it and keep him from harming others," Alexander replied, sounding as pedantic as a professor bored with his own lecture.

If I believe you, Salvatore thought, still uneasy about the alliance he had formed with virtual strangers. He had not done it lightly, but joining with them could open up a world of possibilities for Adam's future and for his as well.

"I understand the urgency, Alexander, but I know my son—"

"Not your son, Salvatore. He belongs to us," Alexander retorted sharply, finally displaying some emotion.

Anger rose quickly. He might have taken Adam, but his reasons had not been selfish. At least, not at first.

"When *my son* is ready, he will return home."

Determined to have the last word, he hung up.

Rich and powerful men like Alexander Sombrosa always wanted to call the shots, but this time he would play by Salvatore's rules. That meant waiting until Salvatore thought Adam was good and ready to meet the woman who would help Salvatore launch Genesis. Until then, Alexander and his crew would have to wait.

Alexander stared at the phone, rage building inside him until the emotion overwhelmed his control. A blast of power fried the cell phone in his hand and sent a shower of sparks flying into the air.

"I gather it didn't go well," Maya said with a smirk as she sashayed toward him and then leaned her delicious derriere on the edge of his desk.

His son's fiancée was dressed all in black, from the skin-tight leather pants to the diaphanous see-through shirt thrown over a lace camisole that showed off her marvelous endowments. The outfit screamed "Touch me" and he wasn't about to disappoint.

He tossed his melted cell phone onto his desk and swung around to stand in the Vee formed by her open-legged stance.

She glanced up at him, her eyes as black as her outfit and the long silky strands of her hair. A murky red-black aura surrounded her, powerfully large. From the moment he had slipped into the space of her aura, her life force had embraced him. Now as he butted his hips against her core, the energy grew ever more demanding as it awaited another kind of joining.

He cradled her gorgeous heart-shaped face in his hands and whispered, "The human could not convince his son to see you."

"Maybe because I should be the one doing the convincing," she said and smiled again, a confident sexy smile that communicated awareness of her power over men in general and, of course, over him. Maya's unique ability was manipulating sexual energy and she used it quite capably to bend most men to her will.

She released a little bit of that power now, wanting to control him by creating need in him—the clan's Añaru. If she had been a Hunter man and shown such arrogance, he might have killed her for it. But he wasn't about to miss this opportunity, since it was clear she had just fed and his own life force needed recharging.

"Really? You think you're that irresistible?" he teased, playing with her the way a cat toyed with a mouse.

"Your son thinks so," she said as she lowered her hand and cupped him through the fabric of his suit. He sucked in a breath as her skilled hands aroused him and she sent a wave of energy skittering through his body, nearly buckling his knees.

"Do not play with me, Maya," he warned, only willing to let her push him so far.

Her gaze slipped for a second to where she was busy giving him a hand job, then back to meet his, that knowing smile in place again. "Forgive me, Añaru. I did not mean to displease. Maybe a little punishment is demanded?"

As if to prove her point, she slipped off the desk, turned and tilted up her backside, ready for a spanking.

Alexander nearly came right then and there. He was past the first two triads of his life and his control was no longer what it should be, especially with his life force needing a charge. But he wasn't going to pass up a moment like this, even if she was his son's fiancée and the bait for the stupid human's Light Hunter son.

"I am your Añaru and you will obey me. Take off your pants," he said and slapped her backside playfully.

Maya grinned again and with an enticing shimmy and wriggle, skimmed down her leather pants, but not before giving him a peek at the tiny thong beneath before it, too, came off. Leaning on the desk, she spread her legs, providing a view of her cleanly shaven sex, glistening with moisture. As she glanced over her shoulder at him, she dared another inviting little wiggle of her hips.

"My Añaru. I live to obey," she almost purred.

He groaned and his erection jerked. He grabbed it to contain himself as he quickly freed himself from his pants and, with no further preliminaries, drove into her. As their bodies merged, the energy flowed around them and between them, insinuating itself into their lovemaking.

She gasped as he filled her, and the moan that followed was one of pure feminine pleasure. He pumped into her, her soft little cries driving him onward as he rode her. Pounding himself into her, he reached up and grabbed her breasts, squeezing painfully, but she urged him on.

"Añaru, more. Please more," she said and he sought out the tight nubs of her nipples and pinched them hard.

"Añaru," Maya cried out as a climax ripped through her and milked him to his own stunning release.

He dropped onto her, pinning her to the hard surface of the desk, his breathing heavy, as he said, "You are a bitch, Maya."

She laughed, unfazed by his comment, probably because it was true. With a gentle push of energy, she lifted him from her body and skipped away to rearrange her clothes.

Alexander glanced at her and grew aroused once

again, but tamped down his desire. She had fucked the Añaru and not him, Alexander, but the Añaru would not be satisfied with a simple ride.

"Come here, Maya," he said and her eyes widened in surprise at the harsh command in his voice.

"Have I displeased?" she said with a little-girl pout on her magnificent face.

"I am hungry," he said, and nothing further was needed.

As a Shadow Hunter before their Añaru, she knew exactly what that meant. With a defiant tilt, she said, "I just fed—"

"I know." She had clearly drained some human of life energy, judging by the strength of the power that sang through her, as tempting as her body. He laid his hand on the bare skin just above the swell of her breast and focused. Little tendrils of light sprang from his hand, forming a web over the smooth, creamy surface of her skin and then digging deep into her flesh. Like the spider for which the Añaru had been named, the web ensnared her life force, sucking it from her body along the fine strands of light, feeding him with its power.

She moaned then, but with pain, as he transferred her vitality to himself, restoring his energy and driving away the patches of pox-marked skin hidden beneath the fine wool of his very expensive suit.

As he watched, a pox mark erupted at a spot close to his life-sucking tendrils. Even though she had recently recharged, it was not enough to sustain him and keep her own illness at bay. The smallpox virus that had incorporated itself into the Shadow Hunters' DNA when the conquistadores had landed in the New World needed constant feeding to be kept under control. The only way to keep the illness away for any length of time was to feed from a Quinchu, one of the Light Hunters' high priests and priestesses.

Maya realized the pox was emerging, too, as she glanced down and saw the first ugly red pustule form. Her eyes widened with dismay and she laid her hand on his chest and pleaded, "I beg you, Añaru."

If it had been anyone else, the plea would have gone unheard. But it was Maya, and she was key for his plans for Salvatore's stolen son. He pulled back the web of power, interrupting his feeding. He would find someone else later that night to fulfill what remained of his unsatisfied need. Maybe one of the unsuspecting humans down below on the city streets.

"Thank you, Añaru," she said as she stepped away as if to make sure he would not resume his snacking.

"Alexander. My name is Alexander," he said, almost weary of his role as the head of the local Shadow Hunter clan. Unlike his father before him, Alexander cared little for the job of governing. He only enjoyed the benefits that flowed from it. Over the centuries his Shadows had accumulated wealth with their assorted powers, providing him with a lavish lifestyle and sensual pleasures like his little tryst with Maya.

She narrowed her eyes and considered him, stepped close and cradled his jaw. Passing her thumb across his lips, she said, "Until later, Alexander." She brushed a quick kiss on his lips and left in a hurry, clearly not wanting to risk that he would change his mind and start feeding from her once more.

Alexander watched her go and then sat back down at

his desk. The smell of fried electrical bits reminded him of the earlier phone call and he considered his options.

He could kidnap Salvatore's Light Hunter son. If the rumors were true, he was the son of a powerful Quinchu couple, which meant that he likely possessed their great strength.

But Alexander wanted Adam to be cooperative. Getting him together with Maya at the right time was key to what both he and Salvatore wanted—a new generation of Hunters filled with amazing abilities. With Adam's Equinox upon him as he neared the end of his first triad, Alexander hoped that a union with Maya would produce a child that could be used to eliminate the human pox that had contaminated his race millennia earlier and stolen so much from them.

But success in that mission meant partnering with Salvatore, who had a similar wish for Adam. If their plan didn't work, Alexander could just suck the life from Adam and fuck Maya again himself, perhaps breeding that amazing power into whatever little brat came from such a union.

The latter would be the easier thing, and Alexander recognized that, sadly, easier was what he usually did. It was one of the reasons he and his son Christopher were so distant.

Christopher was more like his grandfather, industrious and overachieving. His son loathed Alexander's easygoing and sometimes careless ways, believing that they were leading to the decline of their Shadow Hunter clan.

His conscience pricked by the likely condemnation that would result if he acted rashly, Alexander tabled the thought of draining Adam. If there was to be an end to the curse staining the Shadow Hunters, it would be through him and through Salvatore's Genesis project, so he cautioned himself to be patient.

At least this one time.

He would wait for Salvatore to keep his end of the bargain and deliver a willing Adam—ideally, close to the Equinox when Adam's fertility and power would be greatest. It was in these years in and around the first triad of life that a Hunter was meant to mate. Even though Adam had not grown up with the benefits of a Hunter clan, either Shadow or Light, there was no escaping the nature of their race.

The hunger for power would grow in Adam until he found his mate and created new life. Powerful life, if he was paired with an equally strong female Hunter.

Genesis, Alexander thought, kind of liking the idea of playing God.

CHAPTER
3

Tighter. That's it, Bobbie. You can do it," the physical therapist urged as Bobbie Carrera struggled to squeeze the flat rubber circle. She had managed to almost get her hand closed around the flexible ring when the muscles in her forearm and hand spasmed, forcing her to release the grip trainer.

Frustration slammed through her, but her PT was quick to respond with positive encouragement.

"Not to worry, Bobbie. Your grip strength is improving with each visit. It's just a matter of time—"

"Before I'm back to normal," she muttered.

"Before you're *stronger,* and that's something to be proud of," her PT clarified.

"Right. Stronger," she parroted, reminding herself that normal was a word she could no longer use for herself. Bobbie was never going to be normal again. The IED that had exploded close to her had stolen that possibility along with so many others. She flushed away the pity party and focused on the next set of exercises her PT had planned for today's session. With each lift, push, and pull, she was slowly growing stronger.

She would be *almost* normal, she told herself.

When her session with the PT was finished, she thanked him, picked up her cane, and gingerly walked to one of the pieces of equipment they had not used during their workout.

She still had over an hour to kill until her brother was done with his internship nearby and could drive her home. Time enough to work what parts of her were still whole, she thought, and proceeded to use a mix of free weights and the exercise machines until sweat dripped from every pore of her body. With the last clank of the weights and her strength waning, she called it a day and headed to the showers.

The locker room was relatively empty, but Bobbie wasn't keen on revealing her body to others. There were too-visible scars from the explosions that had killed almost all of her platoon. Only her platoon leader and ex-lover—Gil Martinez—had survived the attack. Although she wasn't sure you could call being comatose and connected to a bunch of machines living.

She had fared much better, although her doctors had been shocked at that. Besides the wound to her arm, her leg had been damaged and there had been massive internal injuries. To hear the doctors talk, her abdomen had been nothing more than a complex jigsaw puzzle that had taken hours to piece back together.

She gathered up her clothes and toiletries and walked toward the shower stall, where she hung her cane and towel on a hook. She undressed behind the curtain of the stall, prepped the shower, and stepped in. Squirting a fragrant shower gel into her hand from a nearby dispenser, she lathered up, thinking about how lucky she was to be alive.

Alive but alone, she told herself. Lately, as her body grew stronger, so did the urge to not be alone. As she ran her hands across her body, feeling the slickness of the soap along her skin, she recalled how it had felt to be loved. To feel a man's hands along her skin, stroking it. Giving her pleasure, she thought, as she cupped her breasts and her nipples tightened beneath her fingers.

She ran her hands across the tips and between her legs came an insistent tension that needed release after so many months of solitude. That loneliness was weighing on her, growing more demanding with each passing day.

As she caressed her breasts, she slid her hand toward her center to seek assuagement. But as she skimmed her soapy palm down her torso, the ridges of the scars along her midsection seemed as large as the craters on the moon.

For months she had told herself that it didn't matter. In truth, she had been so busy just trying to do the everyday things like walk or pick up a glass that something so far removed as being intimate with a man or having babies hadn't been on her radar.

But suddenly images of her sister Liliana's very pregnant belly flashed through her mind along with the faces of her dead men. Life and death, twined together in her current existence like two serpents, never to be separated.

She had survived, but inside there were parts of her that were lifeless, and nothing could change that. The reality of that stabbed deep, more painful than her many injuries. Drove her to bury her face in her hands and fight back the tears.

Tears would accomplish nothing, she reminded herself. They wouldn't bring back her men or heal Gil. The tears wouldn't give her the babies and happy life she had envisioned for herself before joining the Marines, the American Dream kind of existence that her family had embraced.

Stiffening her spine, she forced herself to rise, finished showering, and dressed in the curtained area outside the stall.

When she had mustered enough control to meet her brother, she took a deep breath and put on her game face, not wanting him to see her upset. She grabbed her cane with her right hand—her left was too weak to be of much help—and hoisted herself to her feet. A slight pulling sensation came along her midsection. She rubbed at the spot directly above the line where she had been stitched back together like a rag doll. The ache calmed and she exited the gym facility.

Outside, the early spring morning held a hint of the summer heat to come. Bright sun drenched the tree-lined parking lot and as a slight ocean breeze kicked up, a shower of white petals drifted down from the flowering maples along the edge of the lot.

Bobbie paused to savor the brightness of the azure sky, fresh spring leaves bursting with life and the ivory blossoms up in the trees falling on her like giant snowflakes. Before her injuries, she might not have taken the time to appreciate the beauty in an ordinary day, but now she did. Now she appreciated every minute of the second life with which she had been gifted.

With a deep breath, she lifted her face to the sun, absorbing the wonder of the day, feeling the energy of it soak into her, revitalizing her tired body.

Then she began her trek across the parking lot to Tony's car. Even though her gait was guarded, she was thankful for the mobility after her first bedridden months back home. She had hated being confined to a hospital bed, and no matter how painful those initial steps, she had been determined to move on her own two feet.

Reaching the other side of the parking lot, she walked toward her younger brother Tony's "baby"—a vintage Chevrolet Camaro that Tony had restored over the years with their older brother Mick's help. Although Bobbie could drive, she still felt a little uncertain at times behind the wheel. Since her PT schedule had coincided with her brother's internship and the gym was across from his workplace, it only made sense to carpool.

As she waited, Bobbie considered the building where Tony was working. It was not what she had expected in what had once been an older and run-down part of town. The office building and adjacent lab and warehouse space were ultramodern and elegant.

SolTerra. Sun and earth, Bobbie thought, as she scrutinized the large sign above the entrance to the gleaming glass and steel buildings. Beside the name was a distinctive logo combining fanciful images of two orbs— probably a Sun and Earth—joining together. The sign was made of what looked like stainless steel and brass and was quite stylized, almost a work of art. The Sun had a number of squiggly rays spreading outward from its surface while the Earth boasted a series of concentric circles and lines. At the place where the orbs merged, the two symbols melded to create a surprisingly harmonious design.

The logo fit the place, she thought, impressed by the way the modern buildings blended with the carefully maintained natural environment around them. A peaceful synergy of man and nature, Bobbie thought.

She leaned against the bumper of her brother's vehicle, careful not to scratch the paint while taking advantage of the relaxing view as she waited for Tony. It was early afternoon and the employee lot was full, but with little activity. Most people were probably at work within the buildings.

As she passed the time, appreciating the serenity of the compound and the warmth of the spring sun seeping into her body, a twentysomething man exited the office building. His head was buried in his phone as he texted while walking, his long strides quickly closing the distance to the parking lot.

Smartly dressed in a charcoal-gray raw silk suit and snowy white shirt, he stood quite a few inches over six feet, with broad shoulders that narrowed into lean hips and those long fluid legs. Sandy hair was stylishly gelled into place and sun-streaked. Handsome, from what she could see of his downturned face as he approached. An aquiline nose, sharp cheekbones, and well-defined jaw rounded out the impressive package.

But there was something even more compelling that drew her—the impression of innate power that radiated from him. Its presence wafted all around him, demanding that she pay attention.

Gil had possessed that kind of power. She supposed that was why he had made such a good leader. The men and women under his command had sensed that energy and respected it. She, on the other hand, had loved taming that power in bed.

This man harbored that same aura of leadership, but in spades, she thought, finding herself more and more intrigued the closer that he came. Her earlier desire rekindled as she imagined how such strength might satisfy.

As he finally raised his head from his phone, their gazes collided. He had eyes the color of the shadows in a rain forest, verdant and filled with mutable hues. His eyes widened in surprise as she continued to engage his gaze, and something inside Bobbie couldn't resist taking a step toward him.

It was almost as if he was a magnet drawing her in, but she wasn't a piece of some malleable base metal, she thought, checking the impulse to continue to his side. Resisting the pull, she leaned back against the car and waited for him to make the next move.

CHAPTER
4

Adam didn't know what to make of the attractive young woman standing in the parking lot, eyeballing him.

He hadn't noticed her when he had first left the building, too involved in the e-mail exchange spewing onto his smartphone. But as he had gotten closer to the woman, he'd discerned a different vibe in the air, almost like the low hum of power emanating from a live electrical wire. That made him pause to search out the source of that buzz, and there she had been.

Tall and rangy, with eyes the color of whiskey, he thought, as he met her arresting gaze. All around her was a bright aura of sapphire blue, more powerful than any he had ever perceived in another human.

He blinked, thinking it had to be a figment of his imagination or possibly glare from the car behind her. Although it was an older vehicle, it was buffed to extreme shininess and the chrome trimmings glinted a silvery blue in the sunlight.

That was it, he told himself, and yet he felt as if there was almost a physical connection stretching across the twenty or so feet that separated them, a connection that she must be experiencing also, he thought, as her aura seemed to brighten the longer they stared at each other. It limned her curvaceous body. An amazingly womanly, but powerful body.

She took a step in his direction and he found himself doing the same, his gaze still locked on hers. All of his attention focused on the fascinating woman just a few feet away. He was so intent on reaching her that he failed to notice the van parked in the visitor area and directly in his path. He didn't observe the side passenger door sliding open, but he couldn't ignore the oversized man who exited to block his way.

Adam was tall, but this man had quite a few inches on him in both height and width. His arms, neck, and chest were massive and corded with thick, powerful muscles quite capable of inflicting serious physical damage. The man stood on legs with thighs as thick as tree trunks and most likely as immobile.

As Adam examined the man's features, he noted the ragged scar running along the man's jawline. The scar was silver with age, but no less fearsome for that.

Adam jerked back a step, feeling threatened not only by the man's physical presence, but also by the blood-red aura of dark energy surrounding him. The air around Adam crackled with it, so potent was the force.

Suddenly a similar sensation raked the hackles along the back of his neck, propelling a chill through his body.

As Adam turned, he realized there was another man behind him, as big and brawny as the first. His body was encircled with a crimson aura that screamed trouble.

"What do you want?" Adam asked. If this was a mugging, he would give them whatever they needed to avoid injury not only to himself, but to the young woman who was suddenly heading his way, her gait hurried and yet awkward.

He realized she was using a cane and physically disabled, but she was still proceeding toward him, unmindful of the threat. That only made her even more vulnerable, which meant he had to act carefully to protect her.

"We want you, Mr. Bruno," the first man answered and laid his thick hands on Adam's shoulders. With that first contact a blast of power surged through Adam.

It was like being stung by a jellyfish, only one with ten thousand volts, Adam thought, as his body jerked from the shock, and burning pain erupted at the spot where the man had grabbed him. With each millisecond that passed, Adam grew weaker. He had to break free before the man drained him of life. Bringing his arms up between the other man's outstretched arms, Adam shoved outward, dislodging the man's hands from his shoulders.

An intense echo of power reverberated from the contact and sparks flew like metal striking metal. The man staggered backward as he experienced the jolt.

Adam was no sooner free than the second man encircled him with his arms, sending yet another shock into Adam's body. The electricity raced through him, bringing more pain and robbing him of strength once again. As his knees began to buckle, Adam summoned his waning strength and tossed the man behind him up and over his body. His attacker landed with a heavy thud on the ground beside his friend, who was still recovering from the earlier blast Adam had released.

Adam somehow stayed on his feet, swaying, his mind disoriented from the electrical shocks, more potent than those from any stun gun. In response, the power inside him screamed to be set free, but before he could command it, the two men were upon him, lethal energy coursing from their touch, threatening to overwhelm him.

Bobbie witnessed the man stagger as his two assailants renewed their hold. She didn't have time to ponder why he wasn't fighting anymore. Instinct told her to act as she finally reached the trio.

She smashed her cane down across the arm of the man closest to her. It was like hitting a concrete block. The force of her blow reverberated painfully up the cane, but she managed to break the assailant's grip.

The assailant grunted in pain and leaned away, exposing his front. Bobbie swung her cane like a baseball bat, hitting him squarely across the nose.

Blood spewed over her and the other two men as he staggered back, holding his face and howling from the blow.

Home run, she thought, and turned back to the fray.

"Bitch," his friend said, and released his captive to launch a hook at her face. She blocked his punch with her damaged left forearm, ignoring the searing pain when his strike landed on weakened muscle and fragile bone. Reaching past the pain, she shot out with her right hand to land a vicious chop to his windpipe that had him backpedaling, gasping for air.

But only for a few precious seconds.

The man charged her, and Bobbie braced for impact,

aware she was no match for someone his size in her current condition but hoping she'd be able to use his momentum and weight against him. But before her assailant could come any closer, the handsome man seemed to come out of his stupor. One moment he was feet away and then in a blur of light, he intercepted the man in midair and tackled him to the ground.

Stunned by his speed, Bobbie watched in awe as their bodies went down hard in a sprawl of arms and legs. But before anything else could happen, the shouts of people running from the SolTerra building toward the commotion caught the attention of their two attackers.

The man on the ground scrambled to his feet and shuffled back to stand beside his broken-nosed friend. The two men hesitated for a moment as if wondering if they could overcome the crowd swarming toward them. But then the taller, older one Bobbie had bloodied jerked his head in the direction of the van.

One moment they were before her and then in the blink of an eye, they were streaks of light disappearing through the open door of the van. With the squeal of tires and burning rubber, the vehicle jerked into reverse and then sped away, sideswiping a few cars at the far end of the lot as their attackers made their escape.

"Mr. Bruno, are you okay?" a security guard asked as he came running up to them, the radio in his hand squawking with chatter.

The guard reached for the young man—Mr. Bruno, Bobbie assumed—but he waved him off and gingerly came to his feet.

"I'm okay," he said, and whirled to face her, concern etched on his features.

When he took note of the way she was cradling her left arm, he said, "Damn it, you're hurt."

Before she could respond, he touched her, barely grazing her arm with the tips of his fingers, lightly brushing the scarred skin that hid muscle and bone ruined by the shrapnel that had torn into her after the explosion.

An intense tingle danced along the path of his fingers, and for a moment, she thought she detected a glimmer of deep blue light where his skin touched hers. As she had before, she experienced the pull of power and a connection stronger than any she had felt before. Beneath his fingers, her skin was growing warmer, and a prickly sensation spread upward, growing more potent.

Her heart raced as the heat multiplied quickly throughout her body. Between her legs desire rose heavy and unbidden. As her gaze met his, the darkening of those changeling emerald eyes suggested he was experiencing the passion also.

She jerked away, unnerved by the sensations buffeting her body, afraid of the inexplicable attraction arising between them, and yet still embarrassed that he had noticed her weakness and touched her injuries. Judging from his clothing and looks, he was a man used to perfection and the finer things in life. Even before her wounds, he would likely have never given her a first glance, much less a second. They were from two different worlds that just skirted each other, interacting only when the one needed their lawns mowed or some cleaning done.

"I'm fine," she lied, the stinging sensation from his touch still alive on her, almost akin to pins and needles. The tingle and heat continued up her arm and she rubbed at it, wishing it would go away, along with the intense throb of want that had blossomed with his touch.

He tracked her movements and seemed almost taken aback by his earlier actions. Self-consciously, he also rubbed his hands together as if regretting that he had touched her. Bending, he picked up her cane and handed it to her, apparently in lieu of a more traditional handshake as he said, "Adam Bruno. And you're..."

"Roberta Carrera." She accepted the cane from his hand and leaned on it heavily. As the unwanted desire fled her body, a dull, painful pressure developed at the small of her back along with a slight pull threading along her midsection. Assisting him in her debilitated condition had taken its toll.

"Carrera?" Adam murmured, wondering if there was some connection to an intern he had recently hired, but before he could ask, he heard a concerned, "Excuse me," from the group of people gathered beside them.

Looking at the crowd, he noticed Tony Carrera battling his way through the pack to stand beside the woman. There was no denying the resemblance. There was also no denying that like his sister, Tony possessed an aura of power, but it was barely visible. Just a slight glow of a faded denim blue, which Adam might not have even noticed under normal circumstances.

But he couldn't fail to detect it now as he considered them. Brother and sister were of a like height and athletically built, although Roberta was an inch or so shorter than Tony's six feet. They had similar faces, with creamy olive skin and brown hair. Roberta's hair was lighter, though, almost caramel-colored, and tumbled down to her shoulders in thick waves.

On Tony the features and coloring were handsome, while on Roberta...

Superb, he thought, and once again had to fight back the intense need that had arisen from the simple stroke of his fingers across her skin. But when he refocused his attention on her face, he detected the pain in her eyes and the tense furrow at the bridge of her nose.

"Bobbie, are you okay?" Tony asked, and laid a hand on his sister's arm.

Bobbie, he thought, thinking that it suited her. There was something too schoolmarmish about Roberta; Bobbie inspired visions of a reckless tomboy, but one who could also dress up like a lady. He'd seen that wild side today as she had charged to his aid, courageous and impulsive.

When Bobbie finally answered her brother, her voice was tight. "I need to get home."

Feeling guilty that she had been hurt because of him and wanting to further explore the unusual connection between them, Adam motioned to his building. "If you need medical care—"

"I'm fine," she said from behind gritted teeth, and took an unsteady step toward the older-model Chevrolet beside which she had been standing when he had first noticed her.

Tony glanced at him uneasily, a combination of concern and condemnation in his eyes, but didn't say anything. Adam was the boss, and in the corporate world Tony could ill afford to upset him, but Adam didn't run his ship like that.

"Please let me know how she is." Adam handed Tony a business card with his personal contact information. With a curt nod, Tony chased after his sister, and as he caught up to her, he solicitously placed his arm around her waist, offering her additional support.

"Mr. Bruno. Is there anything I can do?" the guard beside him asked as the group that had congregated around them started to disperse now that the action was over.

"Please get me the security tapes of the parking lot area for the last hour," he replied and stalked back toward the SolTerra office building. As he did so, he whipped out his phone and texted a message to the engineers he had been supposed to meet to discuss a new hybrid battery technology. He had been excited about their work and possibly acquiring the knowhow, but would have to postpone their meeting until another day. Given what had just happened, the novel process now seemed almost inconsequential.

He needed to find out more about the men who had tried to grab him and why they possessed powers so similar to his. An electric touch and something he hadn't even known he possessed—the ability to race through several feet in just milliseconds. He didn't know how he had done it, but he had, almost as if his body had moved at the speed of light, or just transported, like in an old episode of *Star Trek*.

He needed to explore that ability in greater depth, but just as important, he needed to get to know Bobbie Carrera and understand what kind of woman would rush to his help. What kind of woman carried such an unusual aura, and how could a simple touch rouse such emotions in him?

Want for sure, but also completeness. The nagging unrest he had been experiencing earlier and he had ascribed to an age-related countdown had stopped ticking in that moment when skin had met skin and desire had arisen. With her gone, the emptiness was back, but not for long, Adam thought.

He intended to find out every little thing he could about the intriguing Bobbie Carrera.

CHAPTER
5

Somehow Bobbie made it to Tony's car.

The weird pins and needles were still stinging all along her left arm along with a bit of lingering heat and some discomfort in her abdomen. The worst of the hurt was at the small of her back. The dull pressure there had blossomed into a knot of pain so powerful, tears stung at her eyes.

With just a quick glance as he helped her into the passenger seat, Tony knew better than to ask how she was. He knew she hated being sick and weak. That she hated relying on others, because she wasn't used to needing help. Bobbie had always been the one who took care of others, not the other way around.

As Tony pulled out of the parking spot and drove away, the car rolled up and over a speed bump. The jerky motion sent even greater waves of agony through Bobbie, dragging a long, low moan from her.

"Bobbie? What can I do?" Tony finally asked, shooting a nervous side glance her way.

Tears running down her face, Bobbie could manage only a short request before curling up into a tight ball.

"Just take me home, please."

She gathered what strength was left in her and focused, staving off the pain as best as she could, chastising herself for ignoring common sense to assist some stranger who hadn't really needed her help anyway.

Not really a stranger, but Tony's boss, Adam Bruno, she thought, liking the sound of his name in her head, and remembering the color of his eyes—an emerald green that seemed alive with the nature around him.

Another bounce of the car across a pothole made her grit her teeth in agony and earned a contrite apology from Tony.

"S'okay, Tony. Not your fault," she said, and willed herself to focus on something other than the pain. Adam's face came to mind again and she used him as her focal point, recalling the feel of his touch, light as a breeze against her skin before the contact had become charged with heat and desire. Even now the recollection of that want caused her to dampen and twist with need.

"Tell me about your boss," she asked.

"Seriously? You're thinking about my boss?" Tony questioned, obviously incredulous.

"I'm not dead...yet," she teased, trying to not only lighten her brother's concerns, but keep herself distracted.

"He's rich. Millionaire kind of rich."

"Damn. I knew there was something awful about him," she kidded, dragging a chuckle from Tony.

The throbbing at the small of her back had receded just a bit, and she slowly straightened in the passenger seat. Beside her, Tony turned his head to check a blind spot before shifting into the left lane and said, "He's not your type, Bobbie."

The car's engine purred softly with the acceleration as Tony switched lanes.

"Sounds sweet," she said, aware of how much time and effort her brothers had put into restoring the classic muscle car.

"See, that just proves my point. Mr. Bruno's first car was probably a limo and he would never call a ride sweet."

Bobbie chuckled, although that simple action produced fresh shards of pain along the left side of her back. She bit back a groan and then asked, "Is he a geek?"

"Totally," Tony replied, with a laugh and a quick glance in her direction.

"So are you, bro, and you're not so bad," Bobbie retorted, but Tony didn't answer as he carefully turned down the street for her condo. He parked the car, exited the Camaro, and hurried around the front bumper to help her out of the seat. Each movement brought renewed pain in her back, but luckily the strange tingling sensation in her left hand and arm had abated, as had the equally troubling throb between her legs.

If anything, her hand and arm were feeling better. Maybe even stronger than they had that morning, if that was possible. Which it wasn't, she told herself. It was only the adrenaline racing through her body that was creating such unusual sensations.

"Thanks for the ride home," she said, and gave her brother an awkward one-armed hug.

"Are you sure you'll be okay?" he asked, concern evident on his face.

"A long soak and I'll be fine," she reassured, although she was feeling anything but fine at that moment.

Knowing better than to push, her brother offered up a weak smile and left as Bobbie slowly made her way inside, her gait like that of an arthritic ninety-year-old. She would normally have pushed herself to make the climb to the third story, but the ache in her back was too intense, so she opted for the elevator instead.

Once inside her condo, she walked toward the breakfast bar, where an assortment of pain meds sat on the counter. She bypassed the various prescription medications and instead grabbed the Aleve bottle with her free left hand.

A left hand that was now surprisingly stronger. She tightened her hand on the plastic bottle, and her grip didn't falter. She squeezed harder and harder until the knuckles on her hand were white with pressure and still her grip didn't waver. The muscles remained fluid as she rotated her arm left and right. She lifted it higher, reaching for the sky and experiencing none of the weakness or restriction in movement that had been there before Adam had touched her.

Lowering her arm, she popped the lid on the bottle, spilled out two capsules, and swallowed them dry. Between the pain reliever and the soak she had mentioned, she hoped she would be well enough to join her family later for dinner. Despite all the bad things that had happened in the last few months, being around her family always made her feel better. In large part it had been their support that had pulled her back into this world after the explosion. They had kept her sane when fear, pain, and guilt might have driven her over the edge.

As she glanced around her apartment and caught a fleeting glimpse of the photos of her family on a nearby wall unit, a sense of balance permeated her.

She was almost whole, she acknowledged. She hadn't expected to feel like that for a long time, all things considered. But there were still pieces missing in her life despite all the progress she had made.

As she recalled Adam and the way he had made her feel with a simple caress, she wondered if it wasn't time to risk a relationship with a man. Although she wasn't sure Adam would be a good candidate for that foray back into the dating life. Even without knowing very much about him, she knew they came from vastly different worlds, maybe too far apart for them to have anything in common.

Despite that, she itched to explore her attraction to him, but first she needed that soak. And if during that bath she also daydreamed a bit about the interesting Adam Bruno...

The tension in the room was palpable as the two men stood before him, militarily rigid, hands clasped before them, heads dipped in either deference or shame.

"You say there was another Hunter there? Possibly a Shadow Hunter?" Kellen Chakotay asked as he surged out of his chair, planted his fists on his desk, and leaned toward the two men in his cadre. His captain—Andres Rayu—sported a swollen nose and duo of black eyes while his second in command, Eduardo Rios, occasionally reached up to rub at a purpling mark across his throat.

"We think so." Andres paused and shot an apprehensive look at his partner. "We couldn't be sure. She—"

"A female Shadow?" Kellen said, and from the corner

of his eye examined his wife. She wrung her hands with worry and he understood why. The female Shadow Hunters were known to be particularly lethal, showing no mercy in who they killed in order to replenish their life forces.

Eduardo, who had been unusually silent and distant during the initial report, finally spoke up, but when he did, his voice was sandpaper raspy. It was clear it was costing him great effort to speak. "Could be. She wasn't whole."

"Not whole? Did her body bear signs of the small-pox?" Kellen asked, and walked around to where his man stood. Raising his hands, he brought one to rest along Eduardo's throat injury and chastised, "Why have you not sought help?"

"Ashamed, Quinchu," Eduardo replied, referring to Kellen by the title the Light Hunters used for their priests and priestesses. Only the Quinchu retained the abilities to gather energy that all the Hunters had possessed at one time.

The Quinchus and the murderous Shadows.

Tight-lipped, Kellen reminded, "We are not like the dark ones. We honor all life and relieve suffering."

With that Kellen closed his eyes and tapped the well of stored power within himself, summoning the energies he had collected during the course of the day. Deep in his core, the forces coalesced, the weight of them dragging at his center. With control honed by decades of practice and millennia of tradition, Kellen sent his healing powers into the man with a gentle push. Beneath his palm an orange-red glow shimmered, and Eduardo's body jumped with the discharge. Warmth erupted and then receded as he withdrew the healing energy, but in mere seconds Eduardo released a grateful sigh.

"Thank you, Quinchu," Eduardo said, his voice restored.

Kellen turned to Andres, intending to deal with his injuries, but the captain of his cadre waved him off. "We must deal with the woman first, Quinchu."

"The one you thought might be a Shadow Hunter. Did *you* see the pox on her?" he asked and walked over to where his wife waited on the couch, sat beside her, and laid a calming hand over her nervous ones.

"It was impossible to tell. It all happened so fast," Eduardo advised.

"But she had an aura. A powerful one," Andres supplied, but was quick to add, "We will not fail again, Quinchu."

Kellen nodded and rubbed his forefinger across his lips as he considered what the men had reported. If a Shadow Hunter was nearby, searching as they were, it could confirm that Adam Bruno was who they thought. But based on their earlier report, his men seemed uncertain about the strength of the power the young CEO possessed.

"The man you tracked down—Adam Bruno—did he have the gift?" It would be impossible for Bruno not to be blessed if he was their son Kikin.

Once again his men hesitated, looking back and forth between each other before Andres noted, "He had some power, but it seemed weak. Not like the force you would expect in a man descended from two such powerful Quinchus as yourselves."

Beside him, Eduardo was nodding, in obvious agreement with his captain's assessment.

A deep, tortured sigh escaped his wife. Kellen understood. The report disappointed him, too. If Bruno's gift was weak, it might mean that he was a hybrid—half-human, half-Hunter. Such half-breeds often had abilities far beyond those of their fellow humans, but the hunting gift was not strong enough to be of much use.

And if Bruno was a hybrid, he was not their son.

With each year that passed and each failure to locate Kikin, who was supposed to be their future Quinchu, the hopes of his Light Hunter clan dimmed. Soon their future might be extinguished like the flame on a candle.

"Quinchu," Andres said, sensing Kellen's distress and pulling his attention back to the rest of the cadre, who stood silently by the door. "What do you wish for us to do now?"

"Find out if this woman is a Shadow. If so, we will have to be extremely careful."

"What about the man?" Eduardo asked.

"Watch and wait. We must determine if he is our son before we do anything else."

Clasping their hands to their chests in a salute and bowing their heads, the two men exited the room and the cadre followed, leaving him alone with his wife.

"Could we be so wrong?" Selina asked, the gray of her eyes like storm clouds over the desert they had left time and time again in their quest to find Kikin. This time their journey had been prompted by a grainy photo in a newspaper article. One of the men in the photo had looked like the Texas Ranger who had taken their son nearly twenty years earlier.

Kellen turned, his knees brushing against hers. He pushed back a stray lock of hair and tucked it behind her ear. Her hair had once been a wealth of coppery brown, but even there worry had taken its toll. Brash streaks of white salted the strands.

"The years may have faded our recollection of his powers, *Warmi*," he said, using her ancient name instead of the modern ones they had adopted to hide their true origins.

"Nothing could take away my memory of Kikin's aura. It was unique. Powerful," Selina replied, her tone brooking no disagreement.

Kellen knew better than to argue with his strong-willed wife. "We will know soon enough, my love. If it is Kikin, the strength of his power will be growing as he nears the Equinox."

For the Hunters, each third of their life brought changes. The years immediately surrounding the initial thirty—the first triad—represented the zenith of a Hunter's powers and fertility.

"But if the Equinox comes upon him, he may die or injure another without our help," Selina said worriedly.

"He is young enough that his change may not happen until he is with us and can mate with the Quinchu from the Ocean clan."

Selina dipped her head and cradled the sharp line of Kellen's jaw. "What of the woman with the aura? What if she is one of the Shadows?"

With a careless shrug, Kellen replied, "We do what we always do. We kill her."

CHAPTER
6

One of his security people had delivered a thumb drive with the video Adam had requested barely an hour after the incident. Adam slipped the thumb drive into his computer, then hesitated, his mind replaying that initial shocking jolt of power as the first man had laid hands on him. Would the video from the security system show that thunderbolt or any of the others that followed? he wondered while worrying about the secrecy of such a revelation.

With a quick wave of his hand, the video began to play on the large-screen television at the far side of his office, and Adam rose to stand in front of it.

The image of him leaving the building, absorbed in his phone messages, played on the screen. Shortly thereafter, the first glimpse of Bobbie, leaning against the car in a simple white T-shirt molded to ample breasts and curve-hugging jeans, grabbed his attention. The video had not picked up her intense cerulean aura.

While the video had not documented the evidence of her power, it had recorded Adam's initial reaction at his first glimpse of Bobbie, the quick glance followed by a slower obvious double-take. Part of it had been because of the waves of energy he had sensed surrounding her. But it had also been plain ol' male appreciation: Bobbie Carrera was a very attractive woman.

That thought fled quickly as he viewed each development on the screen. Even now, safe in his office, the memory of the men's touch brought fear, making his gut clench and causing sweat to gather at the base of his spine. Very little on the video gave testament that there had been anything different about the men or about Bobbie.

Except for possibly the streaks of light as he had intercepted the one man midair and then again when the men had disappeared into the van and raced away.

Adam paused the video at that point with a sharp slash of his hand. Approaching the large-screen television, he realized that part of a license plate was visible. But you didn't have to watch a lot of cop shows to know that either the cars or the license plates involved in crimes like these were usually stolen.

Adam shut off the television and returned to his desk, frustrated that the recording hadn't yielded anything new or valuable.

As he plopped into his chair, he thought about all the possible reasons for the attack.

It hadn't been a simple mugging. The first man had said that they wanted him, so it was more likely it had been a kidnapping, but why? Because he was like them or for some human kind of reason?

Money? he considered. As of that morning, he was

worth close to ten million, thanks to a surge in the Sol-Terra stock price, but he wasn't sure if someone would take such a risk in broad daylight. There were far richer people in the area, and without his approval, no one could move funds out of the various accounts in order to pay any ransom.

A grudge? he thought, not that either he or his company had received any complaints against them. But then he recalled how distraught his father had been lately. Adam had thought the anxiety had to do with one of his father's cases. But now, after what had just happened, it occurred to him that it was possible that his father had been aware of some kind of risk to Adam and had been keeping it a secret to avoid worrying him.

There was only one way to find out, but before he asked Salvatore he had one other possibility to eliminate—that Bobbie was somehow connected to what had happened. It just seemed too convenient that she should be there with her aura at the same time as the two men with their obvious energy signatures.

Adam turned to his computer. He closed his eyes and pushed forward with his energy, commanding the machine to begin a web search using just his power. Within moments he had gotten dozens of hits for Bobbie Carrera and the other members of her family.

The images and information surged from the computer into his brain, where he processed the data at speeds far faster than that of any human.

High school yearbook pictures of Bobbie were posted on a friend's Facebook account. She hadn't changed much in the six years since graduating. That would make her about twenty-four, he calculated.

There were articles from the local papers about the Carrera clan. Besides Tony, Bobbie had two older siblings, and her parents ran a popular Mexican restaurant in nearby Bradley Beach, not that he had ever eaten there, although he lived and worked nearby. Adam continued surfing through all the digital data spewing out of the computer until he encountered a short article about Bobbie and her platoon. Sixteen men dead in an IED attack. Only Bobbie and her platoon leader had survived.

The graphic images of the aftermath jolted him, breaking his mental connection with the computer. Emotion had once again disrupted his control. Resuming the search through more traditional means, he continued reading the article about Bobbie and her men.

She had survived, but broken, he thought, recalling the evident pain on her face after the incident and the sensation of scarred skin and bunched muscle beneath his fingertips.

He shouldn't have touched her, especially not in his wired condition after the attack. Too late he had noticed the leakage of energy from his fingertips. The recollection rekindled the sensation of Bobbie's skin beneath his fingers.

So warm.

Amazingly alive.

He imagined moving his hand from her arm to the fragile skin where her shoulder met her neck. Trailing it downward to cup those generous breasts outlined so beautifully by her simple white T-shirt. Taking off that shirt. Would her nipples be dark as berries and taste as sweet?

He sucked in a shaky breath as he hardened and readjusted the fabric of his pants over his erection. He forced his mind from such thoughts, reminding himself that he barely knew her despite the intense synergy when he had touched her.

But her obvious physical distress and courage in the face of that had reached deep inside him that afternoon, prompting a surge of emotion and energy. It had danced along his fingertips as he skimmed his hand along that injured flesh. Before today the few times he had accidentally released his power had been shocking. Literally.

Since learning of his abilities, he had guarded his touch, fearful of it after he had innocently created havoc with just the brush of his hands. Shapeshifting, blasts of power, or just vibrations could occur when he came into contact with other living things.

Today had been different from anything which had transpired in the past.

He'd wanted to help her, and with that want had come the unexpected—a gentle kiss of energy wherever his skin had met hers, a living and demanding connection like none he had ever experienced. Desire, unforeseen and demanding.

His gut tightened with the possibility that he could just as easily have hurt her if he had lost command of his power. As it was, she had clearly been in pain from her actions during the attack.

The attack.

Those words drove away the last of his passion and pulled him back to his worries, including those about Bobbie.

Bobbie, he thought with a sigh, recalling the intensity in her whiskey-eyed gaze. He hoped she hadn't caught his disappearing and reappearing act when he shot through the air to wrestle one of the assailants to the ground.

As for him, he needed to find out more about the two men and whoever was driving the van. But for right now, his immediate goal was to discover more about the woman he could not forget. Swiveling in his chair, he faced his computer and accessed his company's employment records. He located Tony's personal info and with a mental command dialed his intern's cell number. Tony picked up on the third ring.

"Tony, this is Adam Bruno," he said, and heard Tony shushing the people in the background. From the clink of plates and glasses and the murmured conversation, along with the occasional blare of a horn, Adam guessed that his employee was at some kind of outdoor restaurant.

Perhaps his family's restaurant in Bradley Beach?

"Mr. Bruno. Sorry for the noise. I'm at work. Is it an emergency?"

Work? Adam wondered, then realized he had said it aloud when Tony quickly replied, "At my parents' restaurant. I help out here at night. Do you need something?"

"I hadn't heard from you about your sister."

"I didn't think you were serious about me calling you."

Adam had thought himself fairly in touch and responsive to his employees, but clearly his perceptions were off.

"Is Bobbie okay? Is there anything I can do?" he said, striving for the kind of tone in his voice that would leave no doubt about his sincerity.

The muffled sound of Tony speaking was followed by a more distant female voice. Bobbie. The distance did nothing to lessen the immediate tightening of his gut and the flare of longing.

"She says she's fine, Mr. Bruno. Is there anything else

I can do for you?" Tony replied, clearly anxious to return to work.

"No. Not at all. Sorry to bother you," he replied, and hung up.

Tapping the edge of the smartphone to the tip of his chin, he considered Tony's answer. His intern was at his family's restaurant and his sister was obviously there as well. He checked the time on the phone. Five-thirty. He hoped that she might be there for a bit longer. He had found her address online, and a look through her home might provide some insights into Bobbie and her life.

Shoving away from his desk to pay that visit, he stuffed the report on a new technology for battery arrays into his briefcase. He still needed to review it after postponing his meeting, and he would later tonight after a little breaking and entering.

Maybe some reading in bed before sleep time. Which was so wrong, he thought. He was in the prime of his life and he was taking a lab report to bed with him instead of a warm and willing woman like Bobbie. Chalk it up to his being very selective about with whom he slept—generally women to whom he had no emotional attachment.

Unlike Bobbie, who had been innocently challenging him and earning him a big fail in the restraint department. Cursing beneath his breath, he grabbed the briefcase and stormed out of his office, one thought in his head.

He had to learn all he could about Bobbie so that he could drive her out of his mind.

CHAPTER
7

Bobbie's home was in a condo unit located on Ocean Avenue in Ocean Grove. High-end for someone who was likely living on a military paycheck.

He parked his car around the corner and stepped out, considering for a moment that he should just approach her to talk about all that had happened. But he wasn't sure she would welcome the kinds of questions he would ask. If he could get inside, he might get some needed information.

He walked across the street until he was standing opposite the condo. Even from a distance he could see it had a plain old mechanical lock, so using his energy to trip the mechanism would be impossible.

Behind him on the street was a row of brightly painted Victorian homes. The homes were situated close together, with small alleys between some of them, the perfect spot for what he needed to do.

As he stood there, the door to the condo building opened and someone walked out carrying a burly black cat, placed the cat down on the sidewalk, and then hurried up the block. The cat immediately made a run across the street and straight toward one of the nearby homes. The feline sat a few feet back from the mouth of one of those alleys as if waiting for someone or something. With dusk falling heavily and the streets relatively empty, Adam easily slipped unnoticed down the alley until he was about a foot away from the cat.

He bent and beckoned to the animal. Luckily it was a people-friendly house cat, obviously well-fed and not all that skittish. As the cat came close, it twined around his legs and then peered up at him with inquisitive golden eyes. Then it meowed loudly before plopping itself at his feet Buddhalike and purring.

Glancing around, Adam realized there was no one nearby.

Perfect.

Bending, he laid his hands on the cat and stroked her. Her purrs grew louder as she continued to gaze up at him with her intense slant-eyed gaze. The vibrations registered against his fingers. Her heartbeat, slow at first, sped up as she sensed the connection between them and grew afraid. He continued his soft caress, trying to calm her as he slowly pulled her feline energy into him.

Within him warmth pooled at his core, and the weight of the power expanded with the addition of the cat's energy. As the transfer of her life force proceeded, the deep sable color of her fur spread onto his hands, and the cat blinked at him once, twice, before closing her eyes and slumping to the brick walk in the alley.

Gently he scooped her up and laid her in a tiny niche where she would be safe from passersby, giving one last peaceful stroke along her body before he severed the connection with her so that she could rest and recuperate.

Using the life force he had gathered, he focused on it and concentrated its unique signature. He forced the feline potency along his nerve endings, which tingled as the transformation took hold. His muscles tightened and shortened and his bones compacted, became denser, in preparation for the change. Intense heat developed in his center and it grew heavier as his body mass pulled inward to shrink the size of his body to that of the cat.

Worried the change was taking too long and he might be discovered, he blasted out the remaining feline energy all across his being and into the immediate space around him.

In the blink of an eye, the intense wave of power finally altered him, and Adam took the form of a black cat.

Slinking out of the alley in his sleek new body, he padded toward the sidewalk in front of the homes. He sat there, gazing up and down the street. He had shapeshifted before, but experiencing the world from a new perspective never ceased to amaze him. The cement of the sidewalk was rough beneath the pads of his paws. As a car drove by along the street, the whir of the tires was loud and vibrated the hairs close to the entrance of his ears.

His transformed body reacted instinctively, jumping away from the noise as the cat's innate responses overwhelmed his sentient ones. He shook his head as a fly buzzed close by and the tags dragging from the collar around his neck jangled with the motion.

So different, he thought. It was the first time he had gone out in public in a nonhuman form. Normally he kept to the confines of his own quiet yard as he tested that aspect of his powers.

Increasing his pace, he hurried to the curb, but as a car came around the corner, he once again jerked back from the street. He slinked between two parked cars and waited, then dashed across when he was sure he would not become roadkill.

He padded straight ahead until he was sitting by the front door of Bobbie's condominium building. He contemplated waiting there, but that could take quite a bit of time, unless the cat's owner was only out for a short walk. A rustle in the nearby mounds of flowers hinted that he might find a field mouse and risk another change, but then the sound of a car door closing snagged his attention.

A bottle-green Sebring convertible with a handicapped tag hanging from the rearview mirror had slipped into a spot near the condo. As he watched, Bobbie eased from the car and grabbed a few things from the front seat. Then she came down the walk carrying the bags and headed straight for him.

Something inside the cat responded at the sight of her, and Adam hoped that was a good sign. Maybe Bobbie was familiar to the animal, which would make this even easier. At the door, Bobbie looked down at him and said, "Have they tossed you out again, Tweety?"

Tweety? What kind of sick person would name a cat Tweety? he thought, a second before Bobbie bent and started rubbing the top of his head. Almost instinctively he craned his neck upward, urging her hand behind his ear as she continued petting him.

Heaven, he thought, enjoying the feel of her short nails

against his fur. He began to purr and then butted his head against her leg, wanting more.

"You're a good girl," she said and stroked her hand along his back.

He twined around her legs and Bobbie gave him one last pat before she stood. "Sorry, Tweety. It's time to go in."

"In" being exactly where he wanted to be. With a big meow, he plopped back down and she opened the door, totally focused on maneuvering through with her bags and cane. So focused that he was able to sneak through the entrance just a second before the door closed.

But Bobbie realized he had followed when she was in the hallway, scooped him up, and said, "Let's get you home."

She tucked him tight to her side, his head pressed close to her breast, and he imagined staying there forever. So did the cat within him, which hinted at the fact that this wasn't the first time Bobbie had come to the feline's rescue.

The close proximity to her had him battling for control. She was soft and warm, but also strong beneath the feminine veneer. The warrior, he thought again, intrigued by the dichotomies Bobbie presented.

But there was also another thing drawing him near— the aura he had sensed earlier. It was both comforting and intoxicating and was creating a synergy he was finding difficult to ignore. Inside him, his core did a slow whirl and he fought it back, needing to maintain control to keep his altered shape.

Bobbie stopped at a door on the lower floor of the condo and knocked.

No answer.

She waited for a minute or so and then knocked again.

When there was no response, she mumbled, "Some people shouldn't have pets."

With him tucked against her, she continued to the end of the hall and a small elevator where they rode up to the third floor. Her condo was in the middle of the building and she placed him on the ground to enter. When the door opened, the cat's instincts acted before he could, and he darted into the room.

"Make yourself at home," she teased, the laughter evident in her voice.

He quickly snuck to a spot beside the sofa, where he sat and watched as she efficiently emptied the bags and put away the few groceries she had purchased. When she was done, she headed down a hall, and soon the sound of running water drifted out.

Strangling the thought of her beneath the water, he allowed himself to explore her home.

It was like visiting the tropics after leaving Antarctica.

Unlike the gleaming steel and cold stone environment in the SolTerra offices and his home, Bobbie's condo was animated by color and life. A bouquet of lively pink tulips in a bright sea-blue vase sat in the middle of a bistro table near the kitchen.

On a low wall unit that delineated the area between dining room and living room were framed photos. He jumped up onto the wall for a better look, acrobatically landing on the far edge before delicately winding around the frames on its surface and examining each one.

Bobbie and her family. A group photo of soldiers in uniform along a broken cement fortification. The platoon with which she had served, he assumed. Wedding photos of two different couples. With the physical resemblance of the groom in one and the bride in the other, he had no doubt they were her older siblings.

He plopped down and surveyed the rest of the area from his perch on the wall unit, from where he caught sight of the various prescription bottles on the surface of the breakfast bar. He jumped down, determined to find out more, and then leaped up to a stool by the bar before taking another, shorter jump onto the counter. As he peered at the bottles, it was evident that they were full and he wondered why.

Had she just refilled them, or was she the kind to tough out the pain? Even though his one encounter with her had been brief, he could answer his own question.

Bobbie was the kind to rough it no matter the discomfort she was in. She wouldn't like to be medicated to the point of numbness. She would want to live even if it meant enduring hurt. That was plainly obvious from the life and color present in the apartment.

Which begged the question of what kind of life he was living in his cold sterile environs. Maybe that was why she intrigued him so. The emptiness inside him had recognized she could fill the void with her vitality.

He dropped back to the floor and scurried down the hall, bypassing the bathroom and doing a quick run through a bedroom, which seemed relatively unused although it contained some free weights and an exercise bike.

As he entered the second, larger bedroom, it was clear this was where Bobbie slept. He could smell her in the air, and as in the other room, there were family photos on the neatly organized surface of a dresser. On a nightstand beside the bed sat a paperback novel, a romance, he realized from the binding, and it made him smile to think that beneath the skin of the warrior lurked a closet romantic.

He raced back out of the room, but hesitated by the bathroom this time. The door was ajar. He could easily slip inside to catch a glimpse of her, to replace the fantasies he'd had that afternoon with reality, but honor kept him on the other side of the door.

He was already violating her privacy with his little foray into her personal space. He would not push it any farther.

As he hurried back toward the main living area of the condo, another photograph on the wall unit suddenly grabbed his attention, along with two framed medals. The photo and medals were on a second shelf instead of in the more visible position along the top.

He peered at the medals and discovered that Bobbie had been awarded not only a Purple Heart, but also a Silver Star for valor during battle. A memory popped up from the data he had skimmed earlier, making him recall the article that had mentioned how Bobbie had saved the lives of several of her fellow soldiers. It totally fit what he knew of her so far.

He wondered if one of the men she had saved was the one wearing the uniform in the photo beside the medals. A smiling and obviously happy Bobbie sat in the lap of a handsome Latino man. He had his hand around her waist possessively and a gleam in his eye that spoke volumes. A surprising jolt of jealousy surged through Adam, creating a sudden quiver in his center. He tried to tamp it down, but fighting back the sentiment brought only more problems as something gave in his body. It was followed by a pop of bone shifting in a joint.

He had been so involved with his little expedition that he had not been conscious of the power he had been consuming to maintain the animal form. Only now did he realize that he had taxed his powers beyond his limits. Jealousy had put the final nail in the coffin, making him lose command of the situation.

Strangling a moan as the pain of the transformation raced throughout his body, he moved closer to the front door so he could make his escape. He sought out his own life force and urged it along his nerve endings so that he would have some kind of influence over the change. The fur receded swiftly and his body elongated. Pain ripped along muscles that loosened back to their normal length. Bones rotated and popped into place as they assumed their regular positions. As he shook off the animal vitality he had consumed, his body filled out.

Seconds later, with a final shudder and shove of energy to his extremities, he restored his true form and that of every item that had been on him before he had morphed.

Light-headed, his body bathed in sweat, he leaned against the wall and sucked in a few deep breaths to steady himself, drawing on what little energy remained at his core to provide support against the weakness in his body.

The sound of the water shutting off in the shower propelled him to find the strength he needed to retreat. Careful not to make a noise, he opened the door and rushed out into the hallway. Resting against the wall, he took another few deep breaths until he had stabilized. Then he hurried out, needing to deal with so many things.

He had never morphed for as long a time as he had tonight, and it had left him feeling weak. He was normally quite robust, since he was careful about maintaining his energy levels. He would have to recharge the energy he had spent on the shapeshifting, energy that had already been taxed by the blasts from his attackers. Plus, he had to process all that he had learned from his short online peek into Bobbie's life and even shorter visit to her home.

Despite the brevity of those contacts, Bobbie continued to intrigue him, but tonight's episode had proven one thing to him: Allowing emotion to interfere was a dangerous thing. The jealousy that he had experienced due to the photo had nearly undone him at a very sensitive moment.

He suspected it wouldn't be the last time that emotions related to Bobbie would challenge him. She called to him emotionally and her aura drew him on another level. If he couldn't handle the feelings both of those roused, he might put her at risk.

That was the last thing on Earth he wanted to do.

Bobbie had clearly been through enough on her own without him adding to her misery.

CHAPTER
8

Adam stood on the second-floor balcony off his bedroom, staring at the waves churning up against the shore. The moon was full, bathing everything beneath it with shades of almost white to silvery gray. A storm was brewing tonight. Besides the smell of the rain that was on its way, he sensed the growing energy gathering in the clouds above him.

Closing his eyes, he lifted his face to the skies and inhaled deeply, as if by doing so he might suck in all that turbulent power. Maybe some long-ago ancestor, the one from whom he had inherited his abilities, had been able to gather such storm forces. So far Adam had not been able to harness powers in that fashion, but maybe tonight with the experiment he planned to run he would find a way to tap the intense energy of the tempest, much as he was able to do with the creatures around him and the smaller bits of free-floating energies in the cosmos.

As a child Adam had shied away from gathering such

forces, aware that he lacked the ability to control what he did with them. But he had learned some restraint as a teenager, and he had begun to experiment. He discovered that each living thing he touched possessed its own unique energy signature. Trial and error had helped him to improve the process by which he could round up that energy and use it for a number of purposes.

Anything electrical was within his control with just a thought. With a simple touch he could take on a new shape, which oftentimes gave him a fresh perspective, he thought, recalling that night's adventures in his animal form. Every bit of energy he absorbed brought a new awareness to him.

Like the sensation of Bobbie's skin beneath his fingers, pulsing with life.

Adam sucked in a breath as he imagined how the rest of her might feel pressed against him. So warm and feminine.

What would it feel like to be one with her physically? Or to share that energy and spirit and create a unique synergy of their respective powers?

Tamping down the desire that was becoming almost painful, he opened his eyes and stared up at the skies.

If there was a God up there, why hadn't He allowed Adam to understand what his purpose on this Earth was supposed to be? It still frustrated Adam that he hadn't been able to put some of his powers to any real useful purpose. And now he had a new one to consider—his ability to skip across distances in the blink of an eye.

He shoved off from the balcony railing and headed indoors, away from the impending storm that matched the mounting disturbance inside him. He stalked from his bedroom along the lengthy hall lined with empty rooms and then jogged down the stairs. On the first floor he barely spared a glance at the large open floor plan some designer had thought appropriate for a man of his wealth and importance. To Adam the house and all its luxurious contents had been just things to impress prospective investors in SolTerra.

It would never be a home without more, he thought. Without the joy and love he had seen radiating from Bobbie's face in the photos resting on her wall unit.

He hurried down the stairs to the basement, where he had his home office and laboratory. Placing his face close to a retinal scanner securing the glass door, he waited for the system to validate his identity. When the magnetic lock disengaged, he walked into the state-of-the-art facility that rivaled those at his SolTerra location. To the uninitiated, it might seem as if they had discovered Dr. Frankenstein's lab, but to Adam it represented the possibilities of what his company could do.

For all that *he* could do with enough power. Power that he was lacking right now.

He had to recharge himself.

Normally he did so by meditation to absorb free-floating energy particles in the atmosphere, or with occasional experiments testing the life forces of other living things. In the last few months, however, the growing call of the power had led him to try bigger and better ways of hunting the energy. In doing so, Adam had learned that he seemed to have a natural affinity for all things electrical—funny, in a way, given the work he had chosen to do with SolTerra. It had made him wonder if that hadn't been some kind of subconscious choice all those years ago when he had decided to devote his studies and work to alternative energies.

Regardless, his company had been developing new methods of harvesting forces in nature, and tonight he would not only test one of those methods, but also attempt to use it to restore the vitality he had lost.

Adam rushed over to the computers and engaged them by placing his thumb against another reader. His father had taught him the value of defending against intrusion and to never second-guess an opponent. If someone got through the first door, he still wouldn't be able to access his network without clearing another hurdle.

A panel of monitors jumped to life after the system confirmed his identity. Each screen contained different bits of information, from the sensors tracking the incoming storm to the readings from his last energy-harvesting session. The end result of that experiment, the withered remains of the small purple foxglove plant, sat on the worktable.

He had chosen the foxglove for its known medicinal values, and to his surprise, the readings he had gotten from the plant had been higher than those from the plain old potted fern he had used as a baseline. That had served to put him on notice that he might want to somehow gather those different healing energies.

But he wasn't the one needing healing, he thought, recalling Bobbie's pained expression and the guarded way she had moved after the run-in with the men.

Too bad his only power seemed to be to take and not to give, he thought, with a last look at the emaciated plant. He had only sipped a bit of its life force, but it had been too much for the plant to handle. The power he had gathered had not even been enough to allow for any physical change from the energy.

Not that he had any intention of shifting into your average garden-variety petunia. Too many remnants of the borrowed life force often came over during such an exchange, like the flight instincts of the cat that evening. He had no idea what would happen if he shapeshifted into a nonsentient form.

Tossing the pot into a wastebasket, he sat down at the computer and viewed the radar reports on the incoming weather. The brighter orange and red markings delineating the strongest cells in the thunderstorm were moving quickly and would soon be directly above his Spring Lake residence. With a wave of his hand over a button, he released the lightning rods built into the uppermost story of his home.

Almost as soon as he had done so, the low rumble of distant thunder warned that the tempest was growing nearer. For months Adam had been monitoring such storms using high-speed video. Shooting over fifty thousand frames per second, he had been able to detect the smaller ribbons of electricity that actually composed what the eye saw as only one huge bolt of lightning.

He had also discovered another interesting phenomenon. With him maneuvering the lightning rods by remote, he was actually able to reliably draw the bolts to those devices. It was as if his natural affinity was beckoning the energy to join with him.

Acting quickly, Adam engaged the junctions that would funnel any electrical strike he attracted to a series of sophisticated energy cells and capacitors. The purpose of the collection was twofold. If the array could collect and keep the charge, SolTerra might be able to develop a new source of energy to be marketed.

If he could then personally absorb the power from the energy cells, he hoped to be able to take that force and calm the growing need within him. Afterward, he might be able to direct it to something or someone else without causing harm. Unfortunately, his control was sporadic, even after so many years of trying. Plus there was the recent phenomenon he had been experiencing, which created intense static in his brain and pain if his energy levels fluctuated too greatly.

He suspected that part of the problem was the source of his power. Man-made power did not produce the same results in his body as natural supplies from the cosmos or other living things. As for his shapeshifting experiments, he chose his subjects carefully and made sure he didn't take too much of their vitality, hence his need for alternate ways to recharge his power.

An insistent beep-beep-beep intruded from a nearby computer. The weather service was issuing a severe thunderstorm warning.

Perfect, he thought, and flipped one of the monitors to the security camera watching the rooftop. He shifted the camera's orientation with a joystick, training its view onto the two lightning rods. Then he grasped the remotes for the rods, directing them toward the storm, focusing his attention on the rods while occasionally shooting a half-glance at the video from the high-speed cameras recording the experiment.

Anxiously he waited, his heart drumming in his chest and his core growing warmer as he absorbed some of the free-floating electrical energy increasing with the approach of the storm.

A flash of light brightened the night sky in the distance, followed several seconds later by the crash of thunder.

Another minute passed.

Another flare of light. More distinct. Closer this time. The thunder followed within a few heartbeats, its vibrations thumping against his senses.

The storm was nearly overhead.

Less than a minute later, the first zigzag spike of lightning blasted into one of the metal rods. A second followed ferociously.

Adam turned from the sight of the strikes, their images alive on his retinas as he glanced at the screen tracking the energy levels in the battery array. Only a slight rise. Not nearly enough for the cells to be used as a power source.

Anxious minutes passed before he pulled another bolt of lightning to the rod, and this time it ramped up the readings, as did a fourth hit. Each strike increased the power levels in the cells, but the storm was shifting by too quickly. As fast as the squall had moved in from the land to the west, its fury sped eastward out to sea.

Turning on a different camera, Adam observed as the lightning brightened the inky night sky over the ocean, blinding white silver bursts racing down to midnight sea.

With the storm gone, he checked the readings on the batteries, smiling with pleasure as he noted they had not only finally picked up a substantial amount of the charge but were also retaining it. Tonight's crucial success storing the energy meant he would finally be able to proceed to the second part of his experiment.

The personal part of his research.

He removed his shirt and sat on a stool by his worktable. Carefully he wired himself to an EKG unit, a pulse oximeter, and a computer, which would monitor his vital signs while a second workstation was set to track any fluctuations in energy within his body.

In the event of any drop in his vital signs or dangerous electrical surges, he had programmed the system to engage various safety overrides to prevent any damage to him or the battery array.

Running a quick check of the networked peripherals, he nodded in satisfaction and issued a series of short mental commands to the computer. Before him the monitor flashed off and on as the image of the sea at night with the fading storm was replaced by the program showing the energy levels in the batteries.

He engaged the vital sign checks, and a third monitor provided information from the various wires he had stuck onto himself. Assured that all was in order, Adam picked up the leads connected to the bank of batteries and started a video camera to record the experiment.

With a deep breath, he braced himself and thought, *Computer, engage batteries tenth power.*

A tingle immediately commenced in his palms, like the sensation of holding a small hand massager. Within his gut came a sympathetic vibration, but Adam was uncertain if it was truly power gathering within him or wishful thinking.

The power levels on the battery meter dipped, but his vital signs and energy flow remained normal. The latter was a disappointment, since even during the earlier experiment with the foxglove he had detected a spike of power in his body as he had sucked the plant's vitality.

Determined to see some change happen, Adam rose

from his desk to the open space behind it to push the experiment to the next stage.

Computer, engage batteries half power, he commanded silently.

There was no denying the stronger force pulsing against his palms. It danced up his arms from where he held the leads and coursed through his body, creating a dense ball of heat with more intense pulsations deep in his core.

He glanced at the monitors and watched as the battery levels dimmed, but those within his body steadily increased. His pulse and other vital signs jumped slightly as his core accepted and stored the energy taken from the lightning. As he glanced at his hands, the tendrils of power were visible, encircling his wrists and the leads, writhing and dancing in a vivid display of royal blue and silver light along his hands and up his forearms, like a string of flashing Christmas lights wound around his extremities.

Adam had to find out just how much more power he could absorb, and he instructed the computer to ramp up the delivery to 75 percent.

The surge yanked him off his feet, charging every cell in his body. The heat that had solely been at his center moments earlier raced through his body and overtook him completely. Wired from the power pulsing through him, Adam could barely focus on the data before him. As had been happening with the unexpected bouts lately, his mind became filled with static from the forces zooming along his extremities and core as he became part of the electrical current circulating from the batteries. Before his eyes, rays of light danced across his vision and he followed them, watching as they swirled around his body and into him, like tree roots digging deep into the soil, their colors almost iridescent against the blinding brightness creeping into his vision.

Have to get control, he thought, and mustered enough cognition to see the rapidly draining power levels on the array and the dangerous spikes of energy in his body.

His vital signs were jumping erratically now.

Heart, breathing, and pulse were all reaching critical levels, or at least he thought so; the waves of power were clouding his eyesight. Noise filled his brain and pressure built until he thought his skull would explode.

In the distance, because he felt disconnected from the world around him, Adam heard a warning alarm from one of the units connected to him.

Have to shut down, he thought.

Fighting against the power searing through him, he tried to speak and instruct the computer, but couldn't. The muscles in his body were spasming uncontrollably from the current racing in and out of his being, passing through him as if he were insubstantial or maybe because he was now a part of the circuit. One with the power.

Let go of the leads, he thought, as lightning brightness obliterated what he could see, but his body refused to cooperate. Summoning the last of his fading consciousness, he managed one final word.

Release.

CHAPTER
9

The energy streamed through them like a tsunami crashing across the shore. Kellen and Selina braced themselves, absorbing the flood of power that the humans in the area would not even notice. But the energy would be felt by all the Hunters within several miles, awakening them to the existence of a great presence—another Quinchu, and a powerful one at that, considering the size and strength of the energy wave.

"It's him, isn't it?" Selina asked, covering her husband's hand with hers. The wave of energy had touched her deep inside, rousing memories of Kikin and how his aura felt as he nestled beside her. Inside her as a baby, she thought, laying her hand over her belly as she experienced a phantom kick.

Kellen nodded, wanting to believe the power had emanated from their son, but uncertain, given the earlier reports from his cadre captain and sergeant. "If it is, we must act quickly. If the Shadows arrive—"

"We will lose him." *Again*, Selina thought, but couldn't say so out loud. For so many years her husband had blamed himself for the loss. She would not add to his misery.

They would not lose their son again.

A muscle jumped along Kellen's jaw, vibrating with anger. "We will find him. We will take him back."

The continuation of their clan depended on locating their missing son. Kikin should possess the ability to gather energy to feed those in the clan who could no longer replenish their life forces. At fifty-two, Kellen and Selina were into the last decade of their second triad and could no longer meet all the clan's demands. Their powers were gradually diminishing, and because of that their Hunter clan declined in number as illness and time eroded their life forces.

While Hunters were stronger than humans in many ways, they had their weaknesses as well. Lately it seemed as if those debilities were taking the forefront, necessitating the infusion of energy from a Quinchu like their missing son.

But the safety of the humans also depended on keeping the Shadow Hunters away from Kikin, especially now that he was close to the Equinox. With such power, the Shadows would multiply in number and would need to drain more humans in order to keep the smallpox from ravaging their bodies.

"What if they find him before we do?" Selina asked, mirroring his own concern.

"Then it'll be war once again."

War. It had cost them so much last time. So many lost lives, both human and Hunter, he thought.

But there was no choice. They had searched for far too long not to accomplish their mission.

Kikin had to be found and brought back into their fold, no matter the cost.

How do you explain the unexplainable?

Avoidance, Bobbie thought later that night as she left a voice mail message canceling the physical therapy sessions she had scheduled for the rest of the week. She wasn't ready to deal with giving reasons to her therapist for her sudden and seemingly miraculous recovery. Rotation, strength, sensation, and responsiveness in her left arm and hand were almost all back to normal. She wasn't going to complain, but she was going to try to find out what had happened.

There was only one place to start: Adam Bruno.

She could have asked Tony for Adam's private number, but she wanted to speak with him face to face and check out whether the weird connection she had felt this afternoon had been real or a byproduct of the adrenaline pumping through her body because of the attack. That meant she had to find out where he lived.

She assumed an Internet search would be a bust, but people were sometimes careless about their privacy, especially with the proliferation of sites such as Twitter and Facebook.

Snap off a photo with your cell phone and post it and you could inadvertently be providing more information than you thought. A license plate in the photo or business in the background could give away your location. During her stint as a sergeant in Iraq, she had been forced to caution more than one unsuspecting soldier about such risks when they were snapping photos during their downtime. Plus, she had limited options for where else she could get more information about Adam, so she might as well give the Internet search a shot.

Easing into a chair at the dining room table, she typed "Adam Bruno" into Google and, just for kicks, hit the "I'm feeling lucky" button. No personal info, and as she had expected, the first hit was for the SolTerra website. Interestingly enough, Adam did a regular blog. She read through the first few entries, enjoying his easygoing style and the passion for his work that was evident in his posts.

The blog had a number of photos; the pictures were recent and shot by him personally, according to the information embedded in the files.

In a photograph displaying a series of solar panels, one of the buildings in the background looked familiar. She blew up the image and confirmed what she thought—it was an active adult building in nearby Spring Lake.

It made sense that he might be a local boy, considering that the SolTerra offices were in Neptune. But that still didn't put her any closer to tracking him down, and Bobbie didn't think she could sleep if she didn't at least try to speak to Adam tonight. She was too wired, her brain processing dozens of scenarios for all that had occurred during the attack and its aftermath.

As a Marine, she had been taught to consider all variables and plan for the future, and that training didn't just poof off because she was no longer on active duty.

She surfed for more info, and as she drilled through the pages that came up in the search, one caught her eye. A fancy home and garden magazine had done a photo shoot of Adam's digs. She recognized the house, sporting

solar panels like those in the blog photos, immediately—
she and her older brother Mick used to jog right past the
home on Ocean Avenue in Spring Lake.

She shut down her laptop and grabbed a lightweight
jacket. The weather had cooled, thanks to that night's
earlier storm. Hurrying as much as she could, she took
the elevator down to street level and was soon on her way
southbound along Ocean Avenue. It was a longer way to
go, but she didn't want to risk that she would somehow
pass the house.

Keeping a cautious pace, she drove through the various shorefront towns for several miles. She slowed at the
border of Spring Lake to look for his house, but realized it
was quite some distance away yet.

She continued past her sister's family's multi-million-
dollar beach-style home. The porch lights cast a welcom-
ing glow on the front steps, but beyond that the downstairs
was dark. Brightness in the front bedroom hinted at where
her very pregnant sister Liliana and newlywed husband
might be. She pushed away the pang of loneliness and
regret that she would never have the same joy, choosing
instead to rejoice in Liliana's happiness.

Pressing onward, Bobbie soon spotted Adam's house
just up on the right. Lights blazed beside the front door
and all along the first floor, alleviating any concern that
she might be waking him with her visit. But no car was
visible in the driveway or in front of the home. Probably
in the garage, she thought, as she pulled up to the curb.

Nervous sweat erupted along the palms of her hands
as she sat there, slightly more hesitant now than she had
been earlier. But she wasn't someone who let fear control
her. Ever.

Bravado gave her the impetus she needed to ease from her Sebring. She approached the door slowly, not that she could rush if she wanted to, determined to confront him. She pressed the doorbell and it rang. She waited, but no one answered.

Strange, she thought, and glanced through the sidelight on the door. Every light in the house was on, so where could he be?

Walking back down the steps and toward the garage, she stood on tiptoe and peered through the intricate glass panels near the top of the doors. A car was inside the garage: a very sweet merlot-colored Bentley convertible. Maybe there was room for playfulness in the workaholic Tony had described.

As she turned to head back to the front door, headlights caught her attention. Someone was pulling into the driveway, illuminating her as she stood by the garage. Snagged, she thought, and hoped that whoever was visiting was friendly.

The driver of the car shut its engine off, but kept the headlights on, placing Bobbie at a distinct disadvantage. She could barely see past the glare of the twin beams as the driver stepped out, keeping behind the protective cover of the door.

"Who are you?" the man called out.

"Roberta Carrera," she answered, shielding her eyes with her left hand to try to get a glimpse of the new arrival.

The headlights snapped off and the person eased from behind the door. He was an older man, late forties, she guessed, powerfully broad across the shoulders, but thickening at his waist to a middle-aged paunch. His dark hair showed signs of emerging gray at the temples.

As he took a step toward her, he reached into the jacket pocket of his dark suit and Bobbie tensed, shifting her weight to the balls of her feet in anticipation of an attack. She was relieved when the man only pulled out a badge, which gleamed dully in the illumination from the lights along the walk.

"Special Agent Bruno," he snapped precisely.

Adam's father, although the two men did not look alike in any way. Adam's face was all sharp angles, while this man's was rounded and more indistinct. His eyes were a muddy brown compared to Adam's stunning emerald. Even their hair color set them apart, as this man's was much darker than the sun-streaked dirty blond of Adam's.

When Adam's father reached where she stood, he asked, "What are you doing here?"

"I came to see Adam, but he's not home," she said, and motioned to the front door.

Worry furrowed the lines of his brow. "I spoke to him right around dinnertime, and he said he was staying in to do some work."

Brushing past her, he mimicked her previous action of checking the garage and muttered, "His car's here."

Before she could say anything else, he was racing up the walk to the door. Bobbie followed, leaning on her cane heavily as she rushed.

Bruno didn't ring. He had a key, it seemed, as he reached into his pocket and unlocked the door. He stepped into the foyer and paused, Bobbie slipping in to stand beside him.

"Adam?" he called out, and when there was no answer, he reached behind his back and pulled out a nine-millimeter pistol.

"Do you have a cell phone?" he asked.

Bobbie nodded and motioned to her pocket.

"Stay here. If I'm not back in two minutes, call 911," he commanded. Gun drawn, he entered the house and did a quick sweep of the floor before heading up the stairs.

Bobbie waited, impatient and feeling useless. She was familiar with the procedure for securing a location. She had done it dozens of times in Iraq and during an assortment of training sessions.

Since the first floor seemed secure, she walked farther into the house and realized why some fancy home and garden magazine would want to feature it. Expensive tan leather sectionals filled the large space of the living room and were offset with recliners in deeper shades of cocoa. Here and there was a splash of color in some throw pillows and a large abstract painting. On a nearby wall hung an immense plasma television, and beneath, cabinets displayed a wealth of audio/video equipment behind smoky black glass doors. Carefully selected accessories in black and silver completed the décor.

The room struck her as cold. Impersonal. More of a showcase than a place where someone lived.

But the neatness of it eliminated some of the worry about Adam's seeming disappearance. A burglar would have trashed the place or taken the pricey electronics. If another attack had occurred, she had no doubt Adam would have put up a fight and the space would not be as orderly as it was.

As she inched down the hallway, she heard something. She worked her way toward the sound coming from a door adjacent to the kitchen. She stopped and pressed her ear to the thick wood.

Voices, or rather, *a* voice. Artificial sounding.

She cautiously opened the wooden door and immediately detected the smell of burning plastic and metal. Like an electrical fire. And the voice again, not quite human, repeating one word.

Release.

Release.

Release.

"Special Agent Bruno," she shouted, and his footsteps pounded heavily on the stairs as he hurried from the floor above. When he noted the smell that had wafted out to the hall, he wasted no time in rushing past the door and down to the basement level.

Bobbie followed, hop-skipping down the stairs as fast as she could, cursing her injuries and the cane that knocked against the wall, rebounding and almost causing her to trip.

At the foot of the stairs was a small landing and, ahead of them, a glass door leading to what looked like a laboratory. As Bruno opened the door, the odors hit them, much more powerful than at the top of the stairs—burning plastic and a faint chemical smell.

They raced in and stopped dead. Bruno stood beside her, gaze locked on the scene before them, apparently unsure what to do.

Staring at the smoldering piles of what looked like a battery array, Bobbie had no such qualms. A fire extinguisher hung on the wall and she shuffled to it, yanked it from its mount, and returned to where Bruno still stood. She thrust the extinguisher against his chest with a tersely worded command and pointed a finger at the batteries.

"Go keep that from igniting."

Then she rushed to where Adam lay unconscious on the floor.

A number of electrodes and wires were connected to Adam's bare chest, and he held leads that fed back into the batteries. Grabbing the insulated wires, she yanked the leads out of his hands. Tracking the path of the other cables with her gaze, she stared at all the monitors and medical apparatus and realized each and every piece of equipment was dead.

Her one hope was that Adam wasn't also.

Laying her fingers along the side of his neck as she knelt beside him, she detected a pulse, strong, although racing. Beneath her fingers came that unnerving buzz of power. She ripped her hand away.

The smell and fumes in the room began to sting her eyes and burn the back of her throat. She had to get Adam out of there in case any of the vapors were toxic. Cupping the side of his face, she leaned closer.

"Adam. Do you hear me, Adam?" She stroked his cheek with her thumb, ignoring the prickling sensation against the pad of her finger. It was the rasp of his evening beard and nothing else, she told herself, even as her heartbeat kicked up a notch.

"Adam, wake up!"

His eyelids barely fluttered and she shifted her finger along his skin and murmured his name once again. That seemed to finally awaken him.

"Bobbie?" he said groggily, and tried to sit up, but was wobbly.

Bobbie slipped her arm around his shoulders to offer support. Everywhere skin met skin that odd vibration of energy sprang up, maybe even more powerfully than before.

Adam grew agitated and jerked away from her. "I'm fine," he said, but he was clearly not okay. His eyes seemed unfocused, and without her assistance, he wavered unsteadily.

The fumes mixed with the stench from the fire extinguisher and continued to burn like acid in her throat. They could not delay any longer. She ripped away the rest of the leads and electrodes attached to his body, eliciting a complaint from him as they came away with bits of hair, and maybe even some skin, she thought guiltily.

The pain, however, seemed to fully rouse him.

"We need to get out of here," she said, and pushed to her feet. She looked around for his father, hoping he could help them.

Bruno was at the foot of the stairs, staring at her as if he had just seen a ghost.

"Help me," she said, aware that if Adam needed more assistance she was too weak to provide it.

Bruno just shook his head and stared at his son, an almost fearful look in his eyes. *Weird*, was all that Bobbie could think in the short time it took for Adam to turn onto his knees and then slowly rise with her limited support.

"Can you walk?" she asked, and he nodded, but as he took a step, it was hesitant.

She slipped beneath his shoulder to stabilize him, ignoring the rush of power from his body to hers, and searched for his father once more, but Bruno was nowhere to be found. Cursing beneath her breath, she helped Adam to the stairs, where he paused to push a few buttons.

"Exhaust fans," he explained, and took a look at what remained of the batteries. "They're toast."

"Definitely," she agreed, but then he added, "No more danger. The lab will be fine."

She glanced up the flight of stairs. It seemed as if it was a million steps until the first floor. And there was no way they would make it up the narrow staircase melded together as they were.

"I can do it," he said, his voice stronger than it had been just a moment earlier. "You go first," he instructed.

She didn't argue with him. She couldn't brace him if he fell, and if he did and landed on her in her current condition...

Bobbie went up the stairs, Adam immediately behind her. By the time she reached the first floor, he seemed to be more aware and motioned for her to walk to the right.

She did and found herself in a spacious great room. Adam's father was already there, placing a large glass of water on the table. As he noticed them, he came to stand before Adam, but awkwardly, hands jammed in his pockets, as if he was forcing himself not to touch his son.

"Are you okay?" he asked woodenly.

Adam nodded, and his father immediately countered angrily with, "What the hell did you think you were doing?"

"An experiment," Adam replied coolly, and half-turned to face her.

"Are *you* okay?" he questioned, his emerald gaze alive with concern as he laid his hand at the small of her back.

As it had before, his touch awoke something in her body. Where his skin met hers in the gap between her T-shirt and jeans came a slight vibration and then warmth spread outward from that spot, alleviating the slight pain she had been feeling in her back all night long. But then it continued lower, creating the first tug of nascent desire between her legs. When his hand trembled slightly and his gaze darkened, she realized he was feeling it as well.

"I'm sorry. I didn't mean to touch you," Adam said, and ripped his hand away. But he had touched her, and since the moment he had laid his hand on her earlier, nothing could be the same. As if he understood that, he said, "Let me explain."

CHAPTER
10

Adam glanced at her. At that earnest and beautiful face that had intrigued him so from the moment he had seen her. Then he shot an anxious glance at his father. "Dad, Bobbie and I need a private moment."

"Don't you think I want to hear the explanation also?" he challenged.

"This is between Bobbie and me," Adam reiterated calmly.

A bright flush of color stained his father's cheeks and guilt slammed into Adam, especially when Bobbie said, "Your dad is worried. That's only natural after everything that's happened today."

Salvatore immediately picked up on her words. "What has happened today, Adam? Is there something else I should know?"

Bobbie winced as she realized her gaffe, but Adam tried to smooth things over. "I was going to tell you. I just wanted to try to get more information first."

Salvatore marched right up to them, his demeanor full of bluster, but also concern. "Tell me what?"

Adam shrugged, trying to act nonchalant. "There was an incident in the parking lot today. I was mugged by two men and Bobbie came to my aid."

Salvatore jerked his head from side to side as he glanced between them, his agitation clear. "You were mugged? And you didn't think to call me so I could help?"

"It's not the kind of case you handle. Besides, I didn't want to make it public and draw all kinds of attention to myself," Adam replied. That seemed to mollify his father somewhat.

"You're right. You don't need to be in the spotlight," he said, although he quickly tacked on, "I'm going, but we will talk about this in the morning."

With an abrupt nod in Adam's direction and a slight dip of acknowledgment to Bobbie, his father stalked from the room.

"Angry much," Bobbie said, and glanced up at him.

"He's a good dad. He's just not all touchy-feely like you and your family," Adam replied, recalling the easy camaraderie he had seen between her and Tony, and the love present in the photos in her home.

"What could you possibly know about me and my family?" she challenged, that liquor-colored gaze narrowing on him.

"I just assumed, since you and Tony seemed so close," he lied, and walked the short distance to the table where his father had left the glass of water.

"What about your mom? Shouldn't you let her know you're okay?"

"I don't have a mom," he replied, hating the unexpectedly injured tone that emerged in his voice.

"Everyone has a mom, Adam," Bobbie said with a playful kind of exasperation, attempting to lighten his mood.

"I'm adopted. I don't know who she is," he replied, and then quickly changed the subject. His words hid more than they told, and would likely make her question what else there was to his story.

"Can I get you anything?" He pulled out a chair and gestured for her to sit. Within him the energy he had gathered jumped crazily, and he knew he needed something stronger to quiet that nearly uncontrolled power skittering through his brain and body before it created problems.

"Just like that? You can play host after you almost... Would electrocute be an accurate way to describe the idiot thing you did to yourself?"

Her question needed no answer, so he sauntered to a bar tucked into a nearby set of cabinets. Grabbing a bottle of twenty-five-year-old single malt scotch and two glasses, he returned to the table, sat, and placed a glass before each of them. Pouring a few fingers of the liquor into the tumblers, he lifted his and made a toast.

"To my guardian angel."

"More like a harbinger of doom. Every time we see each other something bad happens," she said, but raised her glass, clicked it against his, and took a swig.

She made a face, disgust, not appreciation, and he chuckled. "You like it," he teased.

She took another sip, wrinkled her nose again. It was a cute nose, he decided, taking his time to examine her very expressive face.

"I'm not much of a drinker. It dulls the senses and I've got enough dullness going on as it is."

Whether she knew it or not, she skipped her gaze down her arm and to her leg before shooting it back up to stare at him. "But you changed that. Or at least, part of it."

He shook his head, not comprehending. "Me? How did I—"

"When you touched me. You put your hand on my arm and—"

"I didn't mean to hurt you." He recalled how in his desire to see that she was okay he had skimmed his fingertips along her arm. Lost control over his power, letting it leak out as his emotions overruled common sense.

With a strong shake of her head, she cupped his cheek. Her touch was already familiar and awoke need in him. The aura around her body broadened and grew an even richer blue, spreading onto him as she touched his face. The brightness of it matched the intensity in her golden gaze.

"You *helped* me. See," she said and elevated her left arm, rotated it, flexed, and made a tight fist with her hand. "I couldn't do this before your touch."

"That's not possible." His powers had always taken and not given.

She rubbed her thumb along his lips, and the scattered bits of energy racing through his body gathered into a molten pool at his center, then dipped lower as she scooted to the edge of her chair and inched closer to him.

"When you ran your fingers along my skin, I felt warmth. It turned into sharp tingles and then pins and needles," she explained, and then, as if she wanted to show him, she danced her fingers along the back of his hand.

Her caress awakened him, but not in a healing kind of

way. As she paused and her fingers trembled against his skin, he realized she was experiencing the passion as well.

He wanted to touch her. Wanted to savor the softness of her skin beneath his fingers, but he feared that contact. And not just because he might hurt her. He feared becoming any closer to this woman who was somehow making him want things that weren't possible for him.

"This isn't a good idea, Bobbie."

She stroked her hand up and down his arm and his gut twisted into a painful knot.

"You feel it, don't you? The connection?" she asked, her gaze filled with yearning and confusion. She, too, wanted as much as she feared.

"Whatever this is can only cause problems for both of us." But even as he said it, he pressed closer to her, pulled toward her by so many things: by the strength of heart he sensed; by the femininity encased in her warrior's body, and by the temptation of the power swirling all around her, creating a bond he had never encountered before with anyone else.

"I'm not the kind to run from a problem," she said as she reached up and ran her fingers through his hair, smoothing the short strands into place. The innocent action stoked alive more need and a sensation like static electricity against his scalp. As she quickly pulled away, it was a sign that she had sensed the effects of the power as well.

"I kind of gathered that when you helped me in the parking lot," he said with a chuckle, trying to downplay the way even minimal contact created a charge between them.

"You handled yourself pretty well. You probably didn't need my help."

He hesitated, contemplating just how much to tell her. Too much and he risked the secrets he and his father had kept for so long. Not enough and he maybe left her defenseless if the two men decided to come after her as well.

He opted for disclosure, wanting to safeguard her as much as possible. "Actually, those men were like the two of us. Different."

She shook her head. "I'm not different. I'm—"

She stopped as he ran the tip of his index finger along her lips and made it impossible to deny the sparks that flew from that contact and the way it roused an ache along her sex. The color of her eyes darkened to amber and she licked her lips nervously. "Why am I feeling this way?"

"You have an aura. It's stronger than any I've ever seen, except for possibly the two men from this afternoon," he explained, and because he couldn't stop touching her, he laid his hands on her bare arms, rubbed them up and down, which generated yet more electricity and heat between them. Everywhere he touched, her blue aura danced with silvery light.

Bobbie sucked in a shaky breath, battling the way her body was responding to his caress. Her nipples were rock hard and between her legs an insistent throb had her damp and achy. There was no denying his actions were the reason for it, but she needed to maintain a level head.

"Are you saying I'm like them?" she asked, and laid her hands against his chest. As she did so, another wave of power had her biting her lip against the sensations rocketing through her, which were mirrored in the rain-forest green of his eyes.

"Not quite. Their touch didn't make me feel like this,"

he admitted. Beneath the controlled tone of his voice was a low rumble, like thunder in the distance.

She licked her lips and gazed at him again, noted the concern and ardor battling in his features as he released her and backed a few feet away, creating needed space, but also a strange sensation of emptiness within her.

He continued with his explanation. "When they touched me, it was like I had run into an electrified fence. Intense shocks nearly took me down each time they laid their hands on me."

"But you got away. Did you do the same thing when you touched them?" she asked, and because she seemed to need something to do with her hands, she picked up the glass of scotch and took a quick sip. That perfect nose once again twitched in apparent distaste, although she didn't release her grip on the tumbler.

"I thought there was a jolt when we fought, but I'm not sure."

"Seems weird that you don't know what you can do." Her training as a Marine had taught her to understand her strengths and avoid any weaknesses. Years of training and war had honed that awareness of her abilities.

His lips thinned and she realized how her comment could have been taken as condemnation, so she quickly did damage repair. "In the Marines we were trained to know what we could do. I'm guessing you weren't lucky enough to have someone to help you like that."

"I've had no one." The pain behind the words was ach-ingly alive, so much so that she couldn't ignore it even though the last thing she wanted was to get more involved with him. She'd already had too much of conflict and wanted nothing more than a peaceful and stable life.

But she couldn't ignore his pain, so she closed the distance between them and cradled his cheek. That unnerving chatter of energy greeted her, but she pushed it back as she said, "I'm here now."

Adam's stomach did a somersault while his heart constricted almost painfully. "Now" was so fleeting an instant in time, but he welcomed it. In the brief moments that Fate had tossed them together, the growing emptiness he had been experiencing had abated.

He locked his gaze with hers—that smoky-hot look which ignited heat like that of the finely aged scotch he had tasted earlier. Shifting his face, her palm was soft against the rasp of his evening beard. A memory rose up, of the cat twisting and lifting its head for her caress. The pleasure that followed.

He wished he could do the same. Feel her touch across his skin. Experience the wonder of her kiss, but kissing her...

Kissing her would be insane, he thought in that split second before he made up his mind.

CHAPTER
11

It was like grabbing a live wire, Bobbie thought as his lips closed over hers. And although common sense told her to run, she couldn't deny that death had been too recent a visitor in her life and his touch made her feel alive again.

His kiss sparked sensation all along her body, whipping up the need that had already been simmering between them. Shifting ever nearer, she laid her hand on his shoulder to center herself as her head swam from the force of the desire snaking through her body.

The kiss continued as she met his mouth again and again. He was a wonderful kisser, knowing just when to back off and when to engage; skilled in the way he slipped his tongue in to play with hers and then teased her with a gentle bite of her lower lip.

She moaned at that, imagining his gifted mouth exploring her body. Wanting to discover other parts of him.

She lowered her hand to his chest. His skin was warm

and satiny, the hairs on his chest crisp as she cupped the deep swell of his pectoral muscle. His hard nipple pressed into her palm, and as she splayed her hand across his chest, the rapid beat of his heart drummed beneath her thumb before she moved to strum it across his nipple.

He groaned and the sound rumbled through her, creating an answering vibration between her legs. Making her want more.

"Touch me, Adam," she said, and was unprepared for his response.

"I can't, Bobbie. I can't do this," he said, and pushed away from her. The feet of the kitchen chair squeaked against the tiled floor with the motion and then he was on his feet, pacing before her.

There was no denying he had been as affected by their encounter as she had been. The proof was right there in the strong jut of his erection against his sweats, which made her wonder about his reaction to her request.

"Why not, Adam? If there's one thing I know it's that time is too short not to grab what you want before it's too late."

His gaze was understanding as it met hers. "I don't want to add to your hurt."

"You think you'd hurt me?" she said, and then recalled his earlier words. His response to her when she had mentioned his touch.

Rising from her chair, she took a step toward him, but he held up his hand to keep her away and she felt it then.

Power. Pouring off his hand and creating an almost physical barrier.

"What is this that I'm feeling?" she asked, raising her hand and pressing against that field of energy, watching it glaze over like frost on a winter window beneath her hand. As she pushed onward, it awakened a corresponding glimmer of lighter blue along her wrist and arm.

"It's me, Bobbie. It's why I can't be with you," he said, a wealth of hurt and loneliness evident in his gaze and voice. So much hurt and loneliness that it caused her heart to ache. She might have known hard times in her life, but she had never been alone or lacked for love.

Pressing forward, she experienced the resistance of his energy, but didn't let that stop her. As she muscled her way past the barrier he had tossed up, it was like being swallowed up in a vortex of power. Her body vibrated from the waves as they buffeted her, causing her to grow weak.

She took another step toward him, but faltered, as if she were slogging through a foot of heavy mud with a full pack of gear.

With her gaze locked on his, she realized he wouldn't really hurt her. Whatever weird thing this was, she was safe, although each step she took became increasingly difficult.

"Please stay away," he said, and gave another shove, which sent her reeling backward, near collapse as the rush of energy that came with it seemed to rob her of the last of her strength. Her knees buckled then, but he was immediately there, wrapping his arms around her to hold her close.

"I'm sorry. I didn't mean to do that," he said.

She looked up at him, amazed and yet puzzled. "What are you?"

Sadness darkened the green of his eyes until they were almost black. "I wish I knew."

• • •

The Light Hunters' cadre patrolled the area around Adam Bruno's home, vigilant for any signs of danger, prepared to battle the Shadow Hunters if they arrived on the scene.

All appeared to be quiet, although the residual ribbons of energy from the earlier flood lingered, dancing in the air, as colorful as a brilliant aurora borealis display to those who could see them.

Pity the humans who could not perceive the energy storm's beauty, Andres thought. The captain of the clan's cadre strode beneath the fluttering undulations of power, vigilant. All seemed calm, he thought, as he casually walked a large brown and black dog on what appeared to be a perfectly ordinary evening stroll.

Adam Bruno's home took up the entire block, leaving a great deal of space between him and his neighbors. Lush, carefully tended gardens surrounded the large mansion across the street from the beachfront. White fencing enclosed most of the property, and as Andres turned the corner, he took note of the car parked at the curb in front of the home.

From his surveillance he knew it did not belong to either Adam or the man who had stolen him and claimed him as his son, which made Andres wonder if the woman from that afternoon was already there. Had she been responsible for the release of power by draining the Quinchu? He continued his stroll past the front of the property, his pace slightly more hurried.

The dog beside him whined and looked upward, voicing his concern. Andres dropped to one knee and pulled the dog close, scratching its ruff. "Easy, Eduardo. We must not act rashly."

Eduardo, who had assumed the canine shell from a German shepherd in a yard across the street, shook his head and jumped up and down on his front paws, clearly agitated.

Andres understood the reason for his partner's distress. "If the woman is a Shadow, we will deal with her." If she hadn't already drained the Quinchu of power, that is. If she had, they might have quite a battle on their hands. A fully charged Shadow Hunter possessed enormous power and was capable of great harm. An attack of such a group of Shadows was the reason they had lost their Quinchu's son in the first place.

Andres would not let that happen again.

Rising to his feet, Andres jerked on the chain and urged Eduardo forward until he could see through the large glass windows of the home. Light spilled into the night.

She was inside, sitting on the sofa, the blue of her aura strong as if she had just fed, but not so empowered that she could not be defeated. A second later a man entered the room, walked to where the woman sat and offered her a glass. Then the man plopped down on the coffee table before her, his back to the windows, but there was no doubting who it was.

Adam Bruno, apparently alive, and from what Andres could see, uninjured.

All around him shone a potent aura of energy, way more powerful than it had been earlier in the day. It shimmered in an intense spectrum of blues tinged with threads of silver and red. The field of energy was immensely larger than any Andres had ever seen before. Not even Kellen and Selina, the Quinchus of their clan, possessed such potency. As their son, Kikin's power signature should have been similar, but Adam's was not.

How could he have misread that aura earlier in the day? And was it possible that Adam Bruno was not their missing Kikin, but a Quinchu from some other nearby clan?

Beside him Eduardo began to whine. As Andres glanced down, he realized why. Eduardo was beginning to revert to his true form. Already the dog's thick black and brown fur was receding, allowing glimpses of peach-colored skin beneath. His paws had softened, showing the nail beds and fingertips of a human.

Andres scooped Eduardo up, but could not zap them to the van, since they were too visible. He rushed back to where the remaining members of their cadre waited. The side door slid open and Andres deposited Eduardo onto the bed of the vehicle. Jerking the door closed behind him, he watched as Eduardo's body shook and heaved as the transformation raced along. The elongated snout of the shepherd slid back, flattening into familiar features as his pointed ears also shortened and rounded. The sharp teeth and canines smoothed to human bluntness and soon thereafter came the pop of bones resuming their normal positions as tendons and muscles sang with tension during their elongation. After a low, almost pitiful wail, however, the transformation stopped, leaving Eduardo's lower half shrunken and in the form of the canine.

Drained, Eduardo's head lolled limply to the floor. He lacked the power to complete the transformation, and if he didn't do so quickly, he would die. His body could not pump enough blood through the smaller dog shape to maintain his human-sized organs.

As Andres gripped Eduardo's hand, he realized that Eduardo's life force was even weaker than he had thought. "Hang on, my friend."

Eduardo nodded, but it was a feeble motion. As his eyes rolled back into his head, Andres feared the worst and cursed the day the humans had brought their sickness to the Hunters.

"Hurry home. The Quinchus must restore him immediately," Andres instructed, although he feared Eduardo would not last that long.

"We are leaving?" asked Stephan, the cadre member behind the wheel.

"There is nothing happening right now."

Turning to the other cadre members in the van, he commanded, "Marcus and Lucas. Secure the perimeter in case the Shadows track the source of the power or the woman causes a problem."

The two soldiers left the van and then Andres returned his attention to Eduardo. His friend's grasp was frail and Andres sensed the life force fading from him. Andres knew of Eduardo's reluctance to accept sustenance from other Hunters like him, but it was necessary. They were not powerful energy gatherers and normally relied on the Quinchus to sustain them. Without such feedings, it might take days to recover from even a simple expenditure of energy, like that which had transformed Eduardo into the German shepherd.

Bending close to Eduardo, he urged, "I need you with me if the Shadows attack. Accept what I offer freely."

With that plea to his responsibility to the clan, Eduardo finally opened his eyes and grasped Andres's hand tighter. Opening the gateway to his life force, Eduardo allowed Andres to gift him with a portion of his own limited energy. Although it would weaken Andres, he hoped he would still be strong enough to fight if that proved necessary.

Inside him Andres experienced the pull of power into

his friend. The drain made him nearly light-headed, but as he watched, the last vestiges of the dog vanished, leaving behind a fully transformed Eduardo, his body drenched and trembling from the shapeshifting.

Andres didn't release his grasp, aware that Eduardo needed to continue feeding to survive. He was too weak, and it worried Andres that the transformation had taken so much of his friend's power. It did not bode well for his continued existence.

Within a few minutes of feeding, Eduardo was already better. His color remained pale and a fine sweat lingered on his body, but he was able to take a sip of the water that another cadre member offered him.

It would only be a few minutes more before they were at the oceanfront compound where his clan leaders had taken residence. There the Quinchus could provide Eduardo even greater strength, so that he would be capable of resuming his duties.

Or at least that's what Andres hoped. Andres could ill afford to lose even one man. He would need each and every available soldier in the cadre should the Shadows emerge or if Adam Bruno turned out to be something other than what they believed.

And if that happened...

Lord help both the Hunters and the humans.

CHAPTER
12

Bobbie accepted the fresh glass of scotch without hesitation, needing something to hold in order to still the trembling of her fingers.

Adam plopped down on the coffee table before her, his gaze dark with emotion. "Are you okay?"

Okay? She was attracted to a man capable of all kinds of weird things, who made her body tingle—and maybe not in a good way—and whom someone had tried to kidnap.

"I'm okay, but I don't understand any of this," she admitted, shaking her head.

He nodded, lowered his gaze, and with a shrug said, "Would it help at all if I said I didn't understand it either?"

"No. I'm used to order and control."

A harsh laugh burst from him and he gave an angry shake of his head. "That's all I've ever had in my life and I still feel like I have nothing sometimes."

Another shrug rippled across those broad, beautiful

shoulders. Despite what had happened before, she needed to touch him, and she suspected he needed the comfort also. Laying her hand on his shoulder, she ignored the rash of his power against her palm and trailed her hand up the corded muscles in his neck to cradle his cheek. Urging his face upward, she rubbed the chiseled line of his jaw, where a muscle ticked nervously. "Nothing? You have family and friends, right?"

"Not really. My father was afraid of revealing what I could do to others, so I was home schooled until I got tired of being so alone. I insisted on going to a public high school when I was twelve."

"Twelve? In high school? Must have been rough."

That stark laugh came again. "Luckily I was a big kid. Made it easier to blend in, but I always felt out of place."

And not just in school, she suspected. Even now, as successful as he was, Adam still seemed to be an outsider. In some ways, she understood.

"When my family first came here, we were different. We were determined to show we were worthy of being here. In the Marines, I had to prove myself again, so I know what it's like," she urged, and tracked her thumb down to the perfect cleft in his chin, circled the edges of it, and watched as that shimmer of sky blue rose again along with warmth and need.

"So maybe we've got something in common." The ghost of a smile teased his lips before he raised his hand and grasped hers, moving it away from his body. But he didn't release her hand. A pleasant buzz of connection dallied where skin met skin as he rested their joined hands on her thigh.

"It's almost like the vibes from a massager," she said.

Adam peered down to where their hands lay. The paler blue of her aura had spread over his as if accepting the union. "I wish I knew what it was. I've been trying to find out for years—"

"Years?" she jumped in. "Doesn't your father have information about your background?"

"I'm not really sure what my father does or doesn't know." He withdrew his hand from hers, severing their connection. He couldn't explain to her about all of his father's nasty need-to-know CIA kind of crap. Or maybe he didn't need to, he considered. Maybe she already knew because she was a part of whatever was going on.

"Adam?" she questioned, her gaze traveling across his features as she sensed his withdrawal. She reached for him, but he backed away and the hurt blossomed on her face.

"Did I say something wrong?" she asked.

"You seem to have a lot of questions all of a sudden."

She jerked to her feet, snagged her cane, and gave him needed distance, pacing awkwardly before she rounded on him.

"You think I had something to do with what happened today?"

"Two men try to grab me and suddenly there you are with an aura that I've never seen on anyone else before."

A disbelieving snort burst from her. When she spoke, her body quivered with tension as she jabbed a long, elegant finger in his direction. Each poke caused a shudder against his aura, as if she were physically touching him. "I didn't even know who you were before today."

He rose from the coffee table and approached until he was almost nose to nose with her. "But now you know who I am. What I can do, especially for you," he pressed and, for good measure, skimmed his hand down her left arm again. There was no denying the shock of power that had her jerking away from him.

"Damn you. I didn't ask to be brought into this. I wouldn't ask—"

"Because you've already been through enough conflict?" he asked, and grabbed hold of her waist, but his touch was soothing once again, as his concern for her and compassion for what she had suffered replaced his doubt and fear.

"I'm sorry," he said, but she was shoving away from him, leaning heavily on her cane as she headed for the door.

He chased after her and stepped into her path, forcing her to stop. "I'm sorry," he repeated, and reached for her, his touch gentle, tender, as he brushed his hands up and down her arms, only the most intense control keeping him from any seepage of his vitality.

She tilted her head up defiantly, fire kindling in her hazel gaze. "I had nothing to do with today. I've never seen those men before."

It would take an Oscar-worthy actress to fake the earnestness in her voice or the resoluteness of her features. In that instant he knew he had only one decision to make.

Trust her or continue to be alone.

Dragging in a ragged breath, he held it for long moments before he expelled it shakily and said, "I believe you."

There was no denying what it had taken for him to reach that decision, Bobbie thought.

It was clear from the way his shoulders sagged with

frustration and the shadows in his eyes that stole the life from them. She stepped near and wrapped her arms around him, offering comfort, laying her face alongside his and whispering, "We'll work together to find out what's going on."

"Why would you do that?" he asked, his body still stiff in her arms, his hands hanging loosely at his sides.

She inched back a bit and he glanced at her. So many emotions played across his face that it was impossible to take a read of him. Bringing her arms around, she rested a hand on each cheek, sensing the tingle of power once more, but pushing it away.

"Because I don't want you to feel so alone anymore."

Something broke free in him then. He finally encircled her waist and rested his forehead on hers. Long moments passed as the comfort of the embrace drove away earlier fears and upset. When peace finally overtook them, the contact slowly transformed.

Adam nuzzled his nose along the side of her face. "Thank you for that, but I guess we should work on it tomorrow. You look a little tired."

She turned toward him, her lips brushing along the line of his jaw as she said, "I am. I should go."

"You could stay."

Stay.

The word echoed in her brain over and over.

Stay.

Seemingly a simple action, but not. Staying meant opening up so much more of herself to him. It wasn't just the physical wounds that were still too fresh. Her emotions were a jumble and surprisingly fragile. She had always considered herself to be strong inside and out, but the deaths of her men continued to haunt her, as did the guilt. That made it difficult for her to really feel anything else or trust in her emotions, not to mention that she had been hoping for peace in her civilian life. If today was proof of one thing it was that being with Adam might entail risk. She was unsure whether she could handle that on a daily basis.

"It's too soon," she replied, and with a resigned smile, he nodded.

"I understand. I'll drive you home." He dropped a quick kiss on her cheek and took a step away from her, but she snared his hand.

"I'm a big girl. I can take care of myself."

"I'm sure you can, judging from what I saw this afternoon. But my father raised me to be a gentleman."

She hugged him hard and said, "I appreciate the offer, but I need my car in the morning."

"I'll make arrangements so it will be there first thing," he said. She recognized that he was determined, and in a way, she kind of liked it. It was nice to have someone who cared. With a dip of her head and a playful shake of his hand, she accepted his kindness.

He smiled, a broad and relaxed grin with a playful dimple that only made him even more handsome and caused a hitch in her heartbeat.

"Let me get a shirt and keys," he said. He rushed upstairs and loped back down the steps, shrugging on a pale blue polo shirt that brought out hints of teal in his eyes and hugged the muscles of his upper body. Then they walked hand in hand toward the kitchen. At the far end, by a door that must lead to the garage, his keys sat on the counter.

He snatched them up as they walked out into the space where the Bentley sat, bright, shiny, and almost red.

"Nice car," she said as he walked her to the passenger side.

"It's a sweet ride," he replied, dragging a chuckle from her and causing him to raise an eyebrow in question.

"A family joke. Let's just say, it's comforting to know that you're actually human despite the money."

He arched up the other eyebrow. "Is that a problem for you? The money?"

Facing him, she ran her hand along the side of his head, smoothing down an errant spike of sun-bleached hair. "It is if you're not a nice guy."

He narrowed his gaze and examined her. "Am I a nice guy?"

Bobbie shook her head and chuckled. "So far, Adam. Only time will tell."

CHAPTER 13

Nobody fucked with Salvatore Bruno. Not the assorted slime balls he had dealt with as a Texas Ranger. Not the overseas mobsters whom he had infiltrated in his first stints in his special CIA unit. Not even the other people in his group who had come to understand he could be one badass motherfucker if they messed with one of his investigations.

As he paced back and forth in his bedroom, he contemplated why Alexander had decided that it would be better to snag Adam on his own rather than continue with their plan. Up until tonight, Salvatore had thought that they were all in agreement that it made more sense for Salvatore to introduce Adam to a potential mate and eventually reintegrate him with his people to advance the Genesis project.

He had thought that both Alexander Sombrosa and he were on board—that this was one time finesse would work better than force.

Given Sombrosa's apparent double cross, Salvatore had obviously been mistaken. Which meant that he had to watch not only Adam's back, but his own. He didn't put it above Sombrosa to attempt to eliminate him so that he could do what he pleased with Adam.

To safeguard himself and Genesis, Salvatore needed more information about what had transpired that afternoon so he could set his trap for Sombrosa. Since Adam had mentioned that the incident had happened in the Sol-Terra parking lot, Salvatore used a back door that he had implanted to access the company's network. He quickly found the security videos and reclined in his chair as he fast-forwarded through the day's recordings until he got to the section that showed the attack.

Via the silent color videos, he observed as Adam and Bobbie fought off the two attackers who had emerged from the nondescript van. He snapped off screen prints of the two men. As he did so, it occurred to him that one of them seemed familiar, but Salvatore had a hard time matching the face to anyone he had met in Alexander's cadre. Maybe Sombrosa hadn't been involved in the attempt.

Was the man familiar because he was from an old case? he thought and printed out the photo so he could study the man's face more carefully. Grabbing the photo, he rose and poured himself a scotch on the rocks. He took a long, slow sip, and the warmth of the alcohol traveled down his throat as he returned to his desk, his eyes glued to the photo. Something about the man's face continued to drag worrisomely on his memory.

With a quicker, almost impatient swig of the scotch, he paced, alternating the sips of scotch with a swirl of the ice and liquor in the glass while he searched his brain for a clue.

Suddenly it came to him.

"Shit," he said, and slammed the almost empty glass on his desk. He unlocked the side drawers on his desk and pulled out his files, which included a highly classified National Security Association archive available to only a chosen few. He was one of the select individuals with high enough security clearance, in light of his participation in his clandestine CIA team, a team that had been involved in this particular NSA mission because of the peculiarity of the crimes.

Opening the file, he flipped through the papers and cursed once again when he confirmed why the attacker looked familiar. Twenty years earlier the man had been a prime suspect in one of Salvatore's cases when he had been with the Texas Rangers, a twenty-year-old case involving a series of mysterious murders in the South Texas desert.

Twenty years, Salvatore thought, and tossed back the remainder of the scotch.

Sombrosa had to be involved in the attack. Why else would there be a link to the case in which he had taken Adam from his people? Anger returned at Sombrosa's duplicity, but Salvatore knew he had to keep a cool head. Sombrosa would be furious that his men had failed. If they were still alive—he suspected Alexander dealt harshly with failure—plans were probably already underway for another attack.

Sombrosa would also likely be playing it cool, waiting for a call from Salvatore with a report on his matchmaking progress. Salvatore wasn't going to disappoint him.

As long as Sombrosa thought he was clear of suspicion, Salvatore was one up on him.

Dialing, Salvatore baited the trap, nonchalantly advising Sombrosa that he was still working on setting up the date with Maya and earning a rather offhanded reminder from his supposed partner that time was running out. The reply wasn't unexpected, but its too-blasé tone bothered him.

Not even Sombrosa could be that good a liar, could he? Salvatore wondered.

Before Sombrosa's duplicity, Salvatore had been determined to arrange for Adam's peaceful return to his Hunter clan and the commencement of Genesis. Now another objective would take priority: determining whether Sombrosa was behind the attempted kidnapping. If he was, there was no way Salvatore would trust Sombrosa with both his son and his precious project.

As Adam drove her home, Bobbie kept vigilant for anything unusual, but it was a quiet and uneventful ride to her condo. Adam eased into a spot by her front door and killed the engine, seeming hesitant to leave.

In truth, she wasn't in such a rush for him to go. He fascinated her, and not because of his powers. Possibly in spite of them. She was more interested in finding out about the lonely boy who had grown up into such a seemingly confident and successful man. But then again, adversity often bred strength. She had seen it in the Marines. She had lived it.

"Would you like to come up?" she said, at the same time that he asked, "Can you do lunch tomorrow?"

They both smiled, and because she realized it made sense to sleep on their attraction and take a step back from what had transpired that day, she quickly replied, "I'd love to have lunch."

His smile broadened and a playful dimple emerged on the right side of his face. "I've never eaten at your family's place."

Although she loved her family, she thought about all the conjecture that would occur if she brought in a man. The last time she had done so it had been Gil, at a time when they thought their relationship would lead somewhere. It hadn't, and she wasn't sure if whatever was going on between her and Adam would lead anywhere, either. Because of that she said, "Unless you want a replay of the Spanish Inquisition, we might be better off going somewhere else."

"How about I pick you up at twelve and then we can decide where to go?"

She nodded and opened the passenger door, hesitating, but he quickly put an end to her doubt about how to end the night.

Leaning over, he whispered his lips against hers, the kiss filled with possibilities rather than the unbridled passion of before.

It still managed to curl her toes.

"Number 301," she said with a shaky caress of her hand along his cheek, and forced herself to leave the cockpit of the car.

Adam watched her enter the building and immediately felt her absence, almost as if she was a part of him that had been missing and suddenly found. Ridiculous, he thought. It was just an overreaction to spending too much time working and not enough time with the right kind of women. But as he pulled away from the curb, he couldn't deny that Bobbie was just that—the right kind of woman.

CHAPTER
14

Bobbie had awoken to a beautiful spring day. The cloudless sky was a brilliant cerulean blue, and a refreshing breeze off the ocean had blown away the heat and humidity from the day before. It was too beautiful a day to spend inside.

Bolstered by the renewed strength in her arm and hand, she had taken a long stroll along the boardwalk, enjoying the solitude of the early morning. She pushed herself as long as she could before heading back for a wickedly steamy shower that melted any achiness from her body but only added to the excitement of seeing Adam as she recalled his kisses and imagined where they might lead.

He rang her bell precisely at twelve and she tamped down the rush of eagerness as she advised over the intercom, "I'll be there in a second."

She hurried down in the elevator and out the door to find him leaning against the bumper of his car. The Bentley gleamed in the bright spring sun, but so did he, she realized. An intense aura of deep royal blue shot through with bits of silver and red limned his body. His eyes had gone from that amazing rain-forest green to an almost neon shade.

She approached him, and as she grabbed hold of his hand, the hum of his power greeted her. Glancing down, she noticed a pale blue surrounding her own hand—the aura he had mentioned the night before. Rising on tiptoe to brush a quick kiss across his lips, she playfully whispered, "Does this mean you're glad to see me?"

He left no doubt about that as he encircled her waist with his arm, dragged her close, and kissed her. Warmth and power washed over her, immediately dragging forth intense desire. Almost unable to control herself, she rubbed her hips across the erection nestled tight to her belly.

A low growl erupted from him, rumbling through her body. The vibration strummed the parts of her that were already aching for more. With a shaky exhalation, she put some needed distance between them and said, "How about we walk to lunch?"

He grinned and said, "I think that'll give us time to cool off."

Although Bobbie suspected an Arctic nor'easter wouldn't do the trick, she nodded, grateful that he hadn't questioned her ability to do the walk. She was tired of being coddled all the time.

Holding hands, they pushed away from the car, and as they did so, she said, "I can see it this time. Your aura and part of mine." She glanced down at their joined hands to emphasize her point.

With a measured breath, Adam said, "Emotion makes me lose control."

A second later she could feel him reining his power back in, and the glow that had surrounded him disappeared, as did the weaker shimmer of her aura at their hands. With that, some of the intense need within her abated as well, and in a way she was thankful. She wanted to get to know him better without the specter of need interfering.

Adam breathed a relieved sigh as he gauged that his power was back where it should be, nestled deep inside him and not visible to Bobbie or anyone else. He hadn't realized just how much being with her could affect him. Restraining the power had also tamed the need that had been ravaging his insides from the moment he had laid eyes on her. He supposed that was a good thing, since he didn't want to be a powder keg with a short fuse, ready to blow the moment she touched him.

And she would touch him. Make love to him. He was sure of that, because there was just too much attraction for it not to happen. It was only a question of having it occur when the time was right and not before.

For now, as they walked hand in hand toward the center of town, he would enjoy the kind of quiet human time that couples were supposed to share—something he hadn't done before, but he suspected being with Bobbie would provide him with a lot of delightful firsts.

As they strolled up Main Avenue, they opted to eat at one of the outdoor tables at Nagles in light of the gorgeous day. After they ordered, Bobbie tilted her head up to the skies and with a heartfelt sigh said, "Can you feel that? How wonderful the sun is on your skin?"

He realized that she didn't even recognize that she was gathering power. It was obvious to him from the way the rays of the sun brightened the pale blue of her aura as it grew stronger. It made him wonder why she didn't know and what she was, because as similar as they were, he was certain she didn't possess the same abilities that he did.

"It's beautiful," he said, and trailed his finger along the smoothness of her cheek, which came alight at his touch.

She gazed at him then, those amazing golden eyes alive. "If you keep that up, we may need to get our food to go."

He chuckled and shook his head. "Are you always that direct?" he said, not that he would want her any other way. In the short time he'd been in business, he had spent too much time with people who were too afraid of losing his favor to be honest.

"Life is too short to be anything else." With her words, some of the joy faded from her eyes, and he knew without asking that she was thinking of her platoon. Of the men who would never come home.

The quick service of the waitress spared him from having to reply, because in all sincerity, he didn't know what he could say to her that wouldn't be just like the platitudes she had likely heard thousands of times before. A few minutes of silence followed as they both dug into their meals, but then she brightened up and started asking him the kinds of questions that he suspected most people asked on a first date.

A first date, Adam thought, the idea warming him inside, since it was such a normal concept. He had never done normal, and maybe that was part of Bobbie's appeal. Even knowing what he could do, she wasn't treating him differently.

He answered the routine questions and asked some of

his own, but as he did so, he noticed that her attention was pulled toward the street off and on in a way that was more than just a casual glance. The third time she did it he tracked her gaze and realized why.

A Jeep Wrangler with two men in it crept slowly past the restaurant. Even across the distance separating them he saw a faint hint of murky red surrounding them. Not as powerful as that of their attackers from the day before, but definitely there and impossible to ignore.

"When did you first see them?" he asked, after the waitress had taken away their empty plates.

Bobbie's lips thinned into a tight line and a ridge of worry wrinkled her brow. "About fifteen minutes ago. The first time I didn't think much of it. The second..."

And this made a third, he thought. "Direct and observant."

Bobbie shrugged. She had been a Marine for too long and some things never left you—like being uberaware of your surroundings. Maybe if she had been more aware that Christmas morning in Baghdad her men would be alive, but she drove that guilt away. It wouldn't change the past. It wouldn't help her now.

"*Semper fi,*" she said, and then added, "Always a Marine, Adam. Some things just become part of who you are."

Her hand was resting on the tabletop and he gave it a reassuring squeeze. "Whenever you need to talk, I'm here, Bobbie."

While she appreciated the gesture, she wasn't ready to unload on him. It wasn't in her nature to show such weakness, just as it wasn't in her nature to run from a problem.

Adam was definitely a problem.

Or at least, the people following him were. If they wanted to grab him again, he had to be ready. Or better yet, he needed to head off the attack in the first place, and the one way to do that was find out where their home base was.

"You need to tail the tail to find out who sent them," she said, and he nodded.

"I was just thinking the same thing."

Leaning toward him, she whispered close to the shell of his ear, "They need to think we didn't see them, so act naturally."

"Like this?" He cradled the back of her head in one big hand and urged her close, nuzzled her nose with his before taking her mouth with a kiss that had her forgetting everything but him.

When she finally broke away to take a breath, she murmured, "Like that."

He chuckled, and when the waitress approached with the bill just a second later, the knowing smile on the young girl's face said that at least she had bought the lovey-dovey act.

Adam tossed several bills on the table, rose, and offered Bobbie his hand. She took it, experiencing again that rush of his power that had her heart racing. As they had earlier, they strolled slowly back toward her condo, only this time they were vigilant. She caught sight of the Jeep one other time before they reached the door to her building.

Once there, she walked with him to his car and said, "You're not going back to the office. You have errands to run."

"I do?" he asked, and leaned on the bumper, hauling her close once more.

"You do. Pick up some dry cleaning. Go to the drugstore. You park this very obvious car somewhere and spend a few minutes in each place. I'll be watching, and once I make them, I will call you."

He reached into his pocket and said, "Let me call you now so you have my number."

He did, and she ignored the buzz of the phone in her back pocket. "I want you to make a few stops. I'll make contact when I think it's time and you'll have to find a back way out of whatever building you're in. Then I'll pick you up so we can tail them once they realize you're not coming out."

He narrowed his eyes, considering her. "You learned this in the Marines?"

She shook her head and said, "No, from my brother who had a private security company. I worked in his office one summer before joining the Marines."

"You've had an interesting life, I see," he said, leaned toward her, and kissed her once more.

"Got to make it convincing, is that it?" she teased when they broke apart.

"Totally," he said, and after a brief hug, he stepped away and walked around to the driver's side of his car. She quickly did the same, heading down the block to where her Sebring was parked. One of Adam's people had returned it earlier that morning.

She was about to slip into her seat when her phone chimed to announce a text message. She pulled it out of her pocket. Adam had sent her the address for the dry cleaner.

Perfect. That would allow her to hang farther back in the hope of spotting the Jeep Wrangler.

Texting back "k," she watched him pull away from the

curb, eased into her seat, and waited for a moment before taking off in the same direction as Adam. As she drove, she could see him quite a distance ahead of her, but no sign of the 4x4 that had passed them earlier. She continued, keeping a discreet distance and parking several yards away from the dry cleaner on Main Avenue. She exited her car and approached the display for the store closest to her. As she made believe she was eyeing the assorted clothes in the window, she watched the reflection of the vehicles that drove by, on the lookout for the Jeep.

Nothing, but that didn't mean anything. Maybe the two men had realized that they had been made and were being more cautious. After a few minutes, her phone chimed again. Another text from Adam with his next stop: the Macaroon Shop in Avon-by-Sea. Even though she had just eaten, her mouth watered at the thought of their almond macaroons.

She slipped back into her car, and as he came out of the dry cleaner holding his shirts, she pulled out of her parking spot and drove by him. She kept to the right, moving slowly to keep him in her rearview mirror.

At the bakery he once again stopped, entered the store, and came out with a box while she parked and watched out for the suspicious vehicle. Not a thing, and they repeated their steps, Adam running errand after errand until she finally caught sight of the Wrangler pulling into the parking lot of the local grocery store. It was an establishment she knew well, and after making sure Adam walked in and the two men were waiting for him, she drove to a spot around one corner of the building where there was a little-known entrance, one that was out of the line of sight of Adam's stalkers.

Parking the car, she sent a message to Adam that they had a bite and she would meet him in the dairy aisle, which was immediately adjacent to the seldom-used entrance. She went inside, her steps a trifle slow, as her leg had a cramp from the long period of inactivity as she drove around.

He was waiting for her, and concern swept over his features as he saw her limp. "You okay?"

"Just a cramp. The good news is, we've got them waiting for us."

Adam smiled. "I'm assuming we make them wait a good long time and then follow them."

She nodded. "You assumed right. But if you can get someone to pick up your car, preferably a mechanic, they'll think you're gone and head out faster."

Adam's grin broadened. "You're good. It's nice to know you're on my side."

He dialed and she listened in as he asked the mechanic at his garage to have someone pick up his car, detail it, and return it to his home by six. There seemed to be no argument on the line about schedules, availability, or any of the other things that popped up whenever she tried to schedule service. When he hung up, she said, "I guess money talks."

He didn't fail to notice the terseness in her words. "I helped Mike out a few years ago when he was in a tight spot."

"You gave him a loan," she said, deadpan.

"Mike had an idea for a way to retrofit internal combustion engines to use solar power during low demand performance. I gave him the opportunity to build, patent, and license the technology," he explained, and some of her earlier tension faded.

"Teach a man to fish—"

"And you feed him for a lifetime. Mike doesn't need to work anymore, but he loves my sweet ride," he said with a chuckle.

He was a man full of surprises, Bobbie thought, enjoying their journey of discovery. Snaring his hand, she led him from the store and to her convertible, where she tossed him the keys and said, "We should put the top up. Less visible that way."

When they were ensconced in her car, she guided him back around close to the Jeep Wrangler, where they parked and waited. Mike the mechanic showed up only about fifteen minutes later and loaded the Bentley onto his flatbed.

As the men noticed what was going on, they pulled out of their spot. Adam and Bobbie followed, making the hunters the hunted, following them as they drove south along Main Avenue until they were past Adam's Spring Lake home. They were just beyond the town line when the Jeep turned onto one of the side streets and proceeded until they were back on Ocean Avenue and in front of one of the larger multimillion-dollar mansions that were right on the beach.

They kept on going past the home as the Jeep parked in the circular drive, and the two men entered the home. Even with the bright sunlight, which sometimes bleached out weak auras, Adam could detect the brick-red aura surrounding them.

"They're like the men who attacked yesterday. Same field of power, only not as potent," he advised.

Bobbie scrunched her eyes together, as if trying to make it out, but then shook her head. "Can't see it, but these guys weren't as big and strong as the others."

"Their second string, maybe?" he guessed.

"I guess we did a halfway decent job of taking out the starting lineup," she offered.

"Maybe." Adam made a mental note of the address, intending to go back to his home and find out who owned it. He hoped that might give him a clue to who suddenly had such an interest in him. Glancing at his watch, he realized that their little adventure had eaten up the entire afternoon and that it was almost dinnertime.

"Are you up for a bite?" he asked.

"Only if you offer me some of those cookies from the Macaroon Shop," she teased.

"I'll do you one better. I will prepare a homemade meal for you, complete with the world's most amazing garlic bread—"

"Garlic. Very romantic," she jumped in, and he laughed.

"Okay, nix the garlic, but not the fine vintage from my extensive wine cellar."

"How can you say no to a man who has his own wine cellar?" Humor was ripe in her tones. He liked hearing it.

"We're off, then," he said, driving away from the mansion, but vigilant in case someone else decided to follow them.

CHAPTER
15

Andres glared at his two men, almost unable to believe that they had lost Adam Bruno's trail in broad daylight.

"This is inexcusable. I cannot advise the Quinchus that we are not any closer to bringing their son to them."

"He gave us the slip," said Marcus, the younger of the two foot soldiers.

"You know where he lives. Go there. Watch him and guard against the woman," Andres instructed, and shot a glance at his second in command. He was tempted to send Eduardo with them to make sure they didn't screw up again, but there was a gray pallor beneath the olive tones of his comrade's skin. Even with a feeding from the Quinchus, Eduardo's aura was not as potent as it should have been. It was almost as if his life force was a battery that had been drained once too often and could no longer hold a charge.

No, he would not send Eduardo with them. He had

to keep Eduardo's experience with him in the event the Shadows attacked their temporary enclave. Facing the two men, he said, "Go. Keep me advised of what you see. I will instruct you on what to do."

As the two men left, Eduardo coughed, drawing Andres's attention. "I could have supervised them."

"I need you here, my friend. If the Shadows felt that blast of power last night, they could be out hunting. We cannot risk that they will locate us and we will be too shorthanded to fight."

Eduardo understood. Above all, the Quinchus had to be protected, since they were the source of life for so many in their clan. For him. He could feel the power dwindling in him. Knew his time on this Earth was short even though he had only just completed his first triad.

He cursed the illness visited upon his descendants that had him feeding from other Hunters and the Quinchus like a mewling pup. As Andres clapped him on the back, sympathetic to the vibrations of anger charging his aura, Eduardo said, "I hope this man is Kikin. We have sacrificed too much to be wrong this time."

Andres said nothing. Just grasped his shoulder with empathy and led him to the Quinchus. While they would not like what they were about to hear, it was their duty to report it.

Salvatore swept his binoculars across the grounds of the large mansion from his protection behind the sea grass on the dune. He hadn't really known what to make of his son's rather cryptic attitude that morning when they had discussed his little experiment of the night before and the attack. It was what made him sneak the GPS device onto Adam's Bentley, worried as he was by his sudden weirdness.

That had led him to Ocean Grove and his son's date with Bobbie. For good measure, he had tagged her car as well while she and Adam were having lunch. Of all the things Salvatore had expected them to do, conducting a classic covert surveillance operation had not been one of them. But he had realized that's what they were up to after his tracking software indicated that the two cars were following each other.

Which had led him here to the gorgeous oceanfront mansion.

As he scoped out the various windows visible from the beach, he caught signs of activity in one and zoomed in closer with his binoculars. He immediately observed the man from the photos, the man who had attacked Adam the day before. Beside him was the second perpetrator who had been involved in the incident.

They were clearly speaking to someone, but whoever it was could not be seen.

Interesting, he thought. He had researched Alexander Sombrosa quite carefully and had turned up only one private residence in this area—a nearby mansion in which Alexander's son Christopher lived. Not this location.

Rising from his position on the dune, Salvatore brushed the sand off his black suit and hurried back to his car. He needed to do a little more investigating before he either confirmed or ruled out Sombrosa's responsibility for the attack. Once he did that, he would decide whether to proceed with their original plan or go with the alternate which had occurred to him: use Bobbie as the Eve for his Genesis project.

Adam's attraction to Bobbie was already there, and with modern advances in stem cell and gene therapies, he might be able to harvest just what he needed.

Genesis would proceed one way or the other, and Adam would be none the wiser about Salvatore's deceit.

Bobbie rubbed her belly, feeling replete. As Adam had promised, the meal had been homemade, the wine wonderful, and the company even better. She had enjoyed working beside him in the kitchen, sharing stories about helping her mom and sister prepare a meal, and listening to his story of how Salvatore had patiently shown him the Bruno secret recipes for Sunday sauce, meatballs, and chicken parmigiana.

"That was delicious," she said, and took one last sip of the wine.

"I'm glad you liked it. It's not often I get to cook."

She smiled as she heard what he hadn't said—that he hadn't cooked for many other women in his home. She kind of hoped she was special that way.

"Well, I appreciate it. I haven't really been doing much socializing myself," she admitted, and he grinned, likewise understanding her meaning. A slight pang of guilt gnawed at her about Gil, but then again, she and Gil had been done as lovers long before that morning in Baghdad.

"Do you have room for the cookies?" he asked as he stood and began clearing off the table.

She did, but their leisurely pace in making and eating dinner had already made it a late night. Her stamina wasn't what it used to be, and the drain of the long day was dragging on her.

"As much as I would like a cookie—"

"I know it's late. Take them with you. I'll drive you home," he said, and came to stand beside her. Reaching down, he stroked his hand along her hair before tipping her face up and bending to kiss her.

The kiss, gentle and caring, made her want to reconsider leaving. And then came the even gentler push of his vitality, somehow recharging her flagging energy.

"That feels good," she said, and he jerked away, his aura bright around him, those amazing eyes nearly electric as they settled on her face before he reined in the power.

Certain that he would prefer her silence about his lack of restraint, she rose from her seat and draped her arms over his shoulders. She inched up on tiptoe to kiss him before running her fingers through his hair and murmuring, "Thank you for dinner, but you don't have to drive me home. Again."

He shook his head and smiled, then eased his hand upward to stroke his index finger across the sensitive skin beneath her eyes. "You're not just tired. You're exhausted. I can see it."

"You're going to insist on taking me home."

"Definitely, so there's no sense arguing about it," he said, dipped his head, and brushed a kiss across her forehead.

"I won't argue. You're not going to do anything stupid after you drop me off, like go back to that mansion?"

The question of what to do about the two men had lingered in the back of his brain all night long, creating the start of a monster headache. But he still had no plan. "I need to know more before I do anything."

"Agreed. Just don't go it alone," she said, rubbing the back of his head playfully.

He arched a brow and considered her. "I suppose you want me to call you?"

Her eyes darkened to the color of rich maple. Sadness crept in to replace the earlier light in her eyes. "I'm not sure that I'm ready for battle mode anymore, Adam. I've had enough fighting and death to last me a lifetime."

And yet she had helped him today, he thought, but didn't press. As strong as she was, her emotions were obviously still fragile about that, which was understandable considering what she had survived.

"I'll drive you home so you can get some rest. Maybe you'll feel up to dinner tomorrow?"

The hint of a smile drifted across her lips and her eyes brightened, losing some of their gloom. "Sure. How about my place? I make some mean Mexican food."

That she was willing to let him into her space was a welcome sign. "I'd like that."

After another kiss that had him doubting the wisdom of letting her go that night, he walked her to his car for the drive home.

"They're on the move," Marcus mumbled, and nudged awake Lucas, the other cadre member, in the passenger seat beside him. Lucas was instantly alert, tracking the Bentley Continental as it pulled out of the driveway. The aura of the two people—a deep royal blue and a paler sky blue—was bright in the dark of the night and quite visible since the top was down on the vehicle.

"We should alert our captain," Lucas said as Marcus pulled away from the curb to follow the other car at a discreet distance.

Lucas dialed Andres, who immediately answered. "Do we have a problem?"

"The man and woman have left the house. We're following them."

"Get as much info as you can on the woman. We need to know who she is."

"What if there is trouble? What are our orders?" Lucas asked, risking a half glance at Marcus as he drove the Jeep.

"They are aware of the threat now, so we need to be circumspect. We must not raise alarm until we are ready. The Quinchus wish to approach him peacefully and speak with him," Andres instructed, in keeping with the change of plans they had decided upon earlier that night with Kellen and Selina.

"Yes, my captain," Lucas replied, pumping his right fist to his chest in a salute ingrained in him after decades of service.

Marcus gripped the wheel tightly and turned his head for only a second to ask, "What are we to do?"

"Follow for now and find out what we can about the woman."

"The woman?" Marcus questioned, his voice rising with worry. "What about the man? Adam?"

"The Quinchus have decided to go talk to him, so we must not endanger him."

With a nod, Marcus drove onward. It was not his place to question the Quinchus' orders, but he was a warrior, and the thought of allowing a Shadow to gain the upper hand left him troubled. Trying to contain his doubts, he followed the Bentley as it rolled along the quiet streets of a cool spring night.

• • •

Bobbie glanced in her side-view mirror again. The Jeep was still on their tail. It was the same kind of automobile as the one from this afternoon that they had followed to the mansion in Sea Girt. She had noticed its headlights almost as soon as they had turned out of Adam's driveway.

Glancing nervously at Adam, she realized he had seen the Jeep as well.

"They're back," he said.

"It's time we did something," she replied, and whipped out her cell phone.

Adam quickly reached over and covered her hand with his. "What are you doing?"

"Calling for help. My brother and cousin are cops."

He shook his head vehemently. "I can't have the authorities involved."

All her life Bobbie had respected those authorities, but she understood. For people like Adam, people who were different, the institutions she cherished could be a threat to their existence.

"Let's see if they really are following us. That's a pretty popular brand of car in this area. Make a left up there." Bobbie pulled down the passenger-side sunshade to reveal the mirror. Opening it, she angled the mirror so she could keep a better eye on the Jeep.

After they turned, the Jeep did as well. Understanding what she wanted, Adam made a series of turns, and each time the Jeep matched their actions.

"Unlikely that they're just out for a cruise, wouldn't you say?"

His jaw tightened to iron and through gritted teeth

he said, "This could turn dangerous. I don't want you involved."

Bobbie appreciated Adam's concern, but she could take care of herself, and despite her desire to avoid conflict, she wouldn't leave him alone to fight. "Unless you plan on tossing me out the door of a moving car, I am involved. And it seems to me that we can either run or find out what they want."

Adam shook his head. "They're unpredictable. Different." Deadly, he wanted to say, but didn't want to spook her, although as their gazes skipped across each other as they looked back toward the Jeep, he knew she understood.

"Different like you?"

Adam recalled the shocks brought about by their touch. How they had weakened him. Maybe they were like him that way, but different in a decidedly dangerous way.

"I would never intentionally harm anyone," he answered, and took one hand off the wheel, brought it to her cheek for a fleeting caress.

She looked away apprehensively and motioned to the boardwalk and buildings of the Avon Pavilion just a short distance ahead of them. "Up there to the right. There's room to make a K turn and check them out."

Adam slowed and began the turn, but the Jeep didn't decelerate at all. "Get out of the car," he shouted, and streaked through the air to escape the driver's side as the Jeep bore down on them.

The 4x4 screeched to a halt just a few feet from the bumper of the Bentley as Bobbie hurried around the car to stand beside Adam, who stood in the middle of the road.

"What do you want?" Adam called out.

Bobbie realized the car couldn't pull around them to go straight and the street was too narrow for a quick U turn. The occupants of the Jeep had little choice: either answer Adam or figure out how to make a run for it.

Suddenly, the Jeep surged forward, heading directly for them as they blocked the street.

"No," Adam shouted from beside her, and thrust his hand out, pointing it toward the 4x4. She caught a quick glimpse of light coalescing in the center of his palm before a sphere of silver-blue light exploded from his hand and collided against the front fender of the Jeep. The blast of power deflected the Jeep from smashing into them and shoved the vehicle into a row of parked cars.

Stunned motionless, Bobbie waited beside Adam as the occupant on the passenger side stumbled out of the car, bleeding from a head wound. The man dropped to his knees, obviously in distress.

"He needs help," she said, and instinctively took a step toward him, although Adam shot out his hand to stop her. As his forearm brushed her, a slight shock registered. She glanced at him and realized his aura was visibly huge and glimmering wildly, the threads of silver and red wriggling in a sea of blue, his emerald eyes gleaming a shocking neon green.

The wounded man sagged slightly as she moved, but at the last moment, he shot his hand out in her direction, and before she could react, he released an orb of energy.

Bobbie screamed as the ball smashed into her and tossed her back several feet into the side of the Bentley. Pain lanced through her back with the impact, but the pain was nothing compared to the web of energy circulating through her body. It fried along her nerve endings, making her muscles spasm. Her legs gave way as she lost control.

Adam raced to Bobbie's side in a blur of light and slipped his arm around her. A weird aura of battling red and blue shimmered all along her body as she twitched uncontrollably from the shock and pain ravaging her body.

She couldn't speak. Couldn't warn Adam as the injured man got to his feet and looked toward them, blood oozing down the side of his face. He raised his hand and pointed it at her once again, as if sensing she was the weak link.

Adam sensed the danger from the immense drone of power coming from behind him. He turned, realized what was about to happen, and placed himself in front of her, absorbing the force of the energy blast. He reeled for a moment as the power scorched his nerves, until anger erupted in his core. With a loud cry from deep in his soul, he raised both hands and suddenly there was a direct line of energy from him to the bleeding man, driving him to the ground.

The wounded man jumped and shuddered like a fish in its last dying throes on land, the power from Adam shocking him over and over.

The driver of the van finally came around the front of the vehicle, likewise injured. As he saw what was happening, he tossed an orb of energy at Adam, but it was like being stung by a gnat now that the full capacity of the power stored within him was at play. It had consumed him, and in his brain there was nothing but raw emotion and the static from the power, growing ever more powerful, so strong that it started to bleed into his eyesight, almost blinding him.

It took Bobbie's anguished cry to finally break into his consciousness and drive back the deadly energy. As he regained command he released his hold on the man.

Bobbie had slumped to the ground without his support, the earlier tremors racking her body reduced to an occasional twitch, her once-bright-blue aura shimmering weakly and now tainted by threadlike streaks of red and gold. Her body gave one final jump and then she lay there, sickeningly still.

CHAPTER
16

Ignoring the two men who had followed them, Adam kneeled beside Bobbie, praying beneath his breath that she would be all right. He leaned over her, calling her name over and over again. Her aura sputtered off and on, but at least it was still present, which gave Adam hope.

He fell to his knees, unmindful of the men across the way, as he defensively placed his body between Bobbie and them. Then he eased toward her body and splayed his hand on the thin cotton over her chest. Beneath his palm, Bobbie's heartbeat raced erratically. Only a shallow rise and fall of her chest confirmed that she was still breathing.

"You're alive, Bobbie. Alive." He willed power from his core to his hand and then into Bobbie. Before his eyes, her aura intensified, spread onto his hand like blood seeping through his fingers. A snowy glow developed beneath his palm as the silver and red tendrils in his aura leached downward, rooting themselves in her body. Against his palm came the unexpected draw of energy, making him light-headed as his power was sucked into Bobbie.

Beneath his hand, Bobbie's breathing lengthened, grew more regular. After one abrupt, hitched breath, her eyelids fluttered open, revealing tawny-colored eyes clouded by confusion and pain.

The wail of approaching sirens registered in warning.

Adam withdrew his hand, fearful that others might be able to see the display of light and energy. As he did so, the connection between them provided resistance, as if his hand was covered in tacky glue that kept on pulling him back. With a forceful yank on his power, he broke free and Bobbie jumped, experiencing the disruption.

He helped her sit up and, wide-eyed, Bobbie peered at him, but then her gaze was pulled over his shoulder.

"Bobbie," he heard a man say and looked back to find a policeman headed their way, followed by two other officers. A duo of squad cars, lights flashing, had closed off both ends of the street adjacent to them. A dozen or more people milled about the vehicles, drawn from their homes by the sirens and lights, and maybe even by the noise of the earlier crash and disruption, Adam surmised.

As the officer approached, Adam noticed that he had lots of brass up at his neck and assumed he was in charge.

"Chief Ryan," Bobbie said, and rose from the ground with his help, still shaky from the energy blast that had struck her, but alive.

She knew the man? he wondered for only a moment as his knees wobbled. He lurched back to rest against the fender of the Bentley while keeping her tucked close.

"Are you okay?" Bobbie asked, laying a hand on his arm, but he shrugged it off, afraid of touching her. He barely had his power under control, and weakness had erupted at his core. He didn't know how long he could maintain command.

Hurt traveled like quicksilver over her features until she schooled them. He hated that he was causing her so much pain.

"What happened?" the police chief asked.

Bobbie returned her attention to the officer. "We were turning around when the Jeep came out of nowhere. It couldn't stop in time, lost control, and plowed into the parked cars."

The chief narrowed his eyes as he considered her. Hooking his thumbs through the loops of his black gun-belt, he said, "How long have I known you, Bobbie?"

"Almost all my life," Bobbie said, and shrugged. The simple movement seemed to cause her discomfort as a grimace shot over her features. Adam wondered if it was from her war wounds or from the blast, since every muscle in his body ached and felt stiff. He was uncertain whether his state was the result of being shocked by the weird orbs of power or of offering his energy to help Bobbie.

He rubbed at his arms and suddenly something came to him, almost as if the electricity had jogged loose a memory. He had felt like this once before—the morning he had awoken with his father-to-be next to him.

"Adam? Are you all right?" Bobbie questioned, but she didn't reach for him again, aware that he wouldn't welcome any contact at that moment.

"I'm okay. I just remembered something."

"Something about the incident?" the police chief pushed, his head cocked at an inquisitive angle.

Much as Bobbie had lied before, Adam did as well.

"Yes. There were two men in the car. Hurt. They ran away after crashing."

The police chief didn't appear to buy it. With a stony glare at the two of them, he said, "Why don't you tell me what's really up?"

"It's the truth, Chief. Believe me," Bobbie pleaded as she wrung her hands.

With a resigned sigh, the chief pushed back his hat and scrubbed his baldness. Leaning close, he said, "If I find out there's something else going on, being a Marine hero and having law enforcement connections won't keep me from tossing you in the can, Bobbie."

"There's nothing else to say, Chief," she replied, and the officer didn't press any further. After getting descriptions of the two men in the Jeep, the police chief released them.

"We should go before the chief changes his mind," Bobbie said, and turned to him, but he was torn.

The lies had come so easily to her. And then there was the powerful pull of energy as their auras had merged when he had been helping her. It had felt as if she was draining life from him, but as he met her gaze, there was only concern there. Concern for him.

He held up his keys. "I'll drive you home."

But as he took a step, he felt incredibly weak and dizzy, so much so that he had to lean against the bumper once again. She shook her head and snagged the keys from his fingers. The wobble was back in his knees when he stepped toward the Bentley, but she immediately tucked herself beneath his shoulder, offering support without hesitation. Seemingly back to normal.

The link he couldn't explain came instantly and trickled

energy back and forth between them, providing him strength. Providing her balance, he realized, as he saw her cane lying on the ground by the back of his Bentley. It reminded him of her injuries, as did the awkward steps she took, and yet here she was, offering him assistance.

They neared the passenger side and he rested against the side of the car, taxed by the short walk. As she opened the door, he reached out and cradled the side of her face before tunneling his fingers into her shoulder-length hair.

She gazed at him quizzically, obviously confused, especially considering how he had rejected her earlier advance.

"I'm sorry. I was out of control. The energy was searing my brain and I was afraid of hurting you," he said, and she dipped her head, acknowledging the apology while at the same time still obviously hurt.

"There's a lot we need to figure out," she replied, as needy as he for an explanation for all that had happened.

He nodded and realized that in the scintilla of memory that had returned to him after the incident, there might be the start of an answer.

The question was whether to share it with her.

She had warned him that she didn't want to be involved in another battle, that she'd had enough of war, and there was one thing of which he was certain: This was definitely war.

CHAPTER
17

The emotions swirled around her in the confined space inside the garage, tinting her aura that deep indigo again. As she met his gaze, uncertainty deepened the hue of her whiskey-colored eyes to that of amber syrup.

"Will you be okay if I leave?" she asked after she cut the ignition.

"I will. What about you? Are you okay?" he questioned, concerned about her, given the attack she had survived.

Bobbie shrugged. "A few aches and pains, but surprisingly okay."

"What about the chief? Are you worried about what he might do?" He focused on a spot directly in front of him where an assortment of tools was neatly pegged to the garage wall to try to hide his fear about possible police investigations and to try to combat the headache that had been steadily growing on their ride home.

Her touch came immediately, the brush of fingers

along the tightness of his jaw, urging him to face her once again.

"I am. My cousin and brother are cops in the next town over. The chief will definitely tell them and I'll have to try to explain. But I'm also concerned about you. What happened tonight..." Her hands fluttered in the air, as if she was grasping for the words to finish, but they eluded her.

"I wish I could explain, but I don't know how I did it," he admitted.

Bobbie heard the subtext beneath what he was saying and called him on it. "But you do know something else. Something you're not saying."

He averted his gaze, but she wouldn't let him off the hook, especially not when whatever had occurred had nearly killed them both that night. This time she cradled his jaw more forcefully, since he had not shunned her advance a second ago. She applied determined pressure until he was facing her, unable to avoid what had to be acknowledged, although he tried.

"This isn't a good time to discuss this," he said, afraid of the growing heaviness in his core that warned he had to acknowledge the power within him and that it needed something more.

"When is a good time? When someone is dead?"

Her words catapulted him into action.

"Inside," he barked and surged out of the car, although he faltered for a moment and braced himself on the hood of the Bentley.

She tamped down the worry she felt. If she had learned one thing as a sergeant, it was that sometimes you had to let someone find his own footing. With danger behind them, this was one of those times.

She exited the car more gingerly. Every bone and muscle in her ached, but she wasn't sure if it was from the impact with the car aggravating her injuries or from the electrical blast she had sustained. It was clear he was hurting, given the cautious way he was moving after his initial burst of motion.

Together they hobbled into his living room, but this time there were no civilities. No scotch or offer of anything, which was fine by her. There was only one thing she wanted from him—the truth.

He seemed to understand that, since as soon as they were seated beside each other, he began to talk.

"I don't know how I tossed that ball of energy. I didn't know I could do that," he confessed with a hunch of his shoulders. His hands were fisted on his thighs, his head cast downward.

"Just like you didn't know you could heal?" She reached over and enclosed one fist with her hand, urging him to relax with a gentle squeeze. He shot her a half-glance, slightly more relaxed, although still hesitant. At another squeeze of her hand, he continued.

"I think your powers are more like mine than we thought."

She didn't seem surprised at his comment, but her words were guarded when she spoke. "What makes you think that?"

"Whenever we touch, the power shifts between us, as if it's one and the same." He demonstrated by opening himself up to her, and there was no denying the link that blossomed between them. There was something almost calming about it, although desire shimmered beneath its surface as the prick of power ebbed back and forth.

"How is that possible?" was all she could say.

"Maybe it's the aura that swirls around you. Tony has one that I didn't notice before, but it's not as strong as yours." His uncertainty was painfully obvious.

"So you think it's power like yours?"

A little less hesitation this time. "Maybe, although it feels different somehow."

Bobbie racked her brains, trying to make sense of it. Thoughts spilled out and became words. "Tony, Mick, and I were always more alike. My older sister, Liliana, was always the odd one out. We were athletic and strong. People always looked to us. For help. For leadership."

"Power is innate. People perceive that," he explained, and it made perfect sense to her. After all, she had been drawn to him for much the same reason at first. But now there was a whole lot more going on between them, she thought, the tie between their joined hands still alive, still pulsing with vitality.

"But that doesn't explain what happened with those men. Why you can—"

"Toss balls of energy and heal people? Speed across distances? That's another one I discovered recently." He swiveled on the couch until he was facing her, and his eyes were shadowed again, his turmoil evident.

She leaned close and cupped his cheek. Ran her thumb along the sandpapery roughness of his face in a soothing gesture. "There's more, isn't there, Adam?"

"The blast left my body sore. Achy, as if it was the day after a massive workout or as if I had just recovered from the flu."

She was feeling the same way, but she sensed it meant more to him. "You've felt like that before, haven't you?"

He nodded, and his gaze grew shuttered. "On the day I first met my dad—Salvatore."

There was no denying how difficult it was for him, remembering that day. But then he surprised her, and maybe even himself, by saying, "I think I've seen those energy balls before. When Salvatore found me. Before I forgot who I was."

"Forgot who you were?" she questioned, seeking clarification, because she didn't want to misunderstand what he meant.

"When I woke up, I had no memories of who I was or where I came from. I still don't, except..."

"You remember the energy. The way the men tossed it. The way you returned fire," she put out for him to consider.

He nodded and screwed his eyes shut, as if forcing himself back to that time and those memories, but then he expelled a harsh sigh and shook his head. "I can't remember any more."

"It'll come to you."

"It hasn't come to me in twenty years, Bobbie. What makes you think it'll happen now?" he challenged, obviously frustrated.

"To every thing there is a season, and a time for every purpose. Maybe now it's time for you to figure it all out," she said, paraphrasing an old scriptural passage she'd heard in church.

"You expect me to have faith, but I'm not a religious man," he warned.

"Hasn't there been anyone in your life in whom you had faith?" she asked, but as a river of emotions washed over him and transferred itself to her, she knew the sad answer to that. Because she didn't want to press and cause him more heartache, she rose from the couch.

"It's time I went home."

"Stay," he said, but quickly added, "I've got half a dozen empty rooms, all beautifully decorated by some famous designer whose name I can't even remember. Just choose a room."

Insanely, she knew what room she wanted to choose, but tempered that rashness. It would only create more issues, and much as she had told him, there was a season and a time for everything.

It was not yet time for that. It might not ever be, since the last thing she needed was to get involved in another conflict. But accepting his offer of hospitality was only common sense considering the lateness of the hour and the way her body pained her.

"I'll take you up on that," she said, and a relieved smile erupted on his face.

He rose from the couch and held out his hand. "Let me show you to a room."

CHAPTER
18

If the designer had been going for all-out luxury, he or she had accomplished that admirably.

The sleekly modern stainless steel variation on a four-poster bed was decidedly decadent, possibly because of the plush mattress and gazillion-count sheets. Or maybe it was just the comfort of Adam's well-worn MIT T-shirt, which he'd lent to her as sleepwear.

Not that sleep was coming easily as her mind raced over all that had happened that day. Much as she had after each mission, she considered every event that had occurred, and catalogued the mistakes she had made so as to not repeat them in the future—like exposing herself by standing beside Adam without regard to a possible enemy just yards away.

She had no doubt about that any longer. Whoever was after Adam was the enemy. Her actions had jeopardized not only her, but Adam, who had absorbed the second blast from their foe, protecting her after she had been hit.

He might have been killed. For that matter, she might have been killed.

She had thought that when she returned from Iraq she would be safe; she had already paid too dear a price for God and country. She had hoped to put the past behind her and rebuild the fragments of her life, to lead a peaceful existence. A home-with-a-picket-fence kind of life. Maybe even one with kids, if she adopted, since she could no longer have any of her own.

Meeting Adam threatened that idea big-time. He obviously had enemies. Powerful ones, judging from the number of men at their command and the very expensive mansion they had made their command center. And given the events of the last two days, it was obviously war, which meant the risk of casualties.

Luckily, both she and Adam were fine. This time. She wasn't sure she was ready to sacrifice more. But she had never been one to turn tail and run when the fight was justified.

But was the fight the right thing to do this time? she wondered and ran her hand down the arm Adam had healed. Even now her skin came alive as she recalled his touch and the current that had alternated between them as Adam had saved her life. Those superhuman capabilities were clearly the reason the men were after him. Who wouldn't want to know the secrets of a human energy source like that? Especially one that could heal or hurt or seemingly allow one to vanish into thin air?

No one, except maybe her.

Even with all his apparently fabulous powers, she remained more intrigued by Adam the man. Although he had been alone most of his life, she sensed there was a well of deep emotion, cosmic in size, behind his enigmatic façade. The time she had spent with him over the last two days had made her want to explore the vastness of those emotions, but with caution, because she didn't want to get caught up in the turmoil surrounding him.

As her mind continued to churn, she decided she needed something more to help her sleep. Something to quiet the demons creating such unrest within her. That nervous energy drove her from the bed.

Maybe a soak in the gigantic Jacuzzi in the room's private bath, she thought as she opened the door to reveal polished marble and gleaming chrome plumbing and accessories.

Then she rethought it and stalked as best as she could to the well-stocked bar tucked into one corner, thinking a shot of liquor might quell her nerves, but she couldn't choose her poison. She had never been much of a drinker.

Possibly a novel or DVD borrowed from the entertainment center across the way from the massive four-poster bed? she mused. But as she faced that bed, looming large in the space, its loneliness provided the potential remedy she sought.

Adam lay on the chaise longue on his balcony, soaking up the free-floating energy and feeling the weakness in his core disappear. Opening his eyes, he stared at the midnight sky as dozens of fragmented thoughts and images pummeled his brain. One kept on repeating endlessly: the image of the energy ball striking Bobbie.

But in his mind the powerful orb was coming for him. Driving him back into a hard stone wall. No, not stone. Adobe. Breaking behind him from the force of his impact.

He had collapsed then, onto dry, arid earth. Dazed. His fall stirring up dust that filled his nose and throat, choking him. Making him cough. A metallic taste had filled his mouth.

Blood.

He had battled past the grit making his eyes tear and the dizziness in his head to find the world aflame around him. Fires had dotted the night. Debris littered the ground beside him, beneath him, rough against his skin.

Bodies, he had thought, blinking his eyes to make sure he was really seeing them.

Adam remembered the bodies now, illuminated by the glow of the flames. So many bodies and parts. And the cries of others, not yet dead. His own plaintive wail of fear as the darkness had danced in his vision before claiming him.

Whatever had happened had been far away. In a place hotter and more desolate than the Jersey Shore. A desert.

Maybe close to where Salvatore had taken care of him in the weeks after he had first regained consciousness. It had been a tiny home, not much bigger than ten by twenty. Devoid of many personal touches, much like the homes they would later occupy. But then again, his father had often been gone for long stretches of time in the years after Adam had been adopted. Those absences left little opportunity for decorating, and the absence of any woman in their household had only added to the lack of comforting touches.

As he had over the last twenty years, Adam wondered about the parents who had left him out in that desert. Why they hadn't tried to find him in all that time.

Why his father, with all his connections, claimed not to have been able to locate the people who had birthed him. Or maybe Salvatore had and they were dead. Maybe they had been lying on the sandy ground not far from him, two of the many corpses littering the desert night.

Would those lost parents have been different from Salvatore? Aware of Adam's unique gift and able to deal with it?

His father hadn't been able to handle it or the many demands of a young boy. He hadn't been overly demonstrative physically, and maybe with reason. A few unintentional shocks from Adam had taught him the dangers of his new young son, as had the incident with Spottie, Salvatore's beagle. The dog had recovered, but the fear from that event had lingered for years.

But Adam had to acknowledge that Salvatore had been caring in his own way, recalling the many days Salvatore had spent with him whenever an assignment was over. The nightly calls when his father was on duty, sometimes just a minute long, to wish him good night or find out how Adam's day had been. Not to mention the visits to an assortment of museums and science centers to satisfy Adam's almost insatiable thirst for knowledge.

A caring man like that might keep secret the fact that Adam's real parents were dead, wanting to spare a young boy distress. But would a man like that keep other secrets? Did Salvatore know more than he was letting on about Adam's origins? Maybe even about the group of men who had attacked him, not once but twice?

The squeak of a door opening had him sitting up on the edge of the chaise.

Bobbie stood at the French door to his room, his T-shirt swimming on her thinner physique, but barely reaching to midthigh, since they were almost of a like height.

She had beautiful legs. Long, lithe, and strong. As he tracked his gaze up their length, he noted the first hint of scars on one thigh, and as she discerned what had his attention, she pulled at the hem of the cotton T, attempting to cover the evidence of her wounds.

"No, don't," he said, and walked to where she stood just inside the French doors to his bedroom.

When he was before her, he reached down and placed his hand on her leg, at a spot just below the first hint of injury. He started to brush it upward, but she quickly snared his hand, preventing him from his goal.

"I think a strategic retreat makes sense right about now," she said, and began to turn, but he placed his other hand on her waist to keep her with him.

Wanting to defuse the increasingly tense situation, he said, "He who fights and runs away—"

"I don't want to fight another day, Adam. Which makes me wonder what I'm doing here," she admitted and wagged her head, as if trying to shake the thoughts loose so they might leave her.

"I don't want you to have to fight or run," he said, and inched his hand upward until the first awkward ridge of scar registered against his fingertips. She applied more pressure then against his hand, trapping it against her thigh. He looked up, locking his gaze with hers. It was fraught with emotions he wanted to understand. "Tell me about it. About how you got hurt."

With a stiff hunch of her shoulders, she said, "Not much to tell. Bomb go boom."

He shook his head in exasperation. "If it were only that simple."

"It *is* that simple," she urged, but the tone of her voice was strained, belying her words.

"I remembered something tonight," he began, wanting her to understand and to share in the hopes she would do the same. Maybe by doing so they would both begin to heal. As they had said before, they apparently had a good deal in common.

"I remembered an attack. Or at least that's what I think it was. Someone blasted me with one of those power orbs and I went flying."

She narrowed her eyes as she contemplated him. "But you couldn't have been more than five or six."

"Probably, but suddenly the memory is here in my head," he said, motioning to his forehead before continuing. "The feel of hitting the wall as the discharge threw me. The bodies around me and the smell of fire. Gritty sand, clogging my mouth and nose. Blood. I could taste blood. It's as alive now as it must have been twenty years ago."

And as alive as it still was for her after only several months, Bobbie thought, and reached up, cradling his cheek, as she detected the hurt in his eyes. She shared her own pain, as she suspected he had intended by revealing his own wounds.

"We were sent to defuse bombs to protect the civilians in the area. We hadn't taken more than a few steps from our Bradley when the IEDs went off."

She paused, emotion tightening her throat to the point where it was almost difficult to breathe. Somehow she dragged in a breath, and when she did, it smelled of fire and smoke. It smelled like that Baghdad morning all over again and it was her undoing.

She screwed her eyes shut against the tears and fought back the sobs, her body trembling from the force of her grief.

Adam pulled her tight to him and laid his face against hers. He lovingly whispered in her ear, "It's okay to let it out."

She did, shedding hot tears against his bare shoulder as she haltingly recounted the rest of her story.

"I flew high in the air." She gulped in a rough breath, forcing herself to continue. "When I landed there was so much pain. I couldn't hear because my ears were ringing from the blast. My skin was burning hot."

"There was fire all around you," he said, trying to help her along with her tale.

She nodded. "Fire and the pieces of my men and our equipment. The heat I felt was from some gasoline burning on me and the shrapnel in my arm and leg. From the blood spewing out of my gut where I had been torn to pieces. Then I blacked out."

He eased away from her, cupped her face between his large, powerful hands, and wiped away the trails of tears from her face, his touch amazingly gentle. A calming wave of power drifted into her with his touch. "You survived. No guilt there."

She sucked in another shuddering breath and expelled it roughly. "I was responsible for those men. I ask myself a thousand times over, 'How could I have prevented it? What didn't I see?' "

" 'And why did I live?' You ask yourself that as well, don't you?" He leaned his forehead against hers and that simple contact made her feel not so alone.

"Yes, I do. I feel guilty that I'm not dead, too," she admitted and with that confession, a weight seemed to lift from her soul.

"You said before that there was a time for everything. A purpose. Maybe your purpose was to be here," he said, the sincerity of his words resonating within her.

"Maybe," she said, and finally did what she had been wanting to do all night long.

CHAPTER
19

His lips were warm and hard beneath hers, giving as he accepted her kiss and returned it, loving her mouth with his. She darted her tongue along the edges of his mouth and he groaned, wrapped one powerful arm around her buttocks, and crushed her close. He opened his mouth and invited her in, dancing his tongue along hers, tasting her and moaning as she ran her hands along the sloped line of his powerfully built shoulders.

As she did so she experienced the flush of power leaking from him beneath her palms. Seeping into her from the contact, traveling along her nerve endings to first bring peace before it transformed into more and passion grew.

Trembling, they eased apart, each of them searching the other for any signs of uncertainty. But there were none, Bobbie realized. It was their time, for however long or short it was meant to be. But despite that, she needed him to understand one thing.

"I haven't since ... My body ..."

"Just say the word and I'll stop," he said, and brushed a kiss along the back of her hand. The action created a trail of glimmering sky blue and heat where his lips touched her.

"Thank you."

With a nod, he twined his fingers with hers and led her to the massive bed in the equally large room. So much room for just one person. Too much room, she thought, imagining how alone one could feel in so great a space.

The comforter and sheets were in disarray, a testament to his earlier restlessness, she assumed. With a few quick tugs, he had them back in some semblance of order and turned to face her, his hand held out in invitation. His aura was just a hint of color surrounding his body, but as she slipped her fingers through his, it grew larger and seemed to vibrate in time to the beat of her heart and the growing throb deep between her legs.

His eyes, those amazing eyes, darkened with passion while beginning to shimmer with the first hints of electric green.

She didn't move any closer, wanting to appreciate the sight of him, because the light show nothwithstanding, he was a beautiful man.

He was bare-chested, as he had been the night before, and she didn't think that the sight of him would ever fail to arouse her. She had seen her share of beautifully sculpted men in the Marines.

Adam eclipsed them all.

He was so exquisitely formed, big, long, and lean with defined muscles that just ached to be touched. She did that, running the pads of her fingers all along his chest before drifting them down the center of him to circle around his navel.

As she did so she left a trail of glittering pale blue and heat. So much heat as their power melded, beginning a union that would soon be completed by the joining of their bodies.

Adam sucked in a breath as she drew her finger around his navel, and the ridges of his abdomen became even more pronounced with the motion. Tracing those valleys, she then dipped her hand lower to the low-slung waist-band of his cotton pajamas.

Inching her finger beneath the edge of the fabric, she ran it back and forth along his skin, relishing the flare of heat that was visible in the expanding flush of the royal blue aura moving to envelop her, evident in the very human response as his large, long shaft jutted against the cotton and the softness of her belly.

Her nipples puckered in reaction, and between her legs, dampness pooled in anticipation of that length entering her, filling the emptiness, as her muscles clenched in anticipation.

She covered his erection with her hand at the same time he raised his and cupped her breast through the fabric of the T-shirt, riding his thumb along the sensitive tip. A shudder of pleasure worked its way across her and she glanced at him, offered up a smile.

A flash of a grin skimmed over his lips, hinting at his restraint. She raised herself on the balls of her feet, closing the final inch between them, and kissed him. Whispered against his lips, "I won't break."

"It's the power. I need to control it," he said, almost as if he and the power were two separate entities.

She recalled the many times he had touched her and the desire that had risen up along with the sharing of his energy. The way he had allowed emotion to release the power earlier that night when they were in danger. Somehow she knew the answer to mastering his abilities wasn't about the rigid control he had been forcing upon himself.

"Just go with the flow," she urged against his lips, almost amused by how appropriate those words were for him.

He chuckled lightly, as if recognizing it as well.

Against her came the release of his tension and something else, a stronger hum of energy, which escaped from him and washed over her, through her, bringing a sense of union she had not ever experienced before.

"Your aura's purple," he said as he caressed her breast and slipped his other hand down to the swell of her ass, urging her hips tight to his.

"Is that a good thing?" she questioned as she brought her hands to the waistband of his pants and slowly inched them downward to reveal his magnificent erection. She released the pants, and they skimmed past his lean hips and down his legs. He impatiently kicked them away.

"Very good," he answered, and then groaned as she surrounded him with her hand, stroked it up and down the length of him, the jerk of his erection beneath her palm bringing an almost painful pulse between her legs. Her touch elicited a very obvious response in his energy as his aura darkened to the purple he had mentioned earlier and spilled onto her hand. Between her legs, the throb became even more intense as his vitality surged through her, drenching her sex.

He must have sensed her need. He brought his hand

around and parted her thighs, eased past the cotton of her underwear, and skipped his fingers along the moist length of her. He bent his head to the crook of her neck, where he dropped a line of kisses before taking a gentle bite.

She held his head to her, savoring the press of his mouth. The stroke of his fingers caressed her, building her passion until her body was trembling against his and beneath her hand came the jump of his erection and a slight hint of damp at its tip. She rubbed the moisture all along the head of his penis and he moaned.

"Adam. I can't wait much more."

Adam couldn't wait either, feeling like a schoolboy on his first fumbling date. Bobbie awoke sentiments he had never experienced with another woman. Emotion. Real emotion, and because of that, he wouldn't delay a second longer, but he wouldn't rush it either.

Bending, he swept her up in his arms and, turning, laid her on his bed. Her caramel-colored hair was a dark spill against the celestial blue of his sheets, the white of his T-shirt glaring, but he knew she wasn't ready to shed that garment yet. The wounds were still healing, physically and mentally. It might take a while before she was able to reveal that much of herself, if ever.

He joined her on the bed, gently applying pressure until they were face to face on its immense surface, her damaged leg beneath him, hidden from view. Capitalizing on that, he laid his hand on her good thigh and skimmed his hand up and down the soft skin sheathing rock-hard muscle beneath, the warrior buried within the very feminine exterior.

She brought one hand down to his arousal and the other to his chest, where she lazily rubbed her finger across his hard pap, tightening it into an even stiffer peak. Every now and then a spark of silver escaped from beneath her fingers.

Adam skipped his hand up her thigh and beneath the hem of the shirt, mindful not to pull it upward as she stiffened beside him. As their gazes met, she realized he would honor her earlier request and relaxed.

He brought his other arm around, pillowed it beneath her head so he could kiss her at his leisure, which he did while tenderly playing with her breasts, teasing the tips into rigid peaks, which he tweaked and rotated, drawing a pleasure-filled moan from her.

A second later her mouth was on him, teething and sucking at his tight nipple, yanking a strangled groan from him and a demand for the taste and feel of her on his lips.

He lowered his head, found the tip of her through the fabric. He sucked and bit at her taut nipples until she was clutching his head to her and easing her thigh over his, her hands guiding him to her center.

He reached down and, with a sharp tug, ripped the fabric of her panties and tossed them away. She urged him ever closer with her hands until he rested against her core. At the first sensation of her, warm and moist, he almost came as an upsurge of emotion and power twisted together in his gut. Somehow he restrained himself, dragging in a breath and holding it for only a second, because that was all he could wait to be within her.

Bobbie accepted the first tentative probe. She shifted her hips forward to take in the tip of him, her gaze locking with his as he slowly pressed forward. His width slipped inside her, ever deeper as she accepted the length of him.

His heat marked his passage into her and was followed by a strong and insistent pulse of power that flowed through her body before returning to his.

His aura was totally visible now, a magnificent purple threaded with silver and red that surrounded both of them in a cocoon of energy. His eyes glowed a bright iridescent green, but wonder filled his gaze.

She imagined hers had the same look, since she had never savored anything that felt so right. So perfect. So complete. As she spread her hands wide on his chest, the hum of power seemed to grow, pulling a profound vibration from her core as the threads of silver and red dancing around him shifted and quaked as if alive, then slipped from him into her, causing a catch in her breath until he moved within her, dragging that insistent pulse to between her legs where it grew with each stroke of his body.

She was shaking, her body trembling more and more until it was as if the next pleasurable stroke would splinter her into pieces.

"Adam," she called out, gripping his shoulders tightly, her head thrown back as desire grew, almost overwhelming.

"I'm here, Bobbie," he said, his own voice shaky. The feeling of being within her was amazing, but so was the way his power swam through her, as if they were part of some cosmic current. He could feel the rush within him, escalating, creating the first hint of static in his brain that said he was on the verge of losing command of that part of him. He drove it back, fearful of hurting her.

Instead he focused on the human feel of her, so warm and tight around him. Skin smooth against skin as his body quivered beside hers, caught up in their lovemaking, the grind of his hips growing ever more erratic until it happened.

She screamed his name, her body shattering into a thousand points of light as her climax blasted through her and transferred its energy to him, bringing him to a higher precipice as the noise increased in his head once more.

He needed release, he thought with a sharp groan punctuated by her name, extending her climax with a few powerful thrusts before he came. He spilled himself inside her while the sheath of energy shimmering around them ballooned and shot off flares of light.

His body trembled beside her as he encircled her waist and held her close. The noise in his head abated as the power finally ebbed, leaving behind a peaceful blue ocean of calm that bathed them in its vitality.

Neither of them spoke.

Bobbie didn't think she could, much less find the words to describe what she had just experienced.

She just curled up tight to him, her body still cradling him within her. His arms wrapped around her and hers around him. No longer two disparate forces, but one.

The feeling was both serene and scary.

Scary because there was still so much she didn't know about him. So much that could destroy the tranquility enveloping them at that moment. Maybe even destroy them if they couldn't discover who was after Adam.

As if aware of her thoughts, Adam raked his fingers through her hair and gently massaged her scalp. "Don't think about that now. In time we'll have the answers."

She nodded, but couldn't help wondering what would happen if they weren't the answers they wanted.

CHAPTER
20

The sights and sounds of that Baghdad morning came alive in her dreams again, but instead of the explosions, it was sunburst blasts of energy strafing a dusty dawn. Smashing into pieces anything that dared to stand in their way.

Something landed beside her with a thud.

Bobbie looked down at the bloodied and burned remains of a sandy-haired body. She battled back a gag as the smell of roasting flesh filled her nostrils. Dropping to her knees, she murmured a prayer that it wasn't him.

That it not be Adam.

The skin beneath her hand was familiar. Still warm. A shimmer of the blue lingered. Death hadn't had a chance to steal those remnants of life.

Forcing herself to act, she flipped the man onto his back. A charred and empty hole, ragged flesh, and pink and white shards of bone were all that remained of his face.

She screamed.

Bobbie twitched beside Adam and her long, low wail drove him awake. He cradled her in his arms and she flailed at him, caught in the throes of a nightmare. Her fitful actions and pitiful cries tore at his heart, a place he had thought oblivious to such emotion after its long disuse.

"Bobbie, it's all right," Adam said, holding her close and rocking her like a baby, willing her to wake from her terror. As he did, waves of calming energy drifted from his body to hers. Slowly she came round, her gaze losing the unfocused look of shock and swinging to meet his. He sensed her apology coming, but stopped it.

"It's okay. We're together," he said, tracing the line of her brow to smooth the deep furrow there.

She nodded and tunneled her hands through the short strands of his hair, hauled him close for a deep kiss. One of tortured need, not of passion. This kiss was meant to drive away the demons, and sadly, Adam understood the need all too well. He had felt such want himself more than he cared to admit.

There was no finesse this time. No slow and careful taking.

She was on him before he was completely hard, burying him within her, riding him urgently before a sharp gasp stilled her motion.

Her leg was bringing her pain, he realized. She had taxed it with the wild and frantic motions pushing them to climax. Wanting to soothe, he ran his hand up her thigh, along the ridges of scars and knotted muscle.

She jerked with shock and then paused to track with her gaze the path of his hand and the slight glow beneath his palm. She winced as he traced a finger along one particularly defined scar.

"It's ugly," she said, and grasped his hand, arresting his journey.

"No, it's not," he said, and with gentle strength, he reversed their positions, urging her to her back.

He moved downward, pressed a kiss above her knee, just below the first evidence of her injury. Her body jumped beneath him, but not with desire.

He moved an inch farther, to the first jagged line, silvery pink against the creamy beige of her skin. When he placed his lips there her body arched as if jump-started.

"Adam," she keened as if in pain.

He glanced up at her, met her gaze. Even in the dark of the night the shimmer of tears was evident. He wanted them to be tears of joy.

"You are beautiful, Bobbie. Inside and out. Strong," he whispered against her ravaged thigh, wanting to kiss away her hurt. He slipped his hand over her and as he did so, a glimmering blue-white frost erupted wherever his fingers traveled. He released his power, imagined that energy drifting inward, along all that hurt, driving it away. Healing her.

"I'm scared, Adam," she said, her body alive beneath his fingers, her life force responding to his power, the color of her aura deepening and accepting the kiss of his vitality.

"I won't hurt you, Bobbie. Don't fight it."

A visible shudder racked her body, but she released her control and accepted him, allowed his gift to flow through her wounds.

Her pulse raced as he trailed his hand along her ravaged thigh, the caress of his power alive against her skin, the color bright. Tendrils of silver and red spread along her flesh before disappearing beneath her skin.

"That feels incredible," she murmured, and brought her hand down, cradling the back of his head to urge him on.

With a smile on his face, he continued upward, shifting past the last remnants of injury high up on her hip, dancing his fingers along the center of her as he nestled his body between her legs. He raised the hem of the shirt so he could see the dark nest of curls between her thighs, bent his head, and found the sweet nub. He licked it, which had her arching off the bed and crying his name. No fear or uncertainty this time.

Just undisguised raw need.

Holding her thighs open, he kissed her again and again, tasting her. Driving his tongue into her dampness. Licking all along her lips until she was writhing against the sheets and her fingers tangled in his hair, holding him close. He eased one finger within and her muscles clenched around it. He nearly came himself.

Surging upward, he braced his arms on either side of her body and looked down at her, seeking permission to enter. She raised her hips and invited him in. With one sure thrust, the climax washed over her and pulled him under with her as their forces tumbled together.

He struggled for breath, drowning in her musky scent. In the wet heat of her, milking him. Pulling his seed deep within. His life force surged through her, completing the union.

As he collapsed on her, she held him tight and rained kisses along his face until he roused enough to meet her mouth with his, and they were suddenly both smiling and laughing, the demons driven away. Or at least, some of them, he thought as the fabric of the shirt he had lent her rubbed against his chest instead of Bobbie's smooth, creamy skin.

In time, he thought, bundling her close.

• • •

Kellen and Selina shared uneasy glances as Lucas's body continued to twitch and spasm on the table before them. The once-brilliant red of his aura was fractured by streaks of silver and blue like sparklers glowing in the shadows of a summer night.

"I've never seen such a thing. Such power," Selina said as she walked around the cadre member, examining him in the hope of healing the damage to his life force.

"It's neither Shadow nor true Light," Kellen replied as he, too, sought some cure for their fellow Hunter. He held his hand above Lucas's body, feeling the force of the power against his palm, a constant drone like that of a race car engine at top speed.

"The woman was there and absorbed an energy blast. She has to be Shadow. A human would have died from such a blast," Marcus jumped in, moving closer to his wounded comrade and the duo of Quinchus who continued to circle the kitchen table they had commandeered to more thoroughly examine Lucas.

Their cadre captain strode to Marcus, arms across his massive chest, his face stern as if chiseled from stone. "I commanded you not to engage," Andres chastised him.

Marcus nodded and then quickly added, "We didn't, Captain. We were confronted, and when we would have made our escape, the man fired at us."

"Fired an energy ball?" Eduardo interjected from across the room. He was seated in one of the kitchen chairs, his face pale.

"Silence," Kellen commanded, sensing how the discussion was worrying his wife. Selina had pinned such high hopes on this man's being their lost son. He worried she might shatter if it turned out he was a Shadow, or worse, if he was their son and the Shadows captured him. If their son, Kikin, was responsible for the energy still surging through Lucas, all could be lost not only for their clan, but for all the Light Hunters in the area if he fell to the darkness, such was his power.

"Selina?" he questioned, as his wife stopped at the foot of the table, directly across from him.

She shot him a look, her eyes clouded with worry although her face was shuttered in an attempt to hide her concern. Her voice seemed smaller when she spoke, as if from a great distance. As if some spark of life had left her, and his heart clenched with the thought of losing her. Life without his wife would be interminable.

"We must ground him, Kellen. Act as the conduits to release this force from his body before it totally short-circuits his life energy."

Kellen didn't question her judgment. Through the many decades of their marriage he had come to understand that Selina understood the vagaries of their Quinchu power better than any of them. With a nod, he took a position close to the head of the table and raised his hands, mimicking his wife's actions.

"On three," she said and began the countdown.

"One. Two. Three."

They both plunged their hands through Lucas's splintered aura and grabbed hold of him. At the moment of contact, the energy slammed through Kellen, eclipsing any he had ever gathered and charging him with intense vigor, more forceful than even his current life energy.

As he raised his head, he could see his wife was experiencing it as well. As their gazes locked, they allowed the power to sweep over them, into them, revitalizing their own flagging vitality.

Beneath their hands, Lucas's body stilled as the foreign energy left him. His body and face became peaceful. As Kellen and Selina pulled back, releasing him, his aura returned to its normal crimson hue and his eyelids flickered open. Dazed, he struggled to one elbow and peered around the room at the members of his cadre and the two Quinchus. "What happened?"

Kellen and Selina stepped away from the table. Even across the distance, they sensed the power enveloping them. Their bodies thrummed with its spirit.

Selina was the first to speak, and her tone was stronger than before, far surer than it had been for longer than Kellen could remember. "The man is Kikin, and he's found his focus. His natural affinity is lightning," she said, and raised her hand toward her husband.

As before, Kellen didn't doubt as he grasped her hand. A mother, after all, knew her child better than anyone else.

"Such an affinity is rare, but powerful. That would explain what we are experiencing," he agreed as he sampled the energy buzzing through his body.

"But what about the woman, Quinchu? Could she be one of us?" Marcus asked, directing his gaze at Selina.

Selina sensed no trace of Shadow power within the energy they had just absorbed from their cadre member, but she was still uncertain what abilities, if any, the woman with her son possessed.

"She must have some of the hunting gift, otherwise she'd be dead. But for now, we must focus on bringing Adam back to the fold *peacefully*," she said, leaving no doubt from her tone that she would not tolerate another incident like the one that had happened tonight.

The cadre members dipped their heads and saluted before leaving Kellen and Selina alone. Blissfully alone, Selina thought as she slipped her hand into her husband's, the power within her rousing passion and the need to share her life force.

With a coquette's half glance, she swung his hand playfully. "The night grows short, my love."

Kellen smiled and hauled her close, his eyes beginning to glow brightly as he released his power and it surged into her, nearly bringing her to a climax from its strength.

"Then let's not waste another second," he said, backing her toward the wall, where he raised the long skirt she wore and eased his hand over her naked sex. With another release of power against that sensitive flesh, he pulled a climax from her that had her shaking in his arms and grabbing hold of his shoulders for support.

He met her gaze, shimmering silvery gray as she laid her hands on his shoulders and exacted sweet revenge. He barely had time to push himself into her before the exquisite female energy of her yanked orgasm after orgasm from the both of them as her stronger power looped through them.

He would willingly die like this, snared in her embrace, he thought before her words echoed in his brain.

"So could I."

CHAPTER
21

It surprised Adam to find his father on his doorstep bright and early the next morning.

It also clearly shocked his father to find Bobbie sitting at the kitchen table, hungrily devouring the bacon, eggs, and waffles they had cooked together just moments earlier.

"I called your office, but they said you were taking the day off," his father said, shooting a condemning gaze from Bobbie to Adam.

"Would you like some breakfast, Mr. Bruno?" Bobbie asked, and rose, pulling an extra plate and cutlery from the cabinets as comfortably as if she had lived in Adam's home all her life.

With a curt slash of his hand in refusal, his father turned to him. "What's going on, Adam?"

"Why don't you pull up a chair? Have some coffee." He walked to the table and dropped a kiss on Bobbie's cheek before sitting beside her.

His father's eyebrow shot up at the telling display of

unity, but Adam had never been one to mince words. "Is something wrong, Dad?"

Blustering, his father said, "You're letting the events of the other day—"

"How about the two men in the Jeep shooting lightning bolts at us last night?" Bobbie said, trumping Adam to the big reveal.

"What? What are you talking about?" his father mumbled, and staggered forward, dropped heavily into a chair by the table, his color a deathly white beneath the Sicilian olive of his skin. Worry drove Adam to his father's side.

"Are you okay?" He squeezed his father's shoulder in a supportive gesture.

"Is it true, Adam? What she said? Is it true?" Salvatore pressed, looking not at Adam, but almost through him, as if he were seeing a ghost.

"It's true, Dad. There was another attack last night."

"This should not be happening." His worry was obvious in his tone and in the fretful way he clasped and unclasped his hands like a frail old man. In reality, his father looked as if he had aged a dozen years in the last few seconds, or as if he were Atlas and the weight of the world had suddenly come tumbling down onto his shoulders. It created unease within Adam, and suddenly he was wondering if he really knew the man who had raised him for twenty years.

"Is there something you need to tell me?" Adam asked, and his father snapped out if it, his daze replaced by the kind of sharp-eyed scrutiny Adam recognized well.

"Who else knows? Who else was involved in what happened last night?" His words were sharp, accusing. He cast a caustic eye in Bobbie's direction.

"The police chief is a friend."

"The police are involved?" His father jumped out of his chair, sending it skittering across the kitchen floor.

"Easy, Dad. As far as the police know, it was a simple accident," Adam replied, trying to keep his tone calm. The reaction seemed severe for someone who wasn't involved.

Unless his father knew more about his attackers than he was admitting.

"What do you know? What is it that you're not saying?"

His father raked his fingers through his thick hair. Was Adam imagining it, or were there more traces of gray there? Were they from the worry that Adam had sensed over the last few months, which he suddenly guessed had a lot to do with him?

"I'm not at liberty to say," came the terse reply.

"We were almost killed last night and you're not at liberty to say?" Bobbie retorted, her body tense beside him. But Adam knew his father too well. Salvatore Bruno would never reveal anything before it was time. If they wanted any information, they were going to have to find it out for themselves.

Laying his hand over Bobbie's as it rested on the kitchen table, he shot her a half glance. "It's okay. My father will tell us when the time is right."

He skewered his father with a stony glare. "Right, Dad?"

Like a quick-change artist's, his father's entire persona altered. Salvatore pulled his shoulders back and inclined his head at a determined angle. His smile thinned, becoming a knife-sharp slash.

"I would never risk your life, Adam. I hope you believe that."

Although his father mouthed the words, Adam wasn't quite so certain anymore. His silence alone was jeopardizing Adam's safety. After Adam's reluctant nod, Salvatore executed a militarily precise about-face and exited the room.

"I guess we're on our own," Bobbie said, and twined her fingers with his, her touch more comforting than he could have ever imagined.

Adam turned his attention to her and smiled despite his concern. He didn't want to worry her, but as he took note of her steadfast features, he realized she wasn't the kind to fret. She was the kind of woman who took action, the warrior ready to protect her own, much like he was ready to defend her as he had the night before.

He tightened his hold on her hand and dipped his head in the direction of her plate. "Eat up. We're going to need to be ready for whatever we plan."

A slow, wicked grin inched across her full mobile lips. "Will that plan include some time in your bed again?"

His gut immediately tightened into a knot of need at the thought of making love to her once more. Bending his head, he licked the edges of her lips, sweet from the maple syrup on the waffles. She responded, opening her mouth and running her tongue along his, deepening the kiss and threading her hand into his hair to hold him close. She met his lips and tongue again and again until they finally broke apart, breathing heavily, desire unleashed and needing fulfillment, until common sense intruded.

"Later," he promised.

"Sooner," she replied with a grin.

• • •

There was one rule Bobbie had learned as a Marine that she considered paramount: Know your enemy.

The problem was that they understood little about whoever had attacked them. The one person who she suspected could provide that information—Adam's father—was clearly keeping it close to his vest. Which meant they had to get the information on their own.

The mess that Adam's little electrical experiment had created two nights before had been cleaned up, and luckily the surge protectors on the various computers, servers, and devices had kicked in with the overload, safeguarding the equipment, for the most part. The monitors that had blown out had been replaced the day before by techs from SolTerra.

Adam motioned to one of the workstations. "I can give you access to the security tapes from the other afternoon. You can refresh your memory while I wait for my security chief. I asked him to come by to see if he could help us."

She nodded, needing something to keep her busy while her mind processed all the information she had so far.

Focusing her attention on the video, she played it again and again, examining the actions of the two assailants for some hint of who they were and memorizing their features. As she paused on one frame where both of their faces were visible, she mentally compared their faces to those of the men in the Jeep last night.

Negative match, she thought.

Nevertheless, there was something similar between their two afternoon attackers and those who had tried to grab them last night. All had large, powerful builds and moved with the kind of masculine authority found in military men. Considering their MO, it would be too coincidental that the four men were not somehow associated with one another.

"Find anything?" he asked, his fingers stationary on the keyboard, making her wonder what he was doing.

"Just a hunch. They seem to be ex-soldiers, except for the balls of energy. But where would they get that kind of power?"

"They took it from someone or something else," he replied, and swiveled in his chair to face her, a shuttered look on his features.

She mulled over his words, almost fearing what would be the most likely explanation. "Are you telling me that you can like suck the energy from other living things? Or machines? Is that why you were going all Computer Whisperer?"

A deep ridge erupted on his forehead and he glanced at her through slitted eyes. "Sounds awful when you put it like that. Like I'm some kind of vampire."

"Do you? Take energy from other beings?" she put out there, needing to understand more about who and what he was before she became even more involved than she was.

He looked away then, obviously uncomfortable. When he spoke, an underlying hint of anger vibrated in his voice. "I can connect with electrical things directly, and as for living things...I could take their power. I usually don't, except possibly here, when I do my experiments."

She glanced around the room as if seeing it for the first time, now aware of its real purpose. "You were trying to gather energy for yourself the other night."

He nodded. "And test a new battery concept. One which can store electrical energy taken from naturally occurring sources, like lightning."

Much as she had earlier with his father, she got the sense it was only a partial answer, that there was more to his powers and what he did with them that he wasn't saying, and in a way, she understood. Even though they had made love twice and spent the night in each other's arms, they were still essentially strangers. Whatever trust existed was built on the rocky foundation laid down by the events of the last couple of days. Before a more solid footing could be found, they needed to learn a great deal about each other.

"Did it work? The new battery?" she asked, diverting the subject to one that she hoped would be less antagonistic.

Visibly relaxing, he offered up a wry smile. "It gave me enough juice to nearly fry myself and maybe even shoot those power balls."

"You've never done that before?"

Shaking his head, he shifted the chair until they were face to face and knee to knee. "No, I haven't. Just like I never healed someone or made love to a very desirable and very beautiful woman before," he said and punctuated his statement by grazing the side of her face with the light brush of his fingers.

She imagined he could feel the heat of the blush created by his words much as she could once again sense the buzz of power against her skin. "I find it hard to believe you've never made love—"

"Not like last night. Not with someone like you," he immediately clarified, and shifting his hand to her lips, traced the edge of them with his index finger, igniting want with just that simple caress.

Leaning forward, she kissed him—just a barely there

skip of her lips along his, eyes open to watch the changing emotions in his. Seeing the already deep emerald darken, get swallowed up by the blackness of his irises as she continued to tease her lips along his.

The loud ring of the doorbell yanked them apart, drawing their attention to a monitor, which flashed to a picture of someone at the front door.

Adam held his hand over his computer and after an abrupt wave said, "I'm opening the front door, Rand. Come down to my lab."

The man immediately entered and less than a minute later, he stood before them at the entrance to the room, hands clasped together, back ramrod straight. He had a bulldog's face, all craggy and saggy in spots, although she suspected he wasn't much older than fifty. It was a face that had seen a great deal and judging from the salt and pepper buzz cut and his stance, he was either ex-military or ex–law enforcement.

"Rand. Thank you for coming so quickly," Adam said and rose from his chair, motioned for the man to enter.

"No problem, sir. I sensed there was trouble." There was no doubt about his feelings as the man glared at her.

She stood, feeling a kink bunch up in the middle of her thigh, causing her to falter a bit when she faced the man Adam had called Rand.

"Do you have a problem with me, Mr.—"

"Cunningham, ma'am. Randall. Chief of Security," he replied precisely, wasting not a word.

Judging from the neat look of him, with his pristine dark suit, white shirt, proper rep tie, and buzz cut, Mr. Cunningham, Randall, Chief of Security, was not a man of excess anything.

"And no, Sergeant Carrera. I have no problem with you. It's just that your presence was…unexpected," he advised with a measured dip of his head and finally a glance at Adam, an almost parental I-hope-you-know-what-you're-doing kind of look.

"No longer a sergeant, Mr. Cunningham. Bobbie will do," she said and held out her hand to the man.

He took it and after exactly two shakes, pulled it away and said, "Bobbie. Once a Marine, always a Marine, Bobbie."

With those words he made himself clear. He was always faithful, not only to the Corps, but also to Adam, his employer. If she posed a threat, he would protect Adam from her. If she wasn't a risk, he'd have her back also.

"I need you to know you're *my* man on this, Rand," Adam said and came to stand by Bobbie, sending his own message. Randall shrugged shoulders that stretched the fabric of his serviceable dark suit as he clasped his large hands in front of him. "Your father might have recommended me, but you pay the bills, Adam."

"Good to know," Adam replied, and then continued. "We've got photos of the men who attacked us the other day. I want to run them against whatever databases are available."

"VICAP, CODIS, as well as the secret stuff, I'm assuming?" Rand asked without blinking an eye.

"You can do that?" Bobbie pressed.

With a slow dip of his head, he said, "I can, but I'm assuming you don't want it to track back to either you or SolTerra."

"That would be correct," Adam confirmed.

Rand reached into his suit jacket pocket, took out a business card and pen, wrote down something, and then handed the card to Adam. "Someone trustworthy. You'll be able to snoop around all you want without sending up any signals."

"And what will you be doing while we're snooping?" Bobbie asked.

Rand gave an uneasy shrug. "I detected some unusual network activity the night before."

"You're saying someone broke into our systems?" Adam dragged a hand through his hair, clearly distraught.

"Not really a break-in," he said, annoying Bobbie with his obtuseness.

"Can you be a little clearer?" she pressed.

"I think they came in through a back door," Rand advised.

Silence followed for long seconds before Adam pushed away from the workstation and paced back and forth before rounding on Rand. "You're saying it was an inside job?"

With a quick dip of his head, the security chief confirmed it. "Could be a simple case of someone trying to steal trade secrets."

"Nothing simple about that and unlikely given that it happened on the same day as the attack," Bobbie offered up for consideration.

Adam's gaze narrowed, but then he inclined his head. "Get to it, Rand. I'm hoping it does turn out to be nothing more than corporate espionage."

With little wasted motion, Rand excused himself and left.

Bobbie approached Adam and cupped his cheek. "He

seems like a capable man. I'm sure he'll have something for us soon."

"Is it still an 'us,' Bobbie?" he said, and wrapped his arms around her waist.

"For now," she answered immediately, because that was the only thing of which she was certain. For now because she wasn't sure she was ready to live in another war zone, always having to watch her back. For now because whatever was happening between them was still too new and inconstant.

Adam smiled tightly. "I understand. I won't press."

Because she appreciated that, she inched up on tiptoe, swept a quick kiss across his lips, and said, "Let's go visit Rand's friend."

CHAPTER
22

The address his security chief had given him was for a souvenir shop located in one of the older buildings on the Asbury Park boardwalk. Centered between the renovated Paramount Theater complex and the still in a state of disrepair Casino along the southernmost edge of the boardwalk, it was in a high-foot-traffic location. Great for selling T-shirts, but maybe not so great for the apparently clandestine activities in which the store's owner also engaged, Adam thought as he peered at the boardwalk. Even on a Friday in the off-season, there were a goodly number of people strolling, jogging, and bicycling along the strip or enjoying a meal at one of the many food kiosks and restaurants nearby.

"Not quite what I expected," Bobbie said as she did a slow visual sweep of the location, echoing his thoughts.

"I'm with you," he muttered. He opened the door for Bobbie and they walked into the shop. A counter stretched across the entire back width of the space and a young woman sat there working on some kind of sewing machine, feeding a T-shirt through while the needle whirred busily.

"May I help you?" she said as she paused in her work and glanced at them. Adam figured she was in her mid-twenties, about the same age as he and Bobbie.

"We're looking for Sam," he said. A wary look came into her hazel eyes and her shoulders tensed.

"Who's looking for Sam?" The young woman slowly rose and faced them, but she reached beneath the edge of the counter and Bobbie had no doubt about what she was reaching for.

"Randall Cunningham sent us," Bobbie advised quickly and the woman visibly relaxed.

"Dad mentioned you'd be coming," the woman said, pulled her hand out, and stuck it in Bobbie's direction. "I'm Sam Cunningham."

"Cunningham?" Bobbie said as she shook Sam's hand.

"That's me. Samantha Ann Cunningham, although everyone calls me Sam." She faced Adam and offered her hand and then briskly strode to the front door, locked it, and flipped around a sign in the glass door to "Closed."

When she returned to where they stood, she pointed in the direction of a door tucked into the corner of the store, and as they walked through, they entered another area that was almost as large as the space in front.

Work tables held an assortment of electrical items as well as about half a dozen pinball machines. At Adam's questioning look, Sam said, "I repair them for the pinball museum down the boardwalk. Aren't many of us who know how to do that anymore."

"Fascinating," he murmured as he walked past the

classic machines, which were in various states of repair, and reached two tables with televisions and other camera equipment.

"Garage sale and dumpster finds. I have a secondhand electronics store on Cookman," Sam explained.

"An electronics McGyver," Adam said, apparently in awe of the woman's multiple talents.

"You might say that," Sam replied with a gamin smile as they continued beyond those tables to the farthest point in the room. A bank of at least a dozen computers and monitors were busy processing an assortment of tasks. Sam motioned to them and said, "I also host a number of websites, mostly for people who want a little extra security."

"Industrious, aren't you?" Adam teased, and a broad smile erupted on her face, transforming her youngish features.

"Coming from you, Mr. Bruno, that's quite a compliment."

Bobbie experienced an unexpected curl of jealousy at the way the attractive young woman was eyeballing Adam, but she strangled the urge to slip her arm through his and stake her territory. Instead she said, "If we're done with the mutual admiration society, maybe we can get to why we're here."

Sam shot her a half glance out of the corner of her eye, her attention still mostly focused on Adam. "You're here because you need information you can't get legally without a lot of red tape."

Bobbie reached into her jeans pocket, pulled out a thumb drive and handed it to the woman. "There are snapshots of two men on there. Grainy, but hopefully they will be clear enough to run them against the law enforcement databases."

"I can access a number of them." Sam took the drive and stuck it into one of the computers, but before she did anything else, she ran a check of the drive.

"Can't be too careful. Someone hacked the Pentagon in '08 using a thumb drive," she explained, but was soon working on checking the photos. As she did so, she glanced over her shoulder at them. "Anything else I can find for you?"

"Not right now," Adam replied, his gaze glued to the flashing images on the monitors, anxiously awaiting a response. He didn't have long to wait.

The system reported a match to a man who had a misdemeanor assault rap and was a person of interest in connection with a series of murders that had occurred in South Texas. But when Sam attempted to access the files, the system denied her access.

"Whoa. They've been sealed big-time," she said as she typed away, attempting to break into the system, but failing. "NSA big-time," she muttered, and then disconnected, but not before Adam waved his hand over the keyboard.

Bobbie wondered what information he had gotten before the link had been broken. "Were you afraid that opening that file might send up a red flag—"

"And have someone trace it back here," Adam finished.

"Damn straight. Whatever is connected to that file requires a high security clearance."

"Like a CIA agent might have?" Adam wondered aloud, and the tension was visible to both the women.

Sam immediately defended with, "My dad's ex-CIA, but he would have told you if it involved him."

Bobbie laid a hand on her shoulder gently, but it was

enough to silence the other woman, who finally seemed to understand. "I'm sorry, dude. I didn't mean to imply that your dad—"

"My dad was sent to investigate those murders," Adam replied, his tones heavy with emotion.

Bobbie eased her arm around his waist and offered him consolation. "I'm sure there's an explanation for the connection, Adam. We just have to find it."

He nodded and looked at Sam. "Can you help?"

Sam hunched her shoulders. "I won't hack the NSA. Too much of a risk. Besides, there are probably all kinds of newspaper reports about the murders."

"And we can head to a local library and connect to those sources through their computers. This way no one can track them back to us right away," Bobbie said, looking up and meeting Adam's troubled gaze.

Clearly unable to speak, he nodded and took a deep pent-up breath before he released it slowly. Reaching into his pocket, he pulled out his wallet, but Sam raised her hand and said, "No charge for Dad's friends."

Adam smiled then, and removed a business card from his wallet. "Thanks. And if you ever want to stop being a jack-of-all-trades—"

"And master one? Too boring for me," she teased, but took the card anyway. She popped out of her chair, slapped her thighs, and said, "I'll walk you out. I have to get back to finishing an order of T-shirts."

Sam led the way back out and after she opened up her shop again, Adam insisted on buying an entire rack of T-shirts. Understanding that his honor demanded that he offer compensation, Sam replied, "I'm never one to turn down a sale."

Once she had charged him and promised to deliver them to his office, Adam and Bobbie walked out into the beauty of the spring day. Bobbie's arm was wrapped around Adam's waist and she offered an affectionate squeeze to reassure him that all would be all right.

He responded with a forced smile and by dropping his arm around her shoulders. "Did you have a particular library in mind?"

"My library card is for Bradley Beach. There's a nice staff there and computers we can use to search the newspapers and other public files for information on those murders."

With a bob of his head, he said, "Then I guess that's where we go."

The Bradley Beach library was a few blocks off Main Avenue on a quiet residential block. A small Federal-style brick building, it boasted a beautifully manicured lawn and landscaping. The inside was just as well-kept despite its size. A row of maple-colored carrels held computers where patrons could work beside the many bookshelves.

As they entered, the brown-haired librarian at the desk looked up and beamed a smile as she saw Bobbie. She quickly rushed forward and hugged her, and Bobbie returned the embrace.

"It's so good to see you out and about," the pretty young woman said.

"It's good to see you, too, Marge," Bobbie replied, and after a short discussion about family and mutual friends, Bobbie motioned to the computers.

"My computer died and I just needed to look up some things."

Marge gestured to the almost-empty tables and chairs.

"It's too early for the after-school rush, so take as long as you want."

They sat down side by side, legs brushing in the tight quarters of the carrel. Adam laid his hands on the edges of the keyboard, and within seconds, it brought up a series of older articles about the murders. Without shifting a finger, he started flipping through them quickly until Bobbie laid a hand on his to slow him down.

"I can't read that fast," she said, and a flush worked across his cheekbones.

"Sorry," he replied with chagrin. "I'm a speed-reader."

Speed-reader couldn't even begin to describe how quickly he worked, making her realize that Adam had a number of other abilities that were far beyond human.

Within several minutes they had a few articles, including one that contained details about the search for the man and the Texas Ranger working the case: Salvatore Bruno.

"So it seems that my father went out into the desert to the commune where this man lived. It didn't pan out and after another couple of weeks of inquiries the murders went unsolved," Adam finished, his tone distant, almost emotionless, but from beside her Bobbie sensed the tension in his body.

She closed her hand over his and clicked on the mouse to print the article for further review. Lacing her fingers with his, she detected the fine trembling in his body, a testament to the battle he was fighting.

"My father found me in Texas. I remember being out in the desert," he said, voice thick with emotion. Bits of bright green were coalescing in his eyes, and where their hands were joined, a hint of blue aura was slowly emerging.

"Why don't you ask your father, Adam?"

Adam cut her off with an abrupt chop of his free hand. "I can't do that now. I won't until there's no other explanation for what's happening."

Sympathy flickered in Bobbie's gaze before she schooled her features. "Then let's shake some trees and see what else falls out."

"Thank you," Adam replied gratefully, and Bobbie added, "There's more in the article. It seems as if all of the victims had some weird scorch marks."

"Can you search for other instances of those kinds of marks while I look for more on the South Texas murders?" Adam asked, but rather distantly, as if his mind was already at work on multiple things. Then he shook his head and faced her, his attention focused on her like a laser beam, direct and unwavering. "I'm sorry, I'm just a little distracted," he admitted.

"That's understandable," she replied, and smoothed her hand across his chest.

Without further discussion, Adam returned to his computer, leaving Bobbie staring at the back of his head of sun-streaked hair.

She understood his distraction as well as his probable frustration. She couldn't imagine what it would be like to not know your real history or to doubt the motives of the only kin you did know. If there was one constant in her life, it was her family.

She could not comprehend what she would do if she couldn't count on them. Because of that, when she sat down at the computer in the adjacent carrel to look for other possibly related cases, she did so with one huge hope in mind—that she could find a plausible explanation for why Salvatore Bruno was lying to his son.

CHAPTER
23

His son was a brilliant man.

Because of that, Salvatore had no doubt that it was only a matter of time before he and the Carrera woman connected the dots to him, if they hadn't already done so. He had to turn that scrutiny away if his Genesis project was ever going to become a reality.

Adam was to have been the progenitor for the new race. Under other circumstances, Bobbie might have made an excellent Eve—the first woman to mate with Adam. He had some knowledge of the Carrera family, after all, knew they were smart and strong. The birth would have eventually provided them with the necessary stem cells to create even more people with Adam's powers. People that Salvatore and his CIA group chose for enhancement as part of Genesis.

There was just one rub with that scenario. He had discovered that Bobbie was barren and his son's emotional attachment to her could only produce complications.

He should know about how emotion created difficulties. Despite all that he had been taught, he had developed a heartfelt connection to Adam that he could not deny. Adam was his son, and at times the weight of that sentiment complicated the duties he owed to his group and to the deal he had made with Alexander Sombrosa.

But there was no way to eliminate those conflicting obligations at the moment. He hoped that maybe there was a way to balance them, to find the means to advance Genesis without losing the only family he had.

Sadly, he had no uncertainty that accomplishing that might mean sacrificing Bobbie Carrera. Or at least, his son's relationship with the attractive young woman.

Salvatore knew just how to accomplish the schism.

Adam watched the screen as page after page flashed by on the monitor at speeds humans were unable to follow. He had raced through a number of articles on the murders, but had saved the most dangerous link for last: the one to the NSA file Sam Cunningham had located earlier.

He had copied the address for the link with a swipe of his hand before they had left Sam's back room.

With a mental command, he fed the computer the link, but to safeguard what he was doing, he commanded a different image to appear on the monitor. In the background, however, the NSA systems were blocking access to the file. Time and time again he attempted to break the password protecting the file, but with no luck.

Frustration set in, along with the first traces of a headache along the edges of his brain. He broke the link with the computer and leaned back in his chair, beginning to experience a weird fluctuation of energy in his core.

Shooting a glance at Bobbie from the corner of his eye, he noticed her rubbing her leg and swiveled in the chair to face her.

Bobbie massaged the dull throbbing in her leg, which had been growing in direct proportion to the stress headache beating at her brain. She hated long periods of inactivity, and staring at the assortment of newspaper articles and reports on the computer for the last hour hadn't helped her mood.

"Let me," he said, leaning toward her, his hands outstretched to take over her massage, but she captured his hands with hers.

"I'm okay."

He slipped one hand from her grasp and ran a finger along the deep furrow in her brow. "Doesn't seem that way."

With just a flick of his finger, the headache eased and he reached for her again, but she didn't waver from her stance.

At the questioning arch of his brow, she said, "I don't want you to think that I'm only here because of—"

"My money?" he said, deadpan.

"Adam," she warned, but with a hint of laughter in her voice.

"My good looks?" he added, shifting his chair even closer to her. A boyish twinkle glittered in his green eyes and toyed along the edges of his lips, hinting at the playful streak buried beneath his normally staid exterior. She suspected that little boy was one who hadn't emerged very often in his life.

She chuckled and shook her head. "Come on, Adam. You know why."

He shifted his chair back to her carrel and his knee brushed hers, sending a jolt of power through her, making her jump from its potency.

"Sorry. It's tough to be around you and not feel this way."

She smiled and cradled his cheek. The force of his power greeted her palm, much more potent than before. "It seems stronger."

In truth, Adam had sensed the difference as well. The call of the power had been growing in him again all day. It had flitted around the edges of his consciousness, but had been taking firmer root over the last few hours. Being this close to her wasn't helping. He could sense the power trying to escape him and merge with her. Because of that, he needed distance and possibly a way to get rid of some of that excess energy before he lost control.

"I need a break. How about you?"

"I need to stretch." She logged off her computer, grabbed the sheets of paper she had printed, and rose. "How about a walk?"

"I'm game," he replied. He moved quickly, logging off and grabbing his papers. He placed a hand at the small of her back as they walked out of the library, pausing only to drop their materials in the car before their stroll.

But as Adam took her hand, a shock jolted her, making her pull away from him.

"I'm sorry. I haven't had so little control in a long time."

His unease was obvious and she tried to alleviate it. Laying her hand against his chest, she ignored what was almost a painful burn of energy pouring off him. "What can I do to help?"

As he had before, Adam experienced the expanding push of the power, wanting to escape, plus the physical pull of his human side, remembering how they had spent the night. Which reminded him of why he had kept his previous contacts to ones devoid of emotion. He stepped back from her, earning a wounded look, but knowing it was necessary. "I don't want to hurt you, Bobbie. Right now, I'm having trouble handling my life force."

She shuttered her upset and put on a brave face. "I understand. Maybe we should go."

"That makes sense," he said, and they wasted little time getting into the car to return to Adam's home.

They were silent as they drove, but with each mile that passed, Adam took note of the energy building in a way he had not ever experienced before. His core grew as dense as lead and so hot it was as if he was burning up from the inside out.

Bobbie seemed to sense his discomfort and reached for him, but he thrust his hand up to keep her away. Shards of light shot from his fingers and Bobbie jerked back, stung by the release of his power.

"Sorry," was all he could manage, as whatever was overtaking him was making it painful to perform even the most basic human functions. His heart raced in his chest and his head pounded in rhythm to the beat. He saw his house up ahead and was grateful, since bright swirls of light danced in his vision, almost blinding him.

Somehow he got the car into the garage, but as he stepped out, his knees buckled and he fell forward. Bracing his hands on the ground, he struggled against the pressure building inside him, like a balloon being overfilled.

"Adam," he heard, but it seemed muffled as static

jammed his brain, making conscious thought virtually impossible. Fighting for stability, he dug his fingers deep, the cement floor of the garage literally melting beneath his touch.

"Adam," came again, even more distant than before, but suddenly, insistently, another force pressed against his, creating a connection that seemed to be grounding him.

Bobbie cradled Adam in her arms, holding him tight and calling his name over and over as she tried to bring him back. The royal blue of his aura was huge, with angry bolts of red and silver dancing wildly, vibrating against her body. His eyes had gone to that neon green, but were unfocused, and it was clear he wasn't seeing her as she held him.

"Oh, God, Adam. Come back to me," she pleaded, and bent and kissed his forehead, praying she could drive back whatever had overtaken him. His arm flopped up and down, uncoordinated, but then fell over hers. She laced her fingers with his and it came. A wave of energy flowed through her, nearly stealing her breath away, settling in her center and bringing with it myriad emotions and sensations, including almost painful desire.

Between her legs erupted the heavy throb of need as moisture flooded her sex. Her nipples puckered and became so sensitive that even the simple rub of fabric along them brought her closer and closer to orgasm. She moaned and gripped him tighter, so lost in her own battle that she almost didn't realize that Adam had somehow mustered a bit of control.

He turned in her arms, his eyes blazing with a whirl of emotions.

"I need you." His voice rasped like a needle scratching across a record, sounding almost nonhuman.

Maybe because he wasn't, Bobbie thought, but she was in too deep now to retreat. Her body was screaming for release and so was his, judging from the immense ridge of his erection visible beneath the fabric of his pants. She reached down and covered him and his body jumped. Another wave of power crashed through her, yanking another moan as her muscles contracted around emptiness.

Touch me, she thought, unable to voice her wish, and in the millisecond that the thought formed, lightness suffused her body before the world became a blur around her. It was if they were whirling through the air until a second later they landed with a thud on the floor of his living room.

Adam was still in her arms, but he dropped to his back and urged her to straddle his hips. She didn't stop to question the how or why. She needed him too badly, so she covered him, his erection rubbing along her cleft between layers of fabric. The movement sent a jolt through her and she had to still for a moment to keep from climaxing, because she wanted so much more, as did he.

She broke from him only long enough to pull off her pants as he was doing the same, wanting all of him naked beneath her. She needed that connection with him almost as much as she needed to breathe, it seemed.

As she straddled him once more, she reached down, ripped off his shirt, and laid her hands on his chest. Whatever force had trapped him had imprisoned her and the energy seemed to ebb and flow between them. Her nipples ached, they were so tight, but as soon as the thought came, Adam placed his hands on her, caressing the sensitive tips, the sure touch of his hands creating a rush of heat and moisture through her nether lips.

He groaned and murmured, "You're so wet, I can smell you. Smell your need."

As she could smell him, a strange combination of musky earthiness and a bright summer day. She bent her head to the crook of his neck, inhaled to memorize the scent. Put her mouth on that spot and sucked that tender flesh because she needed to taste as well.

The pull of her mouth nearly undid Adam, but it also allowed him to corral the power that had virtually overtaken him just moments before. He focused on her mouth and how she worked at him, knowing it would leave a mark, but uncaring, because he knew he would mark her as well with his life force.

Grasping her buttocks, he urged her upward and then poised himself at her center. The heat and wet of her drenched him, and as he entered her, the power surged between them once again, almost like water sloshing back and forth between two shores. Ebbing and flowing, building passion as she rode him, her soft cries telling him of her satisfaction, the rising force of their vitality becoming almost dangerous as it centered itself at his core, waiting for its release.

He met her gaze, where bright bits of green now shimmered in their hazel depths as his aura joined with hers, the end of his being and the beginning of hers indistinguishable, united as they were in both body and energy.

He knew then she was meant to be his. She was the one who could complete him and eliminate the emptiness he had sensed growing in him over the last several months. His power was meant to be shared with hers and forever bound to her being.

He rose then until they were face to face, body rubbing against body. His erection buried even deeper as she wrapped her legs around his waist.

"We are one, Bobbie," he said and the mass of energy that had built at his center exploded across them, charging every ion in their bodies with its vitality and then liberating its gift through every particle of their being.

Bobbie came, hard and fast, moaning his name, her world alight with the feel of every bit of life around her. It was as if she had been looking at the world through a dirty windshield before and now it was clear and all was bright and amazingly sharp.

Including the feel of Adam beside her. Inside her.

Adam held her tighter as his body jerked within her and his seed warmed her from within. His skin was alive against her with heat. She sensed every nuance of it, from the smoothness of his back to the crisp curls on his chest rubbing against her palms, felt each shift of hard muscle beneath as he embraced her.

Bobbie wrapped her arms around him, buried her face against his shoulder. His scent wrapped around her as her body still vibrated from her release and the wonder of the vitality suffusing her.

He shifted his hands up and down her back, the action soothing. Kissing the side of her face, he asked, "Are you okay?"

It had been so long since she had been okay that she wouldn't recognize normal if it hit her over the head with a two-by-four. But what she did know was that how she felt in his arms right now was far better than anything she had felt in like forever.

"I'm more than okay. I'm wonderful," she said, turning

her face and kissing his cheek. She met his gaze, which no longer had the wild glow of power, although remnants of his aura still bathed them in its royal blue.

He smiled, raised his hand to trace the line of her lips before kissing her, rousing desire yet again with that simple touch, although she also felt drained by what had just happened, as did he, apparently.

"It's too soon. I feel like I need to recharge."

She felt it, too, almost as if what had just happened had cemented a link between them, making her cognizant of everything about him and around him.

"How about a nap?" she asked, thinking that lying beside him body to body was about as close to heaven as it might get and might provide the rest they needed to regain their strength.

"How about a swim?" he suggested, surprising her.

"A swim? In April? Cold much?" she teased.

He smiled, that boyish grin that caused her heart to lurch in her chest. "Trust me," he said.

In that moment, she realized she did trust him. He might be something other than human and could rock her world in ways that were downright inexplicable, but she trusted him. With her heart. With her life.

As his smile broadened, she knew that he knew, and for the moment, all was right in the world.

CHAPTER 24

She stood at the water's edge, shuddering as the frosty wash from a small wave covered her big toe.

Although the early evening air was a balmy sixty-eight degrees, the water was cold enough to turn her skin blue and send a chill through her body as she finally braved a bigger step into the surf.

She didn't understand how Adam withstood the cold, swimming just behind the first break of waves, his long, powerful body cutting through the surface of the water with minimal effort.

She hadn't been to the beach in nearly a year. Her injuries had made walking on the sand a risky proposition. Forget about a swim, unable as she was to either tread water or doggy paddle. It saddened her and made her wonder why she had agreed to it earlier.

Maybe because she had been lost in the wonder of sharing herself with Adam.

She had used to ride these waters, her body knifing

through the surf, tangled up in the sweep of the waves, rolling and tumbling through sand and water before shooting up onto her feet on the wet sand. Longing tore through her to join him, but the water was just too damned cold and her footing still precarious.

Although not as unstable as before.

She hadn't wanted to tell him, although he must have noticed by now. Since making love the other night and since his tender and sincere kiss along her leg, it had gotten better. She still cramped up after long periods of inactivity, as she had earlier that day. And there was still pain, but duller. Not as acutely sharp as before. Plus the weakness, that sense of not really being able to put any weight on it for fear it would crumple like a brittle stick, was gone. Especially after this afternoon.

Whatever had happened between them earlier had left something within her. A feeling of power she had not had before. A link with him that allowed her to sense so many things, both within him and around her. Much as he suddenly seemed to be able to sense her wants and needs.

She hadn't had to ask for help earlier as they had hit the sands of the beach. Without a second's hesitation, Adam had wrapped his muscled arm around her waist to help her navigate the once-treacherous sands. So now there she stood, wearing a pair of his shorts that hung to below her knees and another T-shirt, this one with a Golden Gopher. She had picked it from one of the drawers packed with T-shirts from the various places he had visited.

Another sign that in some ways Adam Bruno was just a plain ol' Joe like the rest of them: a T-shirt collection.

She smiled and watched as Adam caught a wave, as agile as a dolphin, and rode it to the knee-high waters.

When he stood, she sucked in a breath, stung yet again by
his masculine beauty, thinking that on Adam a Speedo
was downright illegal.

He shoved his hand through his hair, raking back the
dripping wet strands, and came to stand before her. In the
growing dusk, the fading sun turned the drops of water
clinging to his body silver.

She felt as if she would die if she didn't touch him and
ran her hand along his chest, his skin slick beneath her
palm and warm. Oh, so warm, despite the icy temperature of the water. She shot a look up at him, wondering,
and he said, "I told you it wouldn't be cold if you went in
with me."

"Do you have your own little blast furnace going?" she
teased, and his grin widened.

"Why don't you find out?"

She looked beyond him to the waves and the darkening ocean. It called to her, and as he raised his hand and
held it out, she slipped her hand into his and followed him
into the water.

The jolt of the cold with those first few steps rattled
her, but then he wrapped his arms around her. With a
strong shove of his legs, he drove them into the waters,
the sea swallowing them up for a moment before they
resurfaced.

Artists called a mix of dark and light *chiaroscuro*, and
that was how it felt to be in his arms, floating in the water.
Hot and cold swirled around her, from his body and the
ocean. More hot than cold, for which she was thankful.

His strength kept her afloat in the relatively calm
waters, and it was a marvelous sensation: the weightless-
ness of the waves and their primal push and pull; the heat

of their bodies pressed together, rubbing with the ebb and flow of the water until the inevitable happened.

Her nipples were tight, chilled by that chiaroscuro hot-cold and the fabric rubbing against them. Against him. Beside her belly came the insistent push of his erection, and as before, she had to touch.

She reached down and covered him with her hand, the nylon slick. Looking up, she watched his eyes darken as she stroked him, and along her body, his skin grew ever hotter. Was it her imagination or were there wisps of steam coming off his shoulders?

"Bobbie," he said with a pained sigh.

"Sshh," she whispered against his lips as she continued her caresses, tracing the length of him with her hand before cupping him. Inching beneath the nylon, she encircled him.

He groaned and tightened his hold along her waist, freeing his other arm so he could run his hand across the tight nubs of her breasts, tweaking and caressing them until she was shaking and the emptiness between her legs needed to be filled.

She yanked down her shorts and then did the same with his Speedo, freeing him from the confines of the nylon. With one swift move, her legs were wrapped around his hips and he plunged into her.

Their gasps filled the air, almost drowning out the susurrus of the waves. Above them a seagull cackled, as if chastising them, but nothing mattered but his embrace.

Completeness.

Contentment.

Peace, she thought, not even moving, such was the overwhelming joy and satisfaction of their union. All around them the ocean shifted and flowed, folding them in its embrace, feeding them with its primordial power the way it nurtured so many beings within its realm.

The energy grew around them, within them.

Bobbie could not deny it or him and how he cradled her, his grasp protective and yet not smothering, the strength in him spilling onto her, into her, making her heart race and her body tremble as their passion grew ever higher until she could no longer keep it at bay.

Her climax ripped through her and she arched her back, driving him ever deeper. She lifted her face to kiss him, swallowing his rough call of completion, embracing those powerful shoulders that held her as if she were just a wisp, providing comfort, support, and love.

For minutes they floated there, savoring the remnants of their release, feeding from the life of the ocean as it caressed them. But soon dusk evaporated, warning them that the night had arrived. With her still wrapped around him, Adam propelled them toward shore, and as his feet brushed the sandy bottom he paused and allowed them time to retrieve their clothing and make themselves decent before they exited onto the deserted beachfront.

Once there, he slipped his arm around her waist and helped her from the wet sand to where they had dropped their towels. Bending, he quickly wrapped the terry cloth around her and tucked it tight, pausing to drop a quick kiss on her lips, because he couldn't seem to get enough of her.

She returned the kiss, as hungry as he was, but slowly tempered her response.

"We should go back. Go over all that research we did," she muttered against his lips, but her tone betrayed the fact that she wished they were going back to do something else.

The reality of it was that they had a lot to do, including getting some dinner, he thought, as his stomach rumbled noisily.

Bobbie laughed and slipped her hand over his abdomen. "I have to warn you now. I'm not a good cook."

He snagged a towel and wrapped it around his middle. He playfully grabbed her hand, and as he urged her back toward his house, he said, "Your family owns a restaurant and you can't cook? How is that possible?"

"That's precisely the reason why. My parents were too busy cooking to teach us," she said, and took a step to block his way. Even in the growing dark, her gaze glittered and a broad smile shone brightly. There was something mischievous in her stance, especially as she laid her hands on his waist and tickled his sides. "Which means we can either go out or order in—"

"Or I can cook." He laced his fingers with hers and offered her his support again as they did the short walk up the beach and across the street to his home.

Inside, he jerked his head in the direction of the stairs. "Why don't you take a quick shower while I see what's in the fridge."

Bobbie didn't argue. The ocean salt was sticky on her skin and the slight drop in the temperature of the nighttime air had chilled her even with Adam close by.

She nodded and stole a kiss across his lips before heading up the stairs and to the bedroom he had so graciously offered her the night before.

Had it only been a night? she mused as she grabbed clothes and headed for the shower. She wasted little time in getting clean, wanting to enjoy her time with Adam.

Donning her own clothes, she skipped down the stairs, determined to be happy.

The sweetly aromatic fragrance of onions and pepper cooking hit her at the foot of the stairs. She followed the enticing odors to the kitchen where Adam was already at the stove, stirring something in a skillet.

Freshly showered, his wet hair was raked back from his face, exposing the marvelously sculpted lines of his features. The straight nose with just the right hint of pug. Chin with a perfectly sized thumbprint cleft. His lips— she could spend hours thinking about those lips—with their sharply defined edges and slight bow at the top. The dimple that emerged when he smiled.

"Hungry?" he asked, his emerald gaze fixing on her, one brow rising sardonically, probably because he had sensed she was eating him up with her eyes.

"How can I help?" she said, but even before he answered she was in motion, carefully walking to the center island in the kitchen where the ingredients for a salad sat on the counter.

"What else did you find on the web?" Adam asked, returning to the matter at hand.

Bobbie broke the lettuce as she spoke, tossing the bits into a colander in the sink. "After you discovered that two of the three murder victims had both scorch marks and smallpox scars, I searched for stories about people with cases of smallpox."

"Which would be odd, since smallpox was eradicated in the late 1970s," Adam said as he stirred the garlic and added red peppers and onions to the skillet.

"That's what I thought also. A single death here and there. Maybe someone thought it was an accident," Bobbie surmised, and rinsed the colander in the second sink in the island.

"But multiple deaths in a short span in Texas sent up an alarm and my dad went to investigate. And then found me."

A hard edge crept into his voice and she walked over, slipping her arms around his waist to offer comfort. "I found a few other cases, Adam. Maybe it's just coincidence that your father found you at the same time."

He offered a noncommittal grunt, so she tried another tack. "I noticed some doodles on your notes."

He nodded and glanced over his shoulder at her. "I sketch and scribble while I work sometimes. Helps me think."

"The doodles looked familiar. Like the logo you use for your company."

He paused as he stirred the vegetables in the skillet. He hadn't given it a thought, but the scribbles were often the same designs over and over. Until her observation, it hadn't occurred to him that the rough sketches were very similar to the fanciful Sun and Earth logos he had adopted for his business.

"I hadn't realized it before, since all I did was give the graphic designers some rough ideas about what I wanted," he admitted, and turned around and walked to the kitchen table where they had tossed the papers they had brought back from the library. He picked up his notes and scrutinized the designs. As with the energy blasts that had shaken loose a memory, the symbols—almost like hieroglyphics now that he thought about it—seemed long familiar, and yet he couldn't remember why.

"Do they mean something to you?" Bobbie asked as

she took over for him at the stove, giving a stir before returning to the island and the salad fixings.

He shrugged. "Maybe. I'm not quite sure."

She smiled. "In time, Adam. Everything will come to you when the time is right."

He hoped so, he thought, as he tossed the notes back down and returned his attention to the meal, dropping in the precisely cut strips of raw chicken, following the recipe his father had taught him. He smiled as he thought of those times they'd shared during the breaks when his dad had been home from an assignment.

Placing the skillet back on the heat, he quickly sautéed the chicken and then added the crushed tomatoes. With a quick dash of some spices, he set the temperature to a low simmer and went to join Bobbie.

Contrary to her admission that she couldn't cook, Bobbie seemed quite capable, he thought as he stood beside her, admiring the competent way she worked. Her fingers were long and elegant, her movements graceful as she chopped and sliced her way through the assorted vegetables on the counter.

He placed his hand at the small of her back and leaned toward her. He filched a slice of carrot from the cutting board, earning a playful slap on the back of his hand.

"Do not interrupt the chef," she teased with a nudge of her hip against his.

Despite her warning, he couldn't help messing with her. There was something about her that brought out a mischievous side of him. If she'd had pigtails, he could imagine that he'd be tempted to dip them in an inkwell to gain her attention.

Except that he had a much better idea of how to get

that, he thought, bending his head to nuzzle the straight line of her jaw with his nose before planting a kiss just behind one ear.

A shudder ripped through her body and she paused with the knife poised directly above the bright orange carrot.

"That's so not fair," she said on a shaky exhalation.

"Really?" he challenged, and gently bit his way down to the crook of her neck and shoulder.

The knife clattered to the surface of the cutting board as she raised her hand to hold his head close and turned in his direction.

"Am I interrupting something?"

They broke apart, the moment shattered by the sight of his father standing at the entrance to the kitchen.

He had thought it a good thing that his father have a set of keys in case of an emergency. Not a wise decision in retrospect, he considered as he reluctantly pulled away from Bobbie.

"I hope you have a good reason for coming here unannounced, Dad."

His father seemed taken aback by Adam's challenge, so much so that he actually fell back a step before squaring his shoulders and glaring directly at Bobbie.

"I guess that depends on whether you think finding out the truth about Bobbie and her family qualifies as a good reason."

CHAPTER
25

I'm not the one hiding anything," Bobbie challenged, in immediate defense mode against any possible attack on her family.

"Why don't you let *my son* be the judge of that."

Bruno didn't wait for Adam to invite him in. He marched to the kitchen table where he flung his brief-case on the surface. Shooting Adam a look, she noted his raised brow at the almost theatrical behavior, but opted not to say anything.

His father was right that Adam had to be judge and jury on this. Her only role was to be an advocate against what she was certain would be lies.

Falling back toward the stove, she shut off the chicken and stood there, watching and waiting as Adam's father yanked a number of folders from his briefcase and spread them out across the tabletop. When he was done and Adam had taken a seat, she finally approached, taking a position just behind Adam, where she could see the assorted materials that Bruno somehow thought were damning to her and her family.

Adam opened and flipped through the first few folders, quickly dismissing them, and Bobbie understood why. They contained mostly financial information, including details she had already revealed to him, like the devastating fire at her parents' restaurant that had nearly left them bankrupt and the long road back to some kind of financial stability.

Adam silently reviewed each file, then stacked them neatly to his right. Bobbie hoped his lack of commentary was an omen that so far nothing had created concern. When there were no files left before him, Adam peered up at his father and said, "Is that all?"

A dull flush suffused Salvatore's face, but he shook his head. "I'm not sure Bobbie should be here—"

"It only seems fair that Bobbie has a right to face her accuser," Adam replied, the glacial tone of his voice creating a chill in her but deepening the color on his father's face.

Obviously flustered, Salvatore fumbled while he pulled two other files from his briefcase, one thicker than the other. He placed that thicker file before Adam first and held on to the second, clutching it tightly to his chest as if fearful it would grow wings and take flight.

Bobbie didn't know what to expect of that immense pile of papers, but as he flipped open the cover she immediately realized what it was: her medical history.

A stunned gasp escaped her and her knees went weak as she wondered how Salvatore had gotten it. So weak she had to grab hold of the top rung of Adam's chair to keep upright.

Adam was immediately on his feet, helping her to sit in the chair beside him before kneeling before her. "Are you okay?"

She would be if he didn't read the file. If he didn't find out about every little intimate detail of how her body had been violated by the IED or learn the truth about what she could no longer be.

"Please don't read that file," she pleaded, clenching her hands to keep them from shaking, the pressure she exerted making them appear nearly bloodless, much as she imagined her face might look, as a sickly sweat erupted along her body.

"Ask her why, Adam," Bruno exhorted, a shark smelling blood in the water.

"Please, Adam. It has nothing to do with what's going on," she said, but there was no avoiding the look in his eyes begging for her to give him a reason to believe her, asking her why she couldn't just tell him, and yet the words wouldn't come to her lips. Couldn't form in her brain, because she feared his reaction. Whether it was pity or disgust or anger, none of the emotions she expected would be welcome.

"Let me save you some time," his father said and swiped the file off the table, then flipped through the pages until he reached the one he wanted. Then he handed the papers back to Adam.

Slowly Adam came to his feet, but he hesitated about taking the file. It took his father thrusting it against his belly for Adam to finally accept the documents. With a last fleeting look in her direction, he bent his head to read.

She knew what was there for him to know. The long pent-up inhalation told her he had seen the information and was processing it. The rough breath that followed, along with his rocking back on his heels, communicated that he had understood and accepted the truth of the prognosis on the paper.

This time when he glanced at her there was no denying the emotion.

Pity. It might have been easier for her to handle anger or disgust.

After a long swallow, he said, "I'm—"

"Don't say you're sorry," she parried straightway. "At least I'm alive."

Unlike her men.

A muscle ticked along the side of his jaw as Adam closed the file brusquely and flipped it onto the surface of the table. Jerking his hand in the direction of the file, and without facing his father, he said, "Now that you've violated Bobbie's privacy, care to explain what that has to do with anything?"

Bobbie stared hard at Salvatore, wanting to lash out at the man, but contained herself. Her anger would accomplish nothing.

"I noticed Ms. Carrera seems to be walking better," he said, craning his head to glance past Adam to her cane as it rested on the rung of a nearby seat.

"Where are you going with this?" Adam challenged.

"Where? I thought that would be obvious to a genius like you." With those caustic words, Salvatore tossed the final report onto the table.

Adam flipped the file open and flinched.

Bobbie glanced over at the papers, but couldn't make anything from them. They were just random bars and lines and what looked like lab results, but of what, she didn't know.

Until Adam's father started his explanation.

"I haven't said anything because I was hoping it was just coincidence that you and Bobbie seemed to have met, but when I did some digging around, I found these test results."

"DNA analysis. My DNA and yours, Bobbie," Adam said, gazing at her, the pity and concern in his eyes slowly switching to accusation.

"I don't understand," she said, and reached for the file, but Adam kept a tight grip on it.

"The last case I worked on—am working on now in a supervisory role—involves Bobbie's brother and sister. I thought it odd that one family could find itself involved in the same case not once but twice. Now I understand," Salvatore said.

Bobbie marched up to him until she was nearly nose to nose with him. "Why not make me understand, then?"

"Your family seems to like collecting people with unusual powers, don't they? Caterina Shaw. Jesse Bradford. Did you plan to add Adam to your family's collection?"

"That's insane! Adam..." Bobbie started to refute the accusation, but as Adam once again flipped through the papers, she could feel the doubt creeping into his mind.

"Bobbie's older brother and sister are married to people who were genetically engineered. Bobbie's sister somehow got your DNA and Bobbie's for analysis."

"Tell me you didn't give it to her," Adam said, gazing at her as if he was seeing her for the first time and not in a good way.

"Of course I didn't. I would not betray you like that. And my family has no reason to do this."

"Except of course to obtain yet another specimen with

unique abilities. Maybe even secure patents on whatever properties can be distilled from my son's DNA. They would be quite valuable and would certainly help your parents with their financial issues. Help you pay for your medical expenses," Bruno reasoned.

"That's a lie. I would not betray you, Adam," Bobbie repeated, reaching for the file to examine it herself, but Adam stopped her by trapping the papers beneath his hand.

As she glanced at Salvatore, his smug smile said it all. She looked back at Adam.

"When could I have given anyone your DNA? I've been with you since the attack. Let me have the file and talk to them. Hear their side of it," she said, but Adam's hand remained on the papers.

"Give it to her, son. I've got a copy."

Adam clenched his jaw so tightly Bobbie thought she heard bones pop. His knuckles were white from the pressure he was exerting on the files and she could feel his anger and confusion within her, creating a swirl of emotion deep in her core from the link between them, a link that suddenly felt as if it was growing stronger. He pushed the report in her direction.

"I don't know, but I think you should go." Gone from his voice was any trace of the day's earlier passion.

Bobbie grabbed the file and strode toward the door to the garage, but as she neared it, she realized she had forgotten the cane, which hung on the rung on one of the kitchen chairs.

She turned and her gaze fell upon it, but so did Adam's.

"You forgot this." He jerked the cane from the chair and flung it at her.

She caught it with her left hand and pain radiated from her palm from the force of his toss. But that pain was minuscule compared to that from the fist squeezing her heart. She bit back her distress and met his gaze directly, unafraid. She had truth on her side. In time that would win out over his father's lies.

Without another word, she left.

CHAPTER
26

When the door closed behind Bobbie, it was if someone had drained the life out of him. Adam plopped down heavily in the kitchen chair and buried his head in his hands, almost overwhelmed by the enormity of all that had transpired.

"I'm sorry, son," his father said, and laid a comforting hand on his shoulder, but Adam shrugged it off.

With a belligerent stare, Adam replied, "You said you had a duplicate of the file."

"Of course, I do. I wouldn't—"

"Let me have the copy," Adam said, his tone flat and somewhat curt while he held out his hand for the documents.

"But, Adam—"

"Let me have the copy." Each word was clipped and cutting sharp.

His father must have realized that although he'd driven Bobbie away, Adam wasn't completely under his control.

With a resigned nod, Salvatore reached into his briefcase and extracted his copy of the file. Adam snared it from his hands and placed it on the table before him.

"Now go," Adam said.

"But, son—"

"Go, Salvatore. Before I lose all respect for you."

His father's face fell, but the action struck Adam as theatrical, much like his behavior while he'd been busy staging his case against Bobbie and her family. But no matter how melodramatic his actions had been, Adam could not afford to ignore the cold, hard facts included in the various files.

Rational or not, he was angry that she hadn't told him her full medical condition. How could she hold back when he'd offered his most vulnerable memories?

And he was furious at the DNA testing, and the risk it presented to his existence, even if there was a measure of thankfulness that the tests had proven what his gut had told him all along—that he was different. Possibly not human, and yet coupled with that was the reality that he wasn't alone. The tests had shown a genetic link between him and Bobbie.

True, they had been together almost constantly, but what if the first attack had been a setup? A ruse to collect a sample of skin or hair. The first night she showed up at his home, was it to collect something then?

So lost was he in his thoughts that it took him a moment to realize that his father still stood there, as if expecting a reprieve from Adam's condemnation. But there would be none. Not tonight at least.

"Go," he repeated again, more forcefully, and this time his father left the kitchen.

Adam waited until he heard the snick of the front
door lock. Then he went to the security system panel by
the garage door and set it, engaging the system so that
the moment any entry was opened the alarms would
trip. He didn't want any disturbances or surprises as he
reviewed the test results and tried to make sense of what
they indicated about who he was and maybe even where
he came from.

Hands shaking and palms wet with nervous sweat, he
flipped open the file.

Alexander Sombrosa glared at his son's soldier, rage
churning in him from so many things. Maya, who had
been standing beside him, side-stepped away as the force
of his anger created dangerous spikes of energy that
jumped out to singe anyone nearby.

"Are you certain of this?" Alexander pressed, unable
to believe that his own son was keeping secrets from
him. Why hadn't Christopher mentioned the possibility
of an incredible source of power they could use to heal
themselves?

"I am sure, Añaru," the foot soldier replied, pumping
his hand to his chest and dipping his head in deference to
Alexander's rank. "It happened two nights ago. Not far
from Christopher's home and near the territory belonging
to the Ocean clan of the Light Hunters. A wave of power
like nothing we had ever experienced washed over us.
Restoring us," he said, and held out his hand.

Alexander leaned close and peered at the seemingly
normal-looking appendage. As he did so, he perceived
the power radiating from the man, so alive and enticing.
He grabbed hold of the cadre member's hand, ensnar-

ing it tightly in his grip. The rush came immediately as
the unique energy flowed into him, and like the spider
for which the Añaru was named, he shot out tendrils of
power, which wove a web around the man's hand. They
sank into the man and spread up his arm, slowly sucking
the life juices from him.

Surprise came swiftly to the man's features. "I don't
understand."

"You owe your allegiance to my son and yet you come
here, telling me his secrets," Alexander said, laying his
other hand on the man's shoulder to tighten the web
around him and speed the transfer of power. Before his
eyes dozens of tendrils of Hunter energy formed around
the points of contact before sinking deep into the man's
flesh to draw yet more vigor from his being.

"Came...to...help," the man pleaded, not that it
would do him any good.

"Añaru. You are draining him," Maya said from beside
him, fear in her voice.

"The energy, Maya. It is incredible," Alexander said,
caught up in the vitality racing through his body, repair-
ing the damage created by the damned human pox. A
faint whimper came from the man as he slowly crumpled
to his knees, and still Alexander held on until there was
not a drop of energy left in the other Shadow's body.

He released his hold and the man fell to the ground,
his lifeless stare still mirroring his confusion.

Alexander brushed his hands together, as if wiping
off something distasteful. Then he faced Maya, and with
a smile, cradled her cheek and released a bit of the life
force.

She shuddered and released a mewl of pleasure.

Beneath the tight fabric of her gown, her nipples hardened into visible nubs.

"Later, my dear," he said, and with purposeful strides he returned to the massive granite and steel desk by the large windows of his office. Pushing the intercom button, he summoned his own cadre captain and within seconds the man entered.

His captain strode in, ignoring the other Shadow Hunter's corpse as he approached Alexander and saluted. "What is your command, Añaru?"

"Select your most trusted man, William. I need him to replace this scum in Christopher's cadre." He negligently flicked his hand in the direction of the fallen Hunter.

William finally glanced down at the body of his former clansman. "Did he displease, Añaru?"

Alexander chuckled. "Not at all, William. He pleased me quite well, but there is something I need you to oversee," he said, and advised his captain about the dead man's report and what he wished William to do.

"I want your man to confirm what's happening with Christopher and I want you to visit Salvatore Bruno. Impress on him that Maya and I are growing tired of waiting."

After he had finished, his captain nodded and saluted again. "As you wish," he replied, and exited, leaving him and Maya alone with the corpse.

She walked toward Alexander, her hips swaying, her aura a dark crimson stained in spots from the smallpox energies woven into her being. As her gaze met his, the desire roused by his earlier touch was evident in her dilated pupils. He knew what she wanted, but he would not satisfy her tonight.

"It's time you went to Christopher, Maya. I want you

to find out whatever you can about this unique power he seeks."

Maya walked straight up to him, not stopping until the hard nubs of her nipples rubbed across the cotton of his shirt. She teased him with a little blast of her sexual energy, but he would not be weak tonight. Not when he had such wonderful vitality flowing through him.

"Not tonight, Maya."

"But I'm so ready for you, Alexander," she said, and to prove her point, she grasped his hand and brought it to the fabric between her legs.

There was no denying her readiness. The heat and wet of her drenched the fabric beneath his fingers and his cock jumped in anticipation, but he fought back the desire.

"Go, Maya, before I suck you dry as well."

Realizing he was serious, she copied the cadre captain's earlier deference. "I will go to Christopher as you wish, Añaru."

What he wished was to be whole again, Alexander thought as she left. He glanced down at his hands and saw perfect skin once more. Until the arrival of Christopher's cadre member, he had barely been keeping the pox away, and then only by feeding regularly from one of the many humans in the city below. But such nourishment had to be controlled to avoid calling attention to the existence of the Shadows. He pivoted swiftly on one heel, away from the sight of the body his cadre would remove later, and to the view of New York City below him.

Such a glorious spectacle, he thought as the glowing lights of the city illuminated the multitude of humans on the streets below, unaware they might become a snack for him or one of the other Shadows. So much life for the taking, and yet still not enough to sustain them for any length of time.

Only the energies from the Light Hunters could offer any real sustenance, and even then, no energy was quite as sweet as that from one of their leaders—a Quinchu.

As for the incredible power he had just drained...

If Adam Bruno was the source of it, he had to get Salvatore to push forward with his Genesis project. Whether by getting Adam together with Maya or taking Adam's energy for his own, it had to happen, and soon.

His hunger and the pox could only be appeased for so long.

Selina sighed and snuggled closer to Kellen, basking in the afterglow of their lovemaking, in a sense of completeness that had been missing for so long, but was almost banished with the discovery of Kikin's whereabouts.

She had no doubt the man who thought of himself as Adam Bruno was their son. There had been a link to something old and familiar when she and Kellen had united to dispel the energies jumbling Lucas's aura. The force had resonated with her, awakening the memories of Kikin as a baby. The pulse of his power as he had suckled at her breast. Resting beside her during an afternoon nap to avoid the high heat of a desert summer.

Kikin's energy signature had been twined all around Lucas's, and it was strong. It would soon be at its zenith as he neared the end of his first triad. The only thing left to complete the Equinox would be for Adam to find a mate, a woman with whom he could bind and share his power. With that accomplished, he would incorporate her strength within him to be whole.

If they brought him…No, *when* they brought him home that would happen with the daughter of the Quinchus of the Ocean clan as had been planned so long ago. So much promise for the future of their son and their Light Hunter clan, she thought. Soon that final patch of emptiness inside her would be gone.

Kellen brushed his hand up and down the skin of her back, the motion lazy and sexy all at the same time. In his arms Selina had always found comfort and satisfaction, even during the bleakest moments when she had been on the verge of losing not only hope, but sanity.

"You're smiling," he said, inching back to examine her face.

It had been so long that she reached up and traced her lips just to confirm it. "Yes, I am," she said and allowed those long unused muscles to shift into an even happier grin.

Despite her joy, a deep wrinkle emerged on his forehead and sadness darkened the emerald of his eyes. Eyes so much like Kikin's. Like Adam Bruno's.

"I don't want you to be disappointed," he said, propping his head up on one hand as he focused on her.

"I won't be." She held no illusions about the welcome she was likely to receive from Kikin, but she hoped that in time he would come to understand what had happened. How many had sacrificed their lives that night to protect him. How many others had fallen in the search to find him.

"We must be patient, Selina. Bide our time."

"You know we cannot delay much longer," Selina said, and cradled his face, swiping her thumb along his cheek and the fine lines age and worry had etched onto his features.

His eyes grew dusky, dimming like the light as night approached. "We risk so much if we act too soon."

"Eduardo. Lucas. Their energies, the energies of so many in the clan, are weakening as are ours. Kikin's power can change that. Has changed that," she said in reference to the energy they had siphoned from their cadre member.

He nodded, and in a burst of speed, rolled over her, pinning her to the mattress, covering her mouth with his and taking her lips in a hungry, almost desperate kiss. The strength of it ripped through her, awakening her as no one else could. She gave herself over to his loving, understanding.

Time was fleeting and he wanted to savor every breath they had left if it turned out they could not bring Kikin home.

CHAPTER
27

Bobbie couldn't remember how long she had delayed in the garage, trying to piece together what had just happened in Adam's kitchen. How they had gone from such a loving moment to the accusations that had followed, shattering the sense of peace and unity they had been feeling. If there had been one consolation it had been that she had seen Salvatore Bruno pulling away only moments after she had gotten into her own car.

Adam had clearly not been happy with Salvatore either, judging from the short duration of his stay, which made her hope that there was still some way of convincing Adam that she and her family had done none of the things Salvatore claimed. That was if she even wanted to.

Being with Adam risked the calm and peaceful life she had envisioned for herself after returning from Iraq. Being with him likely meant being constantly on the defensive and at risk.

But being with him also meant feeling more alive

than she had ever felt and maybe that was worth the
risk to her white-picket-fence dreams. Or maybe together
they could put an end to the threat and have a happily-
ever-after-life-on-the-fringe.

With those thoughts in mind, she pulled into a spot
in front of her condo, determined to regroup and decide
what to do next. As she exited her convertible she dropped
her keys, and as she bent to pick them up, a reflection of
something in the chrome rim caught her eye.

She slipped her hand into the wheel well, felt around,
and encountered a thumb-sized box. She pulled it off.
Magnetic backing had kept the box on the inside of her
front fender.

She had no doubt about what it was: a tracking device.

She had no doubt who had put it there: Salvatore
Bruno.

She had no doubt about why: She was a threat to whatever plans Salvatore had for Adam.

She also had no hesitation about what she had to do
next: determine exactly what Salvatore planned for Adam.
To accomplish that she had to turn the tables on him.

Gripping the tracking device in her hand, she knew
just who could help her do that. She placed it back onto
the fender, not wanting to clue Salvatore that she had discovered it. She would have to borrow another ride. But
for right now, she had to go inside and plan. Find a way
to alleviate the heaviness inside her, threatening to drag
her down.

Misery, she told herself. As deep and debilitating as
that she had felt upon first awakening after the IED explosion. She had almost lost herself then. If not for her family's support, she might have. For that reason alone she

would not question them about Salvatore's accusations. She had no doubt they were all lies and didn't deserve her consideration. She also would not involve them in what was happening. Her older siblings had already suffered enough at the hands of others. But despite that, they had found happiness and moved on with their lives.

She wasn't about to disrupt their happiness with Bruno's unfounded allegations. And she wasn't ready to give up her own chance at happiness without at least giving it a shot.

Bobbie slumped in the driver's seat of the speedy Mustang she had borrowed from one of her girlfriends, waiting for Salvatore Bruno to arrive at the laboratory facilities where her older sister was working part-time. Several months ago she and Bobbie's brother Mick had been involved in taking down a group of rogue scientists operating under the name Wardwell. Bobbie's sister, Liliana, still treated some of the patients who had been used as human guinea pigs.

She sipped her coffee, needing the caffeine boost because she had gotten little sleep the night before. Her mind had been too unsettled to allow for any real rest, and she had felt the weight of Adam's restlessness within her as well, adding to her misery.

Then this morning she had been up and about quite early, taking a walk down to Sam Cunningham's shop, where she had sought the young woman's help with a listening device in the event that her tail of Bruno led her to some possible answers. Instead of large parabolic mikes, which would have been way too visible, Sam had provided a much smaller handheld model she had developed.

Bobbie hoped it would be unobtrusive enough to allow her to listen in on Salvatore.

She scrunched down in her seat and pulled her baseball cap lower, impatiently waiting. She'd heard her sister mention during dinner the other night that the government types monitoring her work visited every day. She hoped Bruno was one of those government types.

It was close to lunch hour when Salvatore's blue Cadillac CTS pulled into the lot. He parked the car, walked to the door, and slid a key card through the lock. When the door slid open, Bobbie resisted the urge to follow and confront. This was one time she had to curb her impulsiveness.

Luckily, she didn't have long to wait.

Within half an hour Salvatore exited, checking his watch anxiously as he walked. He clearly had somewhere to be, and Bobbie was hoping that wherever he went would provide her with some answers.

"I'm trying to make it happen," Salvatore said as William, Sombrosa's new emissary, sat in the passenger seat of the Cadillac. They were parked in front of the Dunkin' Donuts on Route 33 and William glanced around, looking for signs of any unusual auras, satisfied that he saw none.

"It needs to happen faster. Adam's Equinox may come any day now."

"Or in a month or in a year. You don't know when it will happen," Salvatore challenged abruptly, clearly not liking the pressure that was being exerted.

"When it does come, Adam must mate with Maya. That is the only way that their powers can be bound together to guarantee the continuation of the Hunters,"

William responded patiently. To put Salvatore at ease, he released waves of power in direct opposition to those he sensed emanating from Salvatore. Like one kind of sound canceling another, William's unique powers let him neutralize the emotions of both Hunters and humans.

"I am working on it, but something unusual has come up," Salvatore said a little more placidly.

"Should we be worried about it?" William questioned, his voice neutral despite his concern that an obstacle had arisen to their plan.

With a sigh, Salvatore said, "I'm already handling her, William. Just give me another day or so."

Because it would take William at least a day to get Alexander's man planted in Christopher's cadre, it was time that William could give the human. With a nod, he opened the door and stepped out, but then stuck his head back in. "I am patient, but Alexander is not. If I can help you solve your problem—"

"One way or the other, I can handle her," came Salvatore's terse reply.

William smiled and shut the car door. He took a step back and then tapped the roof to signal that he was clear. Salvatore pulled away, and after he did so, William strolled toward the GMC Acadia where his man waited for him. He was stepping into the vehicle when he noticed a flash of blue in a car across the way. Unfortunately, the Mustang peeled out of the parking lot of the McDonald's before he could get a close look at the driver.

He cursed himself for not being more vigilant, but forced himself to push away worry. He had a mission to accomplish for his Añaru. The first step had been completed: The message had been delivered.

He could not dally about finishing the second task. The Añaru expected William to place his man in Christopher's cadre, and he had to do that today so that their alternate plans were in place. If Salvatore could not deliver Adam peacefully, they needed to be ready to grab him. And if the unique power Alexander had sensed in Christopher's man did not come from Adam Bruno, they had to be ready to seize that source of energy as well.

CHAPTER
28

Christopher Sombrosa had long ago given up trying to decipher the motivation behind his father's actions, convinced there was only one reason: power.

Unlike his father before him, Alexander Sombrosa took what he thought he was entitled to, forgoing the innovation and labors that had made his Shadow clan great. Many in the clan had followed that example, content to hunt the humans around them rather than learn about the origins of their abilities.

Christopher was convinced they could improve their skills to gather the energy and keep away the illness that had woven its way into their genetic makeup.

The prospects of the clan had suffered from that sense of entitlement under his father, and Christopher had no doubt it was unsustainable. The Shadow Hunters could only suck the life from so many humans before calling attention to themselves and risking the freedom they had enjoyed for so long.

As Christopher stared at William, his father's cadre captain, and the man beside him, he had no doubt that this move was just another power play by his father. The man who was supposed to join his cadre was from his father's guard, which made Christopher uneasy.

The world of the Shadows was wickedly competitive, with danger an everyday occurrence for those who aspired to the role of Añaru. As his father's heir he was a target and preferred choosing his own men to watch his back. He needed a man whom he could trust, not his father's lap dog.

Or his father's leavings, he thought, shooting a glance at Maya, supposedly his fiancée yet marked by the stain of his father's power.

"You say that Andrew has been relieved from service?" he said to William, and peered at the supposed replacement. Then he shot a glance back at his own captain, Ryan, who stood by the door to his office. Vigilant, but silent.

The replacement remained at attention, with not a twitch or blink to give away what he was thinking. Beside him Maya was likewise immobile, but Christopher suspected that she knew what had happened to his cadre member.

"Suffice it to say, Andrew is no longer with us," William replied, utterly deadpan, but the meaning was clear.

Walking directly up to William, Christopher leaned toward his father's captain until his nose was almost bumping the other man's face. Christopher was several inches taller and broader, but it wasn't the physical differences that made him dangerous.

"Andrew belonged to me. His energy was mine."

He placed his hand on William's shoulder, and with only a scintilla of power, the tendrils of his life force dug into William, weaving into his aura and beginning to suck the energy from the other man.

"Christopher. I live only to please," William implored him, his face growing pale from the drain on his vitality. The first blotch emerged on his cheek and grew to a raised pustule. A second soon erupted as the pox in William's body took over while Christopher sucked his life away.

Christopher could taste the man's fear as William's energy melded with his own. But Christopher was not like his father, acting without thought or responsibility.

"Go, and take this man with you. I will pick my own cadre members," Christopher said and, with a blast, returned the energy to his father's captain.

The pox pustules that had scarred William's cheek a moment before vanished. But rather than make his exit, the man hesitated, as if to attempt to change Christopher's mind.

"Go," Christopher repeated, more forcefully, and his father's men fled the office like whipped dogs.

"You were harsh, Christopher," Maya said.

Even before she was near, Christopher sensed the throb of her sexual energy, a potent pheromone to Hunter men. At one time it had ensnared him and brought him great satisfaction. But lately it no longer satisfied. Despite that, Maya was the strongest of the female Shadows, and with his Equinox nearly upon him, he would mate with her for the good of the clan.

When she was barely an inch from him, she laid her hand on his chest and released her energy, igniting a firestorm of need in his gut.

"Do not play with me, Maya. I am not in the mood," he warned.

She coyly ran a finger up and down the front of his shirt. "Really, my love? You always liked to play," she teased.

"Empty games for an empty heart," he said wearily, and something hardened in her gaze.

"Do you not think that I wish for something different? But this is our destiny, Christopher, even if we both may not like it," she spat, not waiting for his reply. Pivoting on one deadly spike of a heel, she flounced from the room.

As the door closed behind her, Christopher actually experienced a moment of admiration at her honesty. Needing such truth from another area, he sat on the edge of his desk and asked his cadre captain, "What do you suppose this is all about, Ryan?"

"Your father or Maya?" Ryan asked, and arched a brow.

Christopher shook his head and chuckled harshly. "Both, actually."

Ryan shrugged. "Your father is not one to waste even an ion of power, which means he must have drained Andrew."

Because his father was a coldhearted and selfish bastard concerned only with his own needs, Christopher didn't refute Ryan's comments. But that presented its own set of complications.

"Even if all he did was taste Andrew, he would sense the energy from the other night. From the Quinchu."

Ryan nodded and hunched his shoulders. "Which would explain in part why both William and Maya are here—to find the source of that power. But I sense there is something else going on."

"I sense it, too, my friend. My father is up to something, which means we must hurry to find where the Light Hunter is located," Christopher said, and motioned to the map he had pinned up on the wall of his office. He had identified a general point of origin for the energy wave, and his men had been scouring the area. More than once they had detected hints of the power as well as remnants of something else—explosions of energy. Formidable blasts that had left behind a unique signature similar to that from the wave.

"What do we do, Christopher?" his captain asked.

"We keep on looking, but make sure to be vigilant for that weasel William and his man. He is sure to linger as long as possible before disappointing my father."

"Disappointment? Your father will be in a rage if William fails," Ryan said.

Christopher chuckled. "Yes, he will. Which is probably why he sent Maya as a safeguard. He's hoping that at least one of them will provide him with the information he desires."

"So our plan is?" his captain asked.

"To make sure my father does not get his hands on that energy."

"What about Maya?" Ryan asked, a hint of heat in his gaze.

"Do I detect interest, my friend?"

"With her affinity, she's a bitch in heat, Chris. It's hard not to respond when she's around," Ryan advised.

Yes, it was hard not to respond physically, but as for emotionally...It was as he had said. Empty. Because of that, he wouldn't deny his friend if he wanted to satisfy himself.

"Maya was more than ready, Ryan. If she's what you want—"

"Am I crazy to think there may be more to her than just sexual energy?" Ryan asked, surprising him. Sadly, Christopher wasn't sure there was, but better that Ryan find out for himself.

Adam slapped the papers across his thigh, tired of reviewing the reports that his father had provided. He hadn't needed them to know he was something other than human. Seeing the proof of it in the DNA analyses made an already difficult situation almost unbearable.

Except that the tests had shown he was not alone. Somewhere long ago, Bobbie and he had shared some kind of genetic connection.

It would explain so much, he thought. Her aura. The ability to handle the blasts of power. How they had joined more than their bodies when they made love.

Tossing down the papers in frustration, Adam charged up the stairs and into the kitchen. The smells of the dinner he and Bobbie had been preparing the night before lingered in the space.

Bobbie, he thought, experiencing a clenching pain in the center of his core at the thought she had somehow deceived him. Even without her physical presence he sensed that she, too, was suffering upset, presumably from what had happened the night before with Salvatore. A night that had started with the promise that he might have found the person to complete his life and that had ended so bitterly.

Leaning back against the edge of the counter and bracing his hands there, he looked around the kitchen. The room was cold, lifeless, and sterile.

More so with Bobbie gone.

He wondered how it was that she could have made such an impact in his life in just a few days. And whether he was crazy to be wishing that she hadn't been lying earlier. That he could trust her. But if he had faith in her, that meant he had to believe one other incredibly troubling thing: that his father was not telling the truth.

The muscles in his gut twisted, because neither possibility was palatable.

The financial reports his father had provided gave plenty of reasons why Bobbie might be lying, but nothing that he had seen so far about either Bobby or her family suggested they were capable of such deception. In fact, the articles and other items in the files hinted at people who were hardworking, patriotic, and responsible. What he knew of both Tony and Bobbie from his personal interaction with them supported that assessment.

Although two nights ago Bobbie had lied to the police about the lightning-bolt throwing men with surprising ease. But she'd only done so to protect him...hadn't she?

Why hadn't she told him she was barren? he wondered, but then recognized that they hadn't reached the point in their relationship at which couples discussed such issues. He hadn't even wanted to become emotionally involved with a woman because he had feared losing control of his powers and hurting her. Family had been even further removed from his mind.

But he had not hurt Bobbie. If anything, he had helped her. And their lovemaking the day before...

Unusual. Incredibly rewarding. Life-affirming.

At first all he could see was the pain of the power within him, almost ready to explode. But she had reached beyond that somehow. Brought balance and stability and need. When he had released himself to her, the world had shifted, righting itself. With that connection had come even more as they had moved from the garage to the living room without taking a step, something he was still trying to puzzle out.

Closing his eyes, he tried to remember what he had thought in that second and realized that he had been thinking he couldn't make love to her on the cold cement floor of the garage. He had wanted to be somewhere else with her.

He imagined that again, shifting from the kitchen to the living room, and within him his core tightened like a spring being wound and then burst from his center.

He opened his eyes and he was in his living room.

He attempted it again, eyes open this time. After the initial coiling and release, everything around him blurred into streaks of color and light until he came to a jarring stop, this time in the garage.

The images he had just seen brought back visions of the two men escaping into the van and of his rushing to Bobbie's side the other night.

Years earlier, when he had been searching for others who might have powers similar to his, he had run across a man who claimed to be an Aztec *nahual*. The man had possessed an aura, but it was just barely visible. He had tried to prove his abilities as a sorcerer by creating tiny balls of light, but they had been not much larger than a marble. When the man had claimed to be able to move through walls, Adam had discounted it as just another bogus claim.

Maybe the man had possessed more knowledge than

Adam had thought. Maybe, like Bobbie, that man had some kind of ancestral association to the source of Adam's powers. But if Bobbie did have nascent powers that he had awakened by joining with her, did that present a risk to his secrets? Or worse, would it endanger Bobbie's life, if she was not working with the men who had attacked them?

His stomach clenched again and he pressed a fist to it. There was only one way he could think of to end his disquiet.

The Light Hunter sat on the boardwalk railing across from the home of the man his Quinchus called Kikin. Their son, Kikin.

They had charged him with guarding the man and imbued him with an extra dose of their power so that he might maintain his guise for the better part of the night.

As Kikin pulled away from his home in his car, heading northward, the Hunter leaped into the air and with a flap of his wings followed the Bentley convertible.

It had been a long time since he had morphed, and it took all his willpower to focus on the man rather than the sights beneath him. Or on the uplift of a gust of air that made the animal spirit within him want to soar and glide with the currents.

He dropped out of the updraft and flapped his wings, pushing himself to keep the car in sight, not that it was difficult to do. The convertible was unique enough to track even from a distance, especially with the top down, which provided a clear view of Kikin and his unique royal blue aura behind the wheel.

He continued to follow and somehow managed to

catch a fast-moving current that sent him racing forward, directly above and just beyond his target.

Looking back at his Quinchus' son, it seemed to him that Kikin appeared troubled. A deep ridge marred his forehead and his jaw was set in harsh lines.

The strong current pushed the hunter ever ahead, and he had to adjust his wings to fly upward, out of the rush of air, and then swoop back down to keep pace with the car.

The pursuit was taxing, draining his energy as he maintained his Hunter awareness while battling the bird's instincts and driving himself physically. There was a heaviness growing in the pit of his belly that said he might not be able to hold this form much longer.

Up ahead the bright neon sign of a restaurant snared his bird's-eye view, and as he lifted his head, he caught sight of the bright blue aura in another convertible a few blocks beyond the restaurant.

The Shadow woman, he thought.

Gliding upward and back for just a moment to confirm that Kikin was heading in the same direction, he pushed forward, following the woman, her aura an intense beacon in the night.

Within a few blocks she turned off Main Avenue and into a village filled with well-kept Victorian homes. It was a little harder to follow here with the proximity of the homes and the tree-lined streets that hid the passage of her car, providing only occasional glimpses of her beneath the copious foliage.

He pushed upward, hoping that additional height might give him a better view.

It did.

He tracked her as she drove to the edge of town and

then onto the avenue along the ocean. Dive-bombing down, he pursued more closely, just feet above her, until she pulled to the curb and parked.

Settling onto the electrical wires by her car, he watched. The bird's keen-eyed sight enabled him to see much more than he could have as a Hunter. Enough to see the woman head to a row of mailboxes by the main entrance to the building, where she slipped her key into a slot.

Carrera; 301.

It was all he needed to know, he thought, as the woman walked into the building. Although he had defied his Quinchus' orders by following the woman, he didn't think that they would be disappointed with the information he would provide from his detour. The woman was a risk that had to be handled, and now they were one step closer to dealing with her.

He was about to fly off when he noticed Kikin's car pulling into a spot before the building, but his Quinchus' son remained in the seat. His aura deepened, and the threads of silver and red jumped wildly, a testament to his discomfiture. Even if his aura had not given away his upset, it would have been evident from the way his knuckles had turned white from his grip on the steering wheel.

Kikin sat in the car for a few minutes, clearly torn, until he finally pulled away again. With a flap of his wings, the Light Hunter followed. Another cadre member would soon be relieving him, and when he did, he could provide the woman's location to his Quinchus.

Bobbie had been puzzling all day about the information she had gleaned by tailing Salvatore. Adam's father clearly saw her as a problem, but she didn't know why. The references to an Equinox made little sense to her, and even after returning home to do research on the Net, she was no closer to understanding what the two men had been discussing.

But she was sure of a few things, she thought as she got changed for bed. Salvatore was lying to Adam, probably because he wanted to get his son together with this Maya person, whoever she was—judging from the conversation, a woman with whom Adam was to bind his power only…

Bobbie thought it was a little too late for that. Since yesterday's lovemaking she had felt different. Connected not only to Adam, but to so many things around her. It was as if she had been living with blinders on and someone had just ripped them off, exposing her to a world that was filled with more than she had ever thought possible.

Including a link to Adam that was difficult to ignore. She had sensed his anger all day long. Felt his presence right outside her building earlier that night. By the time she had gone to the window to double-check, the only thing she had seen was the taillights of his car as he had driven away, obviously having reconsidered the wisdom of seeing her when there was still so much uncertainty between them.

Climbing into bed, she shut off the lights and forced herself to try to sleep. She needed a clear head if she was going to make sense of what Salvatore was up to and figure out how to convince Adam of it without breaking his heart.

Salvatore might not be Adam's biological father, but she was sure that Adam loved and respected him. He was hurting over the possibility that Salvatore might not be what Adam had thought for so many years.

She closed her eyes, willing her mind to put away all thought so she could rest. But barely minutes later she heard a noise. It was slight, only a hint of a footfall, but her soldier's instincts kicked into high gear.

Bobbie tossed off the sheets and came to her feet in a fighting stance, the swift action taxing her damaged leg and delivering pain throughout her thigh before a blow ever landed. In the shadows before her, close to the balcony doors off the bedroom, stood a woman.

"Who are you?" she said, fists raised defensively, legs spread wide in anticipation. Not that she was sure she could launch a kick as effectively as she could before, but it wouldn't stop her from trying if it was needed.

"I'm Kikin's mother," the woman said, and took a step closer, into a beam of moonlight that illuminated her features, revealing the elegant lines of her face.

Achingly familiar lines, Bobbie thought, but maintained her guard.

"Who the hell is Kikin?" she asked, although she knew the answer even before it was provided.

"The man you know as Adam Bruno," the woman replied, and then stretched out her arm. A glow began in her palm, reminding Bobbie of the attackers who had blasted her. If this woman let loose at this distance, Bobbie would be toast.

Only the woman surprised her by saying, "May I provide us some light?"

As before, the answer came before she could respond. The orb doubled in size, its glow spreading, bathing the woman's face in bright red-gold light.

There was no denying the similarity then between her and Adam. It was there in the shape of their eyes, nose, and mouth. Even down to the thumbprint-sized cleft in her chin. But unlike Adam, the woman's hair was darker, although marked with gray, and her eyes were a slate color, lacking the life of Adam's marvelous emerald gaze.

"How about we go traditional light?" Bobbie said, relaxing her stance only long enough to flip on the lamp beside her bed.

The woman immediately cut off her display of power and dropped her arm, an encouraging sign. Maybe she didn't want to turn Bobbie into a crispy critter.

"How did you get in here?"

The woman pointed to the floor beside her. Light snaked along the ground and then slowly formed into three balls lined up uniformly at her feet, almost militarily neat. Unnaturally still at first, and then suddenly one ball grew larger, elongated, and filled out into the shape of a man. The other balls immediately followed suit. In less than a minute, Bobbie found herself staring at not one, but four individuals.

She had no doubt about the identity of the man beside the woman. He had Adam's sandy-colored hair and verdant gaze. Deep slashes on either side of his face hinted at the dimples that might emerge if he should ever smile.

She also had no doubt about the identity of the two men to his right: their assailants from the parking lot. One still bore the remnants of swelling and bruises from her cane. You had to pick your battles, and she knew she was no physical match for the four able-bodied and superpowered people before her. She lowered her hands and quipped, "I guess you're not here to talk."

Selina was intrigued by the young woman her son seemed to fancy, and not just because of Kikin's interest. The woman's aura was not what she had expected. It wasn't Light or Shadow energy, but despite that she could sense Kikin's force swirling all around her.

While they had been standing there, the woman's blue aura had darkened to maroon, hinting at the emotions she was hiding beneath her unyielding façade. The woman was well-versed in guarding any weakness and clearly had been trained in the martial arts. She would never reveal her feelings or weaknesses, and she would not back down in a fight. All qualities Selina would have appreciated in a mate for her son, had he not been promised at birth to another.

"Well? Are you going to stand there all night staring?" the young woman said, yanking a chuckle from Selina.

Andres and Eduardo took a step toward the woman to teach her some respect, but Selina shot her arm up to block their path.

"Quinchu?" Andres questioned, surprise evident on his normally stoic face.

"Leave us," she commanded her captain and his second in command.

"She is a Shadow—" Eduardo began, but Kellen silenced him with a sharp jab of his hand and confirmed her instruction.

"Leave us. Go wait outside."

With starkly rigid salutes, the two men left them, prompting yet another saucy comment from the woman.

"I guess you don't mind getting your hands dirty," she said, and assumed her fighting stance again, as if deciding that two against one provided her with possibly winning odds.

"Give me your hands," Selina said, and stepped toward the woman, a mistake. But not on her part.

Bobbie jabbed at Selina, who immediately seized her hand and sent a blast of mind-numbing electricity through Bobbie's body. Her knees gave way and she dropped to the floor, but Selina didn't release her hold, although she tempered the strength of the charge.

Bobbie glanced up at her, biting her lip to keep from pleading for freedom. The expression on her face sent a clear message: She would never surrender and leave these people free to possibly hurt Adam.

The woman's topaz gaze blazed with irritation as she leaned close. With a disdainful sniff, she glanced over her shoulder at her companion and said, "She's not a Shadow. She's a hybrid."

The man grunted and stepped toward them. Selina released her hold on Bobbie, who fell back onto her haunches, her body vibrating in reaction to the jolt of power.

"What do you want?" she said, her voice tremulous as she tried to regain control of her muscles.

"We want our son. We want Kikin," Selina said, and stepped back toward her husband, who protectively placed his arm around her shoulders.

"If you want him so badly, why did you abandon him?" Bobbie challenged. "Why show up now and go to such lengths to get him after twenty years of absence?"

Her words struck a raw nerve with Selina, who

flinched. In a voice that was decidedly unsteadier than when she had commanded the two men, the woman said, "We didn't abandon him. He was taken from us."

"Taken? How was he—"

"We were attacked by the Shadows at our desert home," the man said, offering a comforting squeeze at the woman's shoulder before pulling her close to offer greater support.

"What's a Shadow?"

Adam's parents shared a glance and then his mother said, "Maybe it would be best if we sat down for this discussion?"

Tottering as she came to her feet, Bobbie jumped when the man surged forward to assist her, his touch gentle. With his aid and that of Adam's mother as she came around to slip her arm through Bobbie's, they half-carried her to the kitchen table, where they helped her to a chair.

"It's a long story," Selina said, and clasped her hands before her on the oak surface.

Leaning back in her chair, Bobbie said, "I'm not going anywhere."

Selina's voice went from cool-as-steel to honey smooth and soothing as she wove the tale of a different people, whose future had irrevocably knitted together with that of the humans around them.

"Millennia ago my people would rise to the sun and honor its gift of life. In time our leaders realized that there were some amongst us who could harness that gift. Gather it within us," Selina said, and mimicked that embrace, her arms fluid and elegant. Normally Bobbie would have wanted to rush her along, forcing her to get to the point, but there was something almost mesmerizing about her motions and the cadence of her voice.

"Our leaders identified those who could harvest the energy. They came to be known as the Quinchu, since they could sip energy from the sun like hummingbirds taking nectar from flowers. They were tutored and joined with others to enhance that gift and became our priests and priestesses."

"Genetically breeding those with desirable traits," Bobbie added, her tone a trifle harsh, earning an immediate rebuke from Adam's father.

"Has not man hybridized animals and plants for centuries to bring out the best of them?" Kellen challenged, a dangerous glitter in his emerald gaze.

Selina laid a hand on his, and a slight orangey glow arose at the contact, seemingly soothing him.

"In time the Quinchu learned not only to use our Mother Sun's gift, but to hunt for other energies from the cosmos and the living things around us," Selina continued, as if she had never been interrupted, her voice once again calming and inviting.

"If you have such wonderful powers, why are there so few of you?" Bobbie wondered aloud.

"At one time there were many more of us and our people prospered for millennia. We were isolated high in the Andes, close to Mother Sun, and away from the humans down below. In time, some of our people left to explore and find out more about the humans."

"Which explains people like me, I guess. Hybrids," Bobbie said, and Selina dipped her head in agreement.

"We've learned that the Hunter genes are recessive and that they also blend. It's the reason why there are not more hybrids and why their powers vary so greatly. Although in general, Hunter hybrids are stronger and smarter than most humans. It's why they are invariably viewed as leaders. Your strength and ability to conduct energy is one of the highest levels we've encountered," Kellen explained.

Selina must have sensed her uneasiness, for as she had done before, she reached out, took Bobbie's hand in hers, and sent a gentle pulse of power that immediately brought tranquility.

At Bobbie's questioning glance, Selina said, "We can heal as well, but you know that, don't you? I can sense Adam's power within you."

Since there was no denying it, Bobbie nodded. "I was injured in Iraq."

"Humans are always so aggressive and warlike," Kellen interrupted with a disdainful sigh.

"Seems to me that the Hunters do a pretty good job of being bellicose as well. Adam remembers a battle. He remembers death and destruction all around him in the desert. Are you saying it was humans that did that?" Bobbie challenged.

The dull flush that spread across Kellen's cheeks was answer enough, but he still tried to establish a distinction. "That battle, as you call it, was an attack on our complex by the Shadow Hunters."

Bobbie arched a brow and returned her attention to Selina, wanting to hear her melodic, peaceful voice divulge more of the history of Adam's people. "Care to explain why you're different from the Shadow Hunters?"

With a nod and smile she continued. "As I said before, the Hunters kept to themselves. Even those who ventured out amongst the humans guarded the secrets of our people. In time, however, a great blight came upon us—a pox brought to us by those Hunters who had resided amongst the humans.

"It seems that the Hunters were as susceptible as the indigenous tribes to the diseases brought by the conquistadores, possibly more so."

Bobbie furrowed her brow. "The smallpox killed your people?"

A silvery sheen washed over Selina's eyes as she continued, and her voice took on a biting edge. "Those who died were the lucky ones."

"Death is never better, no matter how difficult life may seem," Bobbie parried.

Selina smiled sadly and squeezed Bobbie's hand. "I know you are aware of sacrifice and pain, but no one could have predicted how smallpox would change the Hunters. Only a scant number of our people retained the ability to hunt energy, and it fell on them to attempt to heal those who were sick. The lucky ones died. The not so lucky lived, but could never again hunt."

"And they're the Shadows?" Bobbie pressed, wanting to comprehend their hierarchy and how she and Adam fit into the structure.

Selina shook her head and pressed on with her explanation. "The Shadows descend from those amongst us who were forever cursed by the pox. The illness buried itself in their bodies, becoming one with them. No matter how many times they were healed, the pox returned. Until one day a dying Shadow took hold of a Quinchu, drained her life force, and was seemingly restored."

"Because your energy is the most potent," Bobbie

added, and with another sad smile, Selina finished the tale.

"Stealing every last atom of Quinchu power kept the first Shadow's pox away, and others like him revolted, turning on the Quinchus and the other Hunters."

Kellen finally spoke up again. "Our people have been fighting that civil war for hundreds of years, hiding to avoid the Shadows and maintain our world separate from the humans."

"Humans like me," Bobbie finished his thought. "What does this have to do with me and Adam?"

"Bruno took our son. We want him back with us," Kellen replied curtly, then glanced at his wife uneasily.

"Our people...Kellen and I are growing weaker. Without an infusion of new power, our clan will die off."

"Adam is the source of that power," Bobbie stated.

"Yes. If all had gone as planned, Kikin would have married the daughter of the Ocean clan Quinchus," Selina advised.

"Because of the Equinox?" Bobbie asked, recalling the conversation she had overheard earlier that morning.

"You know about the bonding that must happen?" Kellen pressed.

Bobbie glanced up at him. "I overheard Salvatore Bruno discussing something called an Equinox with another man this morning. He used the word 'triad.'"

"Adam's thirtieth year marks the end of the first triad. But there is no way Salvatore could know about Adam joining with the daughter of the Ocean clan," Selina advised.

"Marriage to another," Bobbie nodded, the quiver in her voice the only clue that Selina's pronouncement bothered her.

"What do you want from me?" she asked, even though she already had a clue.

"Can you get Kikin to speak with us? To let us tell our story?" Selina asked, and finally slouched back in her chair, as if drained by all that she had revealed. As before, Kellen lovingly embraced her, placing a kiss at her temple.

Selina could read Bobbie's thought in her face. If she told Adam about his parents, it might mean that he would be lost to her by virtue of the obligations he would be expected to honor. But if she didn't tell Adam about them, he would never know his true origins. Never experience the kind of love that she shared with her family.

It wasn't an easy choice, but love sometimes meant making sacrifices for those about whom you cared. Even if it would break your heart.

With a shrug, Bobbie finally answered in the only way she could.

"All I can do is try."

Selina and Kellen shared another anxious look, and then Selina reached beneath the scalloped edge of the shirt she wore. As she did so, Bobbie noticed the hint of a scar high up along one shoulder.

"We all have our wounds, Bobbie," she said, and then pulled out a heavy golden medallion on a thick gold chain.

Sliding it off over her head, Selina dangled it in front of Bobbie.

"Kikin used to see this all the time, from when he nursed at my breast to the nights when he was older and climbed into bed with us during a storm."

Bobbie took the medallion and examined it. The geometric design was vaguely familiar, and then it occurred to her where she had seen it before.

"Adam doodles sometimes when he's thinking. The drawings look a lot like this. He used the symbols as a logo for his company," she said, running her hand over the surface of the medallion. The design had been worn almost smooth in spots from wear. If she'd had any doubt about the truth of their story, the medallion with the design that Adam was sure to remember chased those doubts away.

Selina laced her fingers together and with a throaty whisper replied, "Maybe it will jog some memory for him."

"Do you have pictures? Anything that—"

"We never keep such things. There has always been fear that the photos will expose our auras or be used to identify us and hunt us down," Kellen explained.

With a nod, Bobbie gathered up the chain and medallion and clutched it in her hand. Facing them directly, she repeated her earlier promise.

"I can't guarantee anything, but I will try."

CHAPTER
29

Adam no longer trusted him, Salvatore thought, taking another long pull on the glass of scotch as he sat at his kitchen table, flipping through the file for Genesis and wondering how he would ever regain Adam's trust, or if he even wanted to, since he was unexpectedly unsure of the plans he had made with Sombrosa.

Although Alexander's man had radiated calm, there was just something about him and Sombrosa that was suddenly not sitting so well with him. Add to that the fact that Adam had appeared so happy with Bobbie before Salvatore had given him the doctored files.

He had made the Carreras out to be the bad guys, although nothing could be farther from the truth. The only real facts in the files were Bobbie's barren state and the results of the DNA tests. Adam had probably not given much thought to children yet, but someday he would, and Bobbie would never be able to provide him with a family of his own. Children with Adam's unique abilities.

Children who might have been the first step for his project. His grandchildren, he thought, his sense of duty and his feelings for Adam warring with each other as they had on more than one occasion. He had tried to be a good father, had done the best he could. And didn't all good parents push their children to reach their full potential?

Organizing all the papers before him, Salvatore slipped them back into the file for Genesis and then sat there, his hands splayed on the surface of the table.

A serviceable table, he thought, shifting one hand back and forth across a slight dent on the wooden surface. He and Adam had been working on a science project when the power drill had slipped from Adam's young hands and dropped onto the tabletop, creating the impression in the wood.

A few inches away was an inch-long burn mark in the varnish, a testament to another project and a soldering iron that had gone forgotten as Adam and he had gotten to talking.

Salvatore wasn't an emotional man, but as he raised his head and glanced around the kitchen, each place his gaze touched roused a memory of Adam.

His chest tightened painfully with the memories. He grabbed the glass and took another long swig, but it did nothing to relieve the pressure around his heart or the wrenching of his gut.

Guilt, his conscience said. Adam might not be his biological son, but he was for all intents and purposes his child. Twenty years of watching him grow, of protecting him, couldn't be erased as easily as he had thought.

Finishing the scotch, Salvatore poured himself another as he returned his gaze to the file sitting before him.

Twenty long years he had waited for this moment. For the time when Genesis could become a reality.

He should have been ecstatic.

Instead all Salvatore felt was despair.

Adam had barely slept all night, his mind streaming out thought after thought like a tickertape gone wild. Image after image, fact after fact, sped along his synapses, keeping him going long into the night and early morning.

A low, insistent buzz finally roused him from a troubled sleep. His smartphone danced along the surface of his nightstand.

He picked up the phone and came instantly awake at the number displayed by the caller ID.

Bobbie.

Doubt and need snaked around his heart, constricting it painfully as he stared at the vibrating phone in his hand.

And then the buzzing stopped.

Relief and regret replaced his earlier emotions, the latter strong enough to make him want to return her call and find out what she could possibly want that early on a Sunday morning. The phone droned again, flashed to let him know he had a voice mail.

He should disregard it, ignore her and her call, because he was still unsure of so many things. And yet he found himself accessing the message, sending his password with a mental blast while he sat back against the pillows to listen to what she had to say.

"Adam."

Just the sound of his name on her lips tightened his gut.

"I need to see you. Please, Adam. Please call me back."

It was that plaintive plea that got to him, driving

away any doubt about the wisdom of returning her call. He hadn't known Bobbie long, but he had learned one thing during their short time together: Bobbie wasn't the kind to beg. Not even if her life depended on it. Maybe for someone else. Someone she cared about, but not for herself.

Calling himself a fool a thousand times over, he blasted her number into the phone.

Bobbie hadn't expected him to call back. She was doubly surprised that he did so within a few minutes of her voice mail. But if she had any hope that their conversation would be easy, it was quickly shattered by the frigid tone of his voice.

"You said you needed to see me."

"I have something important to discuss with you."

"Why can't we discuss it over the phone?" he challenged.

Bobbie glanced down at the gold medallion in her hand. Its weight dragged at her hand and her heart. "It's the kind of thing I need to explain face to face."

A long hesitation on the line was chased by a harsh sigh and a mumbled curse before he said, "I must be a fool. Where do you want to meet?"

She had hoped to go to his home, but on reflection, it made sense he wouldn't want her there. It was too private, and too many memories lingered of the short time they had spent there together. Somewhere public, she thought, and it immediately came to her where.

"There's a pavilion on the boardwalk in Ocean Grove and some benches across the way from it on the Auditorium grounds."

"Half an hour. Be there or I'm gone," he said, and hung up before she could utter another word.

She would be there, and perhaps Adam would be willing to listen, she thought, the weight of the medallion in her hand reminding her of just how many people were relying on her, the heavy weight in her heart confirming how much she stood to lose even if she was successful.

When Bobbie lost her platoon, she thought she would never recover from that pain. But, little by little, she had recovered and learned to view every day as a gift. She had told Adam life was too short not to go after what you want. And though her time with Adam had been brief, and initially she had feared entering his world, she was certain that the only thing in life she really, truly wanted was to be by Adam's side, forever.

CHAPTER
30

The grounds in front of the Auditorium had grown empty as Bobbie sat on the park bench across from the pavilion. In the summer the faithful would gather in the pavilion for Sunday praise service while sometimes impatient beachgoers lingered along the boardwalk, waiting for the chains to come down along the paths to the beach.

With Memorial Day still a couple of weeks away, those with a religious bent had hurried to the Auditorium for Sunday service, leaving her alone to wait and worry. It had been at least half an hour since the call and Adam's ultimatum.

Was he testing her? Or maybe he was just being cautious, fearful that he would be the subject of another attack. She didn't blame him. She'd had the same sense of urgency when she had first noticed the woman in her bedroom last night.

Before yesterday evening, Bobbie had considered a

number of possibilities about why someone would want to grab Adam. Never in her wildest imagination had it occurred to her that it would be his parents behind the attempts.

She had no doubt about that fact—Selina and Kellen were his parents. It went beyond the physical resemblances and strange powers. It had been the love and despair in Selina's gray gaze. The determination in Kellen's emerald eyes, so much like Adam's.

And the final straw, if one was even needed, had been the medallion tucked into her jeans pocket. She ran her hand over the bulge from the pendant and traced the centuries-old designs etched into the medallion, the circles and lines that looked way too much like Adam's absentminded scribblings and the SolTerra company logo. Even then he had been making a connection to his past and the things buried in his memory.

A flash of burgundy red and the sexy purr of an expensive engine dragged her attention to the street. With the lack of summer traffic, Adam had pulled into a spot directly across from her and adjacent to the pavilion.

She rose from the bench, but couldn't muster the strength to take a step. Her knees were shaking and the vibrations seemed to travel up to her core, fluttering about her stomach.

Placing a hand there, she waited.

He looked around and adjusted the rearview mirror so he could see her. Their gazes connected in the reflection of that surface, his distant, hers hopeful.

With a brisk shake of his head, he finally tossed open the door and stepped out. He stood there, hand on the door. Expectant.

Nervous, she thought, as he did another quick reconnoiter of the area in preparation.

He was dressed in comfortably wrinkled khakis and a light blue shirt that brought out the teal in his eyes. Eyes that were shadowed with slight bruises beneath them as if from lack of sleep.

As he took that first step toward her, she girded herself to silence the nervous flutters, knowing she needed every ounce of strength for the discussion to come, feeling the jump in her center as her body recognized his and responded with anticipation, even desire.

His powerful strides ate up the distance separating them and suddenly he was before her, large and imposing, his unique energy pouring off him and registering along every inch of her skin.

"Adam. I'm glad you came." For an awkward moment she moved to embrace him, but then he leaned back and jammed his hands into the pockets of the khakis he wore.

She understood. If she touched him she might lose her resolve to go ahead with this, but if she didn't, so much could be lost, including Adam's life. That she would not risk for anything, including her own happiness.

"Please sit down," she said, and took a seat herself, hoping he would follow her lead.

Instead he just stood there, glaring down at her, every muscle in his body coiled tensely and ready to spring into action.

"Last night..." She shook her head and plucked at the fabric of her jeans, searching for the right words, but finding none other than the truth. Wagging her head a little more forcefully, she plowed on. "A man and a woman came to my home last night. A man and a woman who say they're your mother and father."

Some emotion other than anger finally registered on his features as he rolled back onto his heels, sucker-punched by her words.

"My mother and father? Impossible."

She did reach out to him then, grazing the skin of his arm with her fingertips, feeling as she had before that crackle of static as skin met skin, awakening the bond that had been created between them. He twisted away from her touch, as if fearing it would make him vulnerable, and maybe it would. She knew she wanted his touch and would do almost anything to be in his arms once again.

"I believe it's the truth, Adam. I wouldn't be here if I didn't trust them and think you should talk to them."

"Talk to them." The words exploded from his mouth and he raked his fingers through his hair, his frustration obvious as he stalked away.

He stopped a few feet before her, his back to her, arms akimbo as he stared ahead at the imposing structure of the Auditorium at the far end of the grounds.

She waited, thankful that he hadn't kept on going, that the distance between them, physically and possibly emotionally, was not too great to span. And if there was a time for action on her part, it was now, she thought, rising and approaching him slowly, cautiously, the way she might a skittish animal.

Pausing barely an arm's length from him, she reached up and laid a hand on his shoulder. Beneath her palm, his body quaked with tension, so powerfully she worried he might come undone from the force of it.

He dragged in a breath, then slowly exhaled. Softly

he asked, "How can I believe? After all this time, how can it be true?"

She hesitated, needing each word that she said to be right, knowing she had an ace in the hole thanks to the medallion in her pocket, but not wanting to use it. She needed more from him—some show of faith that he believed in her, she realized—and with that pause that she took, a low murmur rose from the Auditorium before them.

The loud warble of an organ was joined by joyous voices raised in song. The sounds filled the morning and wafted to them along with something else, a powerful presence, radiating outward and beating against them as they stood there.

She knew then what she would say.

"Do you feel that, Adam? It's the power of faith. Of believing without question because you know in your heart that something is true."

"You want me to believe in you like that?" he challenged, still staring straight ahead.

Her answer when it came was as pure and direct as the notes of the song filling the morning.

"Yes, because I believe in you like that."

With a ragged breath, his head dipped down and beneath her hand came the release in his body. He reached up and laid his hand on hers and then he faced her. Despite his outward acquiescence, his eyes still bore the shadows of doubt, but she hoped that in time they would disappear as well.

"Come with me. I have something to show you," she said. The Adam of old might have had a sexy rejoinder, but not this man, who was still suppressing his emotions.

With a gentle tug on his hand, she urged him to walk with her to his car, and they drove the few short blocks to her condo. They were silent as they did so, preoccupied.

Once they were inside, she led him to the living room and brushed her hand across his cheek, the touch awakening old feelings and needs. "I know you may not believe one hundred percent just yet, but I hope you will soon."

Adam stood there awkwardly, wanting to reciprocate her gesture, but still not totally convinced by her words and actions. "What could you possibly show me to convince me you're telling the truth?"

A quick flash of pain skimmed over her features before she mastered her emotions. Crossing her arms, Bobbie inclined her head in the direction of a nearby couch. "I think you should sit down."

Since he didn't want to delay her big revelation, he did as she asked, his forearms braced on his spread thighs.

She reached into her pocket and extracted something, he couldn't tell what. Then she approached and eased into the spot directly in front of him on the coffee table, their knees brushing as she sat there.

As she raised her hand, he noticed the thick chain of gold spilling downward before she placed her hand before him, palm up, displaying the large gold medallion she held there.

Images pounded at his brain, coming at him almost faster than he could process. Memory after memory of the design etched onto the surface of the medallion.

The softness of a breast beneath his cheek and a gentle voice crooning a song. Long caramel hair and eyes blazing like silver stars. A deeper voice and eyes the mirror of his glittering with laughter.

The happiness of those recollections was immediately replaced by another emotion.

Fear.

He had been holding that woman's hand, running in a low crouch as the explosions sounded around them and the ground beneath their feet shook as blast after blast chased them across the desert. A heartbeat later he was torn from her as hard hands grabbed his shoulders, jerking him away.

"Mama," he said, his voice sounding painfully like that of that little lost boy.

A woman's hand cradled his jaw, the touch so kind-hearted and loving, it pulled him back to the present.

He met Bobbie's shimmering gaze as she pressed the pendant and chain into his hand.

"You remember."

Shaking his head, he clenched the medallion tightly until his fingers grew numb and the edges were cutting into his palm. "Only bits and pieces. Her voice. His eyes."

"You were taken from them," she said, and passed her thumb across the cleft in his chin before skipping it upward over his lips.

"My father. Salvatore. He knew all this time."

"Maybe not. Maybe he thought everyone with you was dead," she said, surprising him by offering Salvatore the benefit of the doubt.

He couldn't.

"He knew. He hid me from them. It explains so much," he said, and for clarified her how Bruno had moved them to the New York area only weeks after first finding him, told her of the many years that Adam had been homeschooled and tucked away from contact with other children, limited to the adults that Bruno had hand-selected.

"I was a prisoner and I didn't even realize it."

She shifted forward, easing into the Vee formed by his legs. She wrapped her arms around him and laid her face against his.

"But it's over now, Adam." She kissed his temple, trailed her mouth down to drop another kiss along the side of his lips as she cradled his face in her hands.

He smiled, feeling freer than he had in a long time, but she was wrong about it being over. Laying his hands at her waist, he grasped it tightly, wanting to keep her near.

"It's only just the beginning, Bobbie. Salvatore has had some reason for keeping me to himself for the last twenty years."

"I'm not afraid of a fight," she said, fire blazing in her amber gaze.

"I don't want you hurt."

She silenced him by shifting her hand to his lips, her palm so soft it invited a kiss there. She shivered beneath his hands and her voice grew smoky as she said, "*Semper fi*, Adam. You can always trust me to have your back."

Again he smiled, but this time it was because the last thing he wanted was to have her back. He wanted her lips and her arms around him. He wanted her in his life as his heart finally acknowledged what had been there all along, but fear had kept hidden.

"I love you," he said, the words mumbled beneath her hand.

A hesitant smile came to her lips and she moved her hand away. "Did you say—"

"I love you. I think I've loved you since the moment I saw you kicking ass in the parking lot."

Her grin broadened, spread across her beautiful face.

She leaned in, brushed a kiss against his lips. "You always say such romantic things."

A chuckle escaped him, but then he grew slightly more serious. "You love me back, right? I mean in the movies, the hero says 'I love you' and then she says—"

"I love you, Kikin. That's your real name, by the way. Kikin Chakotay."

Beneath Bobbie's mouth came the shift of his lips expanding into a wicked smile. "Say that again," he said, and tunneled his hands into her hair to keep her close.

She said each word slowly so that he would have no doubt. "I love you, Kikin."

He groaned and wrapped his arms around her waist, hauled her close and kissed her hard, leaving no doubt in her mind about what he felt.

She welcomed his kiss, meeting his lips over and over. Such hard, yet mobile lips, wielded by an expert, she thought, as he savored every inch of her mouth, playfully bit her bottom lip, and tugged to invite her to deepen the kiss.

Opening her mouth, she accepted the glide of his tongue, danced hers along his and the perfect line of his teeth. She dropped her hand to his chest, rested it there for balance as her world slowly tilted off center. Beneath her hand came that sensation of power. His. Hers. Melding much as they would soon join their bodies.

Of that she had no doubt.

With the back of her hand she rubbed his chest. Caressed the hard nub beneath the thin fabric of his polo shirt.

He huffed out a satisfied breath, lowered his arms to encircle her buttocks and, with a powerful surge, came to his feet with her in his arms.

Opening her eyes, she met his gaze, nearly black with desire. "Over there," she said, and jerked her head in the direction of a hall off the kitchen.

In a blur of light they were at the door of her bedroom, where he paused to glance at her, seeking confirmation that she was sure. She grabbed his shoulders and levered herself up to kiss him, providing the answer that he sought.

With a needy groan that reverberated into her body, he took the last few steps to her bed, gently laid her down, and stood there for a second before he was reaching for the hem of her shirt.

She stopped him then, afraid of the scars he would see, breathlessly waiting for what he would do next.

Gone was the hurry from seconds before as Adam slowly slipped his hand beneath her shirt, past the low waistband of her jeans to the smooth skin of her toned midsection. He splayed his hand there and experienced the awkward ridge of scar at her center followed by her abrupt inhalation.

"You asked me to believe before, and now I'm asking the same. Believe me that all that I see is a beautiful woman whose body is a testament to her strength of will."

Her body trembled beneath his hands, but he pressed forward, running his hands up her middle, dragging the shirt upward as it caught on his wrist. With each millimeter that he moved, he exposed yet another bit of the damage to her body, drew forth his power and willed it downward.

Bobbie was thankful for his restrained and patient caring. As he moved slowly, a tingling warmth sprang to life where his skin met hers. He trailed his hand upward to just below her sternum where all evidence of her wounds ended. Beneath his palm, a silver-blue radiance escaped, and within her, something loosened and relaxed.

She almost feared looking up at him, seeing the pity and disgust on his face, but she had never run from anything in her life. She couldn't avoid this any longer.

Glancing up at him, she searched his features but saw nothing of what she dreaded. There was only love, shining from his gaze, and a shudder of relief ripped through her body.

He placed a knee on the edge of the bed and braced his other hand beside her as he dipped his head and kissed her. "I love you, Bobbie."

"I love you," she repeated.

He smiled then and shifted to his knees, grasped the hem of her shirt with both hands, and helped her remove it. He slipped his hand beneath the straps of her bra to urge it downward. He paused, gazing at her.

"You're beautiful."

Even though they'd made love before, she felt almost shy revealing so much to him and reached up to cover herself, but he shook his head and eased his hands beneath hers, cupped her breasts, and strummed his thumbs over the puckered peaks of her nipples. Between her legs, her muscles clenched and her sex grew damp, anticipating the glide of his body into hers.

She needed to touch him as he was touching her. Impatiently, she grabbed the hem of his shirt and yanked upward. He interrupted his caresses only long enough to rip the shirt off his body and toss it aside. Then he reclined his long, lean body beside hers, slipped closer to bring his lips to her breasts.

Tunneling her hands into the short strands of his hair,

she held him to her as he tasted her, licking and sucking the sensitive tips, drawing the moisture of his mouth around the peaks with his fingers.

Pleasure slammed into her and she closed her eyes and arched her back, focusing on the sensations he was creating and the feel of his body against hers. So much skin to skin free of any emotional or physical barriers. So much vitality beneath her hands as she ran them along the taut muscles of his shoulders and experienced the pulse of power shifting back and forth between them, growing ever stronger as emotion and need rose to ever greater heights.

With a gentle bite he dragged a moan from her and a breathy, "That feels so good."

A very masculine chuckle escaped him and he said, "It's only the start."

He moved downward and she protested with a little moan, digging her fingers against his shoulders and resisting his movement. But then he brought his mouth to the first hint of scar and placed his lips there.

She jumped as if electrified, shocked by the feel of the tiny kisses he dropped down the length of her. The warmth and tingling intensified and she almost didn't dare to look, but then she glanced down. Watched as he shifted ever lower, until he was at the worst of her injuries. His kisses left behind bright bits of silver blue, twinkling like a trail of tiny lights.

Tenderly he kissed the skin along her scars and brushed his hands across her midsection. The shimmer of energy came again as he whispered, "I wish I could take away all the pain."

The realization slammed into her. "You have, Adam. With you I'm whole again."

With her admission came a sense of completeness in
him as well, Adam thought. She was the piece that had
been missing for so long, maybe even since before Salvatore had taken him. As if on some other plane their energies had been divided until the time when it was right for
them to come together once more.

Her words came back to him, powerfully alive.

"To everything there is a season and a time for every
purpose. Until now I was lost, Bobbie, but now it's time I
come home to you."

He surged upward and they kissed once again, sharing
each breath and heartbeat as one until they needed to take
the final step to complete that union and satisfy the power
building in them, which wanted to be shared.

Adam reached down and Bobbie followed the path of
his hands, helping him get rid of his khakis and boxers,
trailing her hand up along his thigh to encircle him.

He sucked in a breath at her caress, nearly undone.
Gently he eased himself between her legs, bracing his
hands on either side of her, gazing down at her and seeing the love and acceptance in her eyes. He allowed her to
lead him to her center, paused with the tip of him at her
entry, the heat and wet of her summoning him.

She dragged her hands away from him to grasp the
sides of his hips and tightened her fingers there to urge
him forward.

Slowly he joined with her, savoring every nuance of
his body sliding into her center. The moist heat surrounding him. The brush of her crisp, curly hairs against his
flesh. The intense slide of skin against skin and the fric-
tion of their energies, seeking a similar joining.

As she raised her knees, deepening his penetration

and cradling his hips, she shifted her hands upward to his shoulders. Wherever she touched, a bright silver gleam lit the way. She smiled at the wonder in the display and urged him down to meet her lips again.

He rested within her as they kissed. Content. Complete. Their merged auras cradled them with their joined life forces, feeding their souls and passion with the power of their union.

Every meeting of their lips was filled with life and love and laughter as they rejoiced, as passion grew ever stronger and he finally began to move within her, pulling her along with him toward ever greater pleasure, the pain of their past, of all wounds both physical and emotional, healed by the strength of their love.

He came first, unable to contain what he felt for her. How she moved him.

He had barely drawn a breath after that explosive release when she was joining him, her body arching upward to his as her desire erupted. She screamed his name and gripped his shoulders, rising upward, her body milking his, drawing him ever deeper.

He imagined what might have been then if things had been different. Laying his hand over her flat midsection, he pictured it rounded with his child, and as her hand slipped over his and he met her gaze, he realized she was imagining it as well.

"I love you," he said, wanting her to understand that nothing could change that.

With a sad smile and tears shimmering in her eyes, she said, "I know and I love you even more for that."

He leaned down and kissed her, the caress one of ten-

derness and understanding, soothing away the hurt that
had intruded on their miracle.

Bobbie held him to her, and as he eased to his side, she
snuggled up against him and laid a hand over his heart.
The beat beneath her palm still raced from their lovemaking, but slowly eased back to normal as they rested
together, as the bright display of their combined life forces
retreated.

Idly she ran her thumb along the crisp hair on his
chest, knowing there was one thing that still lingered over
them, needing to be discussed.

Tentatively, she broached the subject. "Your parents
came here to find you."

"I know," he said, running his hand up and down her
back as he kept her tucked close to him.

"Do you want to be found?"

He stopped the motion of his hand, obviously uncertain. "I do, only I'm not their Kikin anymore. I'm Adam
now," he said with obvious reluctance before continuing.
"I have a life here. A life I want to share with you."

"And they have other plans for you." She understood
the all too common theme. So many parents had hopes
for their offspring that didn't necessarily match their children's wishes. In Adam's case, it was complicated by the
dynamics of his people and their apparent needs.

"I'm not sure what they expect now, but I want to meet
them," he said.

She rubbed her hand back and forth along his chest,
looked up and met his gaze. "My family is my bedrock.
I couldn't have survived without them. But Salvatore has
been your family. What will you do about him?"

Storm clouds gathered in his eyes, shadowing them,

and his lips thinned into a tight line. "I need to deal with him, but not now."

Wanting to dispel the hurt, she cradled his cheek and urged his face down the inch or so to hers. With a gentle pass of her lips along his, she said, "Right now you've got other things to do."

And just in case there was any doubt about what, she brought her body against his.

"Did I ever tell you how much I like that you're an empowered woman?" he teased as he kissed her.

She chuckled and said, "Why don't you show me instead?"

CHAPTER
31

Christopher drummed his fingers along the desktop in frustration and eyeballed his captain.

"Tell me again how it is that your men somehow lost William and his underling."

Ryan lowered his gaze, obviously ashamed of the actions of his cadre members. "They said they got distracted by the pull of incredibly strong Hunter power."

Christopher arched a brow. "Other Shadows?"

Wagging his head, Ryan replied, "No. Light Hunters. And from what they said, it's possible it was the source for which we've been searching."

An amazing font of power, Christopher thought, willing to contain his anger if in fact they had located the Quinchu with such incredible strength.

He heaved away from his desk and over to the map pinned to the wall. As in any military campaign, the possible targets had been indicated on the chart. Blue pins for each possible Light Hunter location, not that he intended to track down those smaller vessels of power. He had a bigger plan in mind, one that would wrest control from his father and lead his people on another path. Motioning to the wall and the red pins denoting where they had sensed that greater Quinchu power, he said, "Where was it this time?"

Hesitantly, Ryan picked up a red pin from the ledge along the bottom of the map board and pressed it deeply into the area denoting the Auditorium grounds in Ocean Grove. The pin stuck out like a sore thumb, nowhere near any of the other red pins, including those encircling the large area that Christopher believed to be the origin of the tsunami of energy from a few nights ago.

As he considered the location of the pins, Christopher muttered in frustration, "Fools. It was the power of the humans gathering together. They may not have a great deal of strength individually, but when they unite it's palpable."

Stalking back to his desk, he plopped down into his leather chair and leaned an elbow on its arm. Scrubbing his jaw with one hand, he considered Ryan as he came to stand before him once again.

He wondered where his father's cadre captain and assistant had run off to, and if Maya had any idea about what his father had planned. Had she revealed anything about the source of the power to his father?

Christopher didn't want to consider what his father could do with such might.

"There's a storm brewing tonight. Whoever the Quinchu is, he could be preparing to gather that strength," Christopher mused out loud. After all, it was what he would be trying to do to boost his Añaru powers.

Ryan nodded, clearly understanding what he wanted. "I'll send the cadre to patrol."

"See to it, Ryan. I also want you to set a guard on Maya as long as she is here," he said, the unspoken message clear.

Failure was not an option. In his father's cadre, everyone understood the price for such a fiasco. For a moment Christopher considered that maybe that was a good thing. But only for a moment, since he was not his father's son.

As Ryan jerked his arm to his chest and saluted him, his features tight with worry, Christopher repeated in a friendlier tone, "I trust you, my friend. I know you will not disappoint if at all possible."

The tension immediately fled from Ryan's body and an easier smile came to his face. "We will find the source and keep an eye on Maya."

Christopher nodded and likewise grinned to further alleviate his captain's concerns. "I have no doubt about the first. As for the latter, am I to assume you will attend to that personally?"

A bright flush erupted on Ryan's face as he stammered, "Doesn't it bother you that she shares her bed with so many?"

Christopher shrugged. "She draws her power from such trysts and I need a powerful mate. It would bother me more if she shared her heart with others, but that's not possible."

Ryan narrowed his gaze to consider him. "And why is that?"

Laughing harshly, Christopher said, "Because Maya has no heart. Now go. There is work to be done."

With another, less rigid salute, Ryan walked away, and as Christopher looked at his friend's retreating back, he had only one hope: that his men would find the Quinchu

288 *Caridad Piñeiro*

before his father's minions did. He could not let his father control such power.

Their bodies were a tangle of limbs. Legs interlaced. Heads pillowed on each other's arms. Fingers twined together and trapped between them, close to their hearts.

"I don't want to move," Bobbie said, contentment deep in her bones.

"Then don't," Adam said, and grazed her forehead with a kiss.

"I'd love to, only nature calls," she teased, and with a quick surge upward to drop a kiss on his lips, she slipped from the bed.

Adam appreciated the fine form of her naked backside as she went out the door. Sitting up in bed, he rearranged the pillows behind him, laced his fingers together, and rested his head against them. His gaze was trained on the door as he anxiously awaited her return.

The sounds of her activity drifted to him. Running water. Bare feet padding along the hardwood floor, but moving away from the bedroom.

The clink and clatter of plates and glasses alerted him that she was in the kitchen, which was probably a good idea, considering they had been in bed for hours, alternately dozing and making love, and lunch was way overdue.

When she returned she was carrying a small tray, tucking it tight to her midsection, hiding what she could from his view, although the rest of her was gloriously naked.

He couldn't resist gazing at the beauty of her breasts with their deep coral nipples before dragging his gaze upward to her even more arresting face. Would he ever get tired of seeing it? he wondered for only a second before the answer came swiftly and unequivocally.

No. He would never tire of her.

A flush erupted across her face and breasts at his perusal, dragging a smile to his lips. He patted the bed beside him. "Come here. I've missed you."

With a wry smirk, she said, "I've only been gone five minutes."

He patted the bed again. "Five minutes too long."

She came over and was about to place the tray on his lap, but that wasn't possible. The sight of her had aroused him, providing a less-than-flat area for the tray.

So instead she leaned over and placed it to one side, then climbed back into bed and straddled his legs, facing him, his erection tucked beneath her center making food the last thing on his mind.

Bobbie clearly had a different idea.

She reached over and grabbed a grape from a bunch sitting on a plate beside some cheese, a dried sausage of some kind, and slices of a crusty Italian bread.

She brought it to his lips and he opened his mouth. After popping it in, she took one for herself and ate it. "Sweet."

Adam gazed at her breasts. "I can think of something far sweeter."

The flush deepened and her hands fluttered over the food for a moment, but then she recovered and prepped him a slice of bread with some of the cheese and sausage. She brought it to his lips and he eyeballed the morsel for only a second before taking a bite, leaving her with a half that she popped into her own mouth.

"Tasty," he said.

With a wicked grin, she shot a glance downward and

rubbed her hips along his. "I can think of something tastier."

Heat erupted across his face and his aura flared brightly. His gut tightened and he almost choked on the bit of food she had fed him before swallowing it hastily.

"Need a drink?" She leaned over, grasped one of the short glasses on the tray, and handed it to him.

"Wine?" he wondered aloud before taking a sip of the merlot-colored liquid, only to discover it was red grape juice.

"Don't drink all that much. Just in case I need the pain meds, although I don't take them often," she explained, growing uneasy and crossing her arms along her mid-section.

He placed the glass back down on the tray, laid his hand at the crook of her neck, and leaned forward. Nuzzling his nose along hers, he whispered, "I can make it better."

Bobbie brought her hands up between them, clasped his face in her hands. She gazed into his emerald eyes, darkening with emotion and devoid of the shadows that had haunted him earlier. "Just having you here makes it better, Adam."

She kissed him then, leaving no doubt about what he meant to her.

He groaned and wrapped his arms around her waist, hauled her close to him, crushing her breasts to his chest with the tightness of his embrace. But as they held each other, emotions stronger than desire rose up.

Peace. Unity.

Adam whispered against the shell of her ear, "I wish we never had to move from here."

She murmured her agreement, but they both recognized this special time together was fleeting. One call would change it all. One call to his parents.

His parents, he thought, unable to believe that after so much time all the wondering and hoping was over.

They had found him. He would no longer be alone, but with that immediately came another thought. From the moment he had met Bobbie he hadn't been alone. Tightening his hold on her, he closed his eyes and let himself sink bonelessly into her embrace. He wanted to savor these moments before the world he knew nothing about intruded.

CHAPTER
32

Salvatore Bruno sat steaming in his car as he waited outside Bobbie's condo. It wasn't just the land breeze, hot and humid like a sirocco, making him warm. It was the fact that Adam was here with her. Had been here with her for most of the day. After everything they had shared, his son had chosen to trust a virtual stranger over him.

It shouldn't hurt so much. Wouldn't, if he had remembered his goal and not gone soft for so many years. Adam was just another assignment, he told himself. But the little voice inside his head screamed "Liar."

He wondered what they had been doing up in her condo for so many hours, not that it took much wondering. Even with her injuries the Carrera woman turned heads.

He was thankful that the sun was beginning to set and a shift in the wind was creating a drop in heat and humidity. The sea breeze helped, but there was that smell in the air that said a storm approached.

Inside Bobbie's condo a light snapped on, and Salvatore fixed his gaze on it, impatiently waiting for his son to emerge. He hoped that if he had just a little more time to chat with him, he could convince Adam that he was mistaken about all that had happened.

So Salvatore sat and waited, and then waited some more.

The storm that had been threatening came and went, refreshing the air and causing another drop in temperature. But it left behind scattered pockets of rain and lightning.

It was nearly midnight when Adam finally emerged from the building, but he wasn't alone. Bobbie Carrera stood beside him, her fingers laced with Adam's. The way she leaned toward him and then skimmed back a lock of his hair spoke volumes about their level of intimacy. The hungry kiss by Adam's car confirmed it, as did the blue glow that surrounded them both, surprising Salvatore.

He had never seen Adam's aura engulf anyone else before. It spoke of a bond far stronger than one based on just emotion.

After the kiss ended, he expected Adam to drive off, leaving Bobbie behind, but instead they both slipped into Adam's Bentley. With a low rumble, the engine jumped to life, followed by the flare of the headlights.

Adam pulled out onto Ocean Avenue, and after a short wait to allow enough distance to disguise his presence, Salvatore started his car and turned onto the street, lights off to avoid immediate discovery.

Adam seemed in no rush, keeping a moderate pace past the homes and inns on Ocean Avenue. Instead of continuing down the beachfront road, he turned westward and up to Main Avenue. Traveling south, he pushed the sports car a little faster through the stretches of mile-long beach towns and past the turnoff for his home in Spring Lake.

Salvatore narrowed his eyes, perplexed by where his son… No, not his son. That ruse was over. Adam was now just the first subject in the long overdue launch of the Genesis project. He could no longer let emotion interfere in what he had to do. In what he had planned for so many years.

Vigilant as he tried to guess where Adam might be headed, Salvatore followed carefully. The Bentley pushed past modest homes, which became a tangle of small businesses before the street reached the end of the town and the lake for which it was named. Barely a quarter mile later, Adam turned eastward toward the ocean in Sea Girt.

A hodgepodge of moderately sized homes developed into multimillion-dollar beach houses and the lovingly restored Beacon House Inn. Across from the inn sat the normally busy Parker House, almost quiet with the late hour as waiters tidied up.

Salvatore pulled over as Adam's brake lights flared to life and his son turned the Bentley into a parking spot across from the Sea Girt lighthouse. The beacon atop the red brick building rotated, piercing the night sky, serving as a reference point for Adam and Bobbie, apparently, since they left their car and headed straight for the lighthouse.

They moved with determined strides that put distance between them and the street quickly, puzzling him, since Bobbie appeared to have little evidence of her earlier limp. The two marched in front of the lighthouse and then disappeared from sight.

Intrigued, Salvatore exited his car and chased after them.

Bobbie and Adam paused on the walkway in front of the beacon, scoping out the beachfront in between sweeps of the rotating light. The night's earlier storm had created a haze along the shore and another approaching front hung over the ocean, threatening. Bright shards of light mixed with muted flashes as the tempest neared.

"It may not be safe along the waterfront if the storm hits," Bobbie said, and Adam peered at her from the corner of his eye.

"It may not be safe period." Adam tucked his hands beneath his arms and squinted into the misty night, trying to make out any shapes along the sand. There were none.

"Maybe you should stay up here. Just in case there's trouble."

Bobbie wagged her head emphatically. "No way, no how. We go together or we don't go at all."

Facing her, he took note of the determined set to her jaw and the defiant tilt of her head. She had on what he was coming to recognize as her stubborn face, and he knew it would be difficult to change her mind. Besides, if truth were told, he had no doubt he could count on her, both emotionally and as his wingman in a fight.

"You stay close. Just in case."

She grabbed hold of his hand, leaned into his side, and rubbed her hand along his back. "Close. I'll have your back."

He grinned then, remembering the last time she'd had his back and his front and virtually every other part of him. Her smile and the glitter in her eyes communicated that she remembered it as well. Pushing onto tiptoe, she swept a quick kiss across his lips before urging him forward.

Adam gripped her hand tightly as they stepped onto the beach. The sand was heavy, soaked from the prior rains. A low-lying mist lingered, swirled around their feet as they pushed ahead.

"They said in front of the lighthouse, right?" he asked, wanting to make sure they were walking to the correct location.

Bobbie looked all around, a furrow of worry in the middle of her forehead. "That's what they said, except no one is here."

They reached the hard-packed wet sand, and the mist continued to eddy around their feet. Suddenly a flash of lightning illuminated the ocean and the sweep of black fins cutting through the surface.

"Dolphins," Bobbie whispered with a note of awed delight.

In Adam's head came a strange buzzing, like static on a radio. He shook his head, trying to clear it, and from the side of his eye caught movement as two seagulls swooped downward. They glided down on the storm breeze onto the sand about twenty feet away from them and strutted back and forth, pecking at the sand. Normal, but something about them seemed off to him.

"Adam," Bobbie said, and tugged at his hand.

He looked at her, but she was intently staring ahead.

Tracking her gaze, he noticed the pod of dolphins again as the lighthouse beacon swept across the water. It was a sight he'd seen more than once along the shore, but these dolphins weren't moving parallel to the beach.

They were swimming straight for them, and as they did so, the drone in his head intensified. This time he understood it for what it was—the hum of power. Coming off the dolphins.

Another pass of the beacon illuminated the surface of the water.

The fins disturbed the surf barely ten feet from shore. A jagged spike of lightning, dangerously closer, lit up the ocean, revealing four black shapes rising out of the water.

Humans. Or at least they would be soon, he thought, taking note of how arms slowly pulled away from the sleek dolphins' bodies. Their noses flattened and the area around their faces became normal.

Darkness descended for seconds before the rotation of the beacon illuminated the now-human-looking quartet striding toward him and Bobbie—three men and a woman dressed in black.

Lightning flashed above them, followed closely by the rumble of thunder, as the incoming storm was now nearly directly overhead.

As the four came ever closer, the push of power was so strong he could almost feel it buffeting him. Their bodies were limned in a soft crimson aura, reminding him of a red sky at night. He took a step back, but Bobbie laid her hand on his arm and softly said, "It's okay, Adam. It's your—"

"Parents," he finished as two of the group, a man and the sole woman, sloshed out of the surf while the two other men stayed back. As another flash of lightning erupted above them, he realized it was the two men who had tried to grab him in the parking lot.

His parents were barely ten feet away when another

flare of light erupted, horizontal lightning, slamming into one of the men lingering near the surf line, tossing him back several feet where he collapsed into the waters.

Adam's parents pivoted quickly in the direction of the spike of light. Adam tucked Bobbie behind him and whirled in the same direction.

Before them on the wet sand, roughly twenty feet away, there were two men instead of the seagulls that had been there just a short time earlier. In the blink of an eye, tendrils of energy erupted at the palms of their hands and wove themselves into bright balls of power.

Adam glanced toward his parents. They were crouched low, standing close together, his father shielding his mother with his body. Another blast came, close to their feet. Too close.

"No," Adam said softly, as memories slammed into him. Memories of this happening once before. Of Salvatore grabbing him, pulling him away as he tried to hold on to his mother's hand. Of a bolt of energy slamming into him as Salvatore dragged him toward a nearby building.

"No," he repeated more loudly, and took a step toward them, so caught up in the past that he failed to see the dangers of the present.

"Adam," Bobbie called out, which was followed by the deeper echo of his name.

Suddenly Bobbie threw herself in front of him.

The blast hit, and Bobbie fell back toward him, but so did another body.

"Dad," he said, as Salvatore tumbled into a heap on the sand beside Bobbie. He lay deathlike while beside him Bobbie's body spasmed from the force of the ball of power.

Fury tore through him, more potent than anything he

had ever experienced. He raised his hands to the skies and cried out his rage as a blast of lightning lit up the night. Descended from the heavens straight into his hands.

With another roar he deflected the power across the sands, striking the two men who had attacked them. Like fireworks in the night sky, they burst into brightly colored embers before his eyes. Just like that, the danger was gone, but the damage was done.

He dropped to his knees beside Bobbie and his dad. Bobbie's aura flickered, veins of silver and red spreading through her like poison. She gazed at him, silently pleading for relief. He was about to touch her when his mother fell to the sand beside him and stayed his hand. "Let me. You do not know enough to deal with the Shadow force tainting her."

Nodding, he shifted away and watched as his mother placed her hands at the uppermost edge of Bobbie's aura. Slowly she inched downward, and the streaks of red and silver were drawn to his mother as if she was a magnet for the poison.

His mother's body trembled as the energy slipped into her, but beneath her hands Bobbie's body calmed, and little by little, her aura returned to its normal sapphire hue. His mother released Bobbie and slumped into his father's arms, obviously drained. As his father held her, Adam reached down and embraced Bobbie, clutching her to him tightly.

"I'm okay," she said, weakly at first, then more strongly. "I'm okay. Salvatore took most of the hit. He jumped in front of you also."

Salvatore. He lay facedown just a couple of feet from them. Motionless.

Together Adam and Bobbie moved toward him, knelt beside him, and carefully flipped him onto his back. Wet sand clung to his face as sightless eyes stared at the night sky. Burn marks marred the front of his shirt directly in the middle of his chest.

Bobbie placed her fingers at his throat, searching for a pulse, then shook her head.

"I'm sorry, Adam." Tears fell down her cheeks, shimmering thanks to a weak flash of lightning from the passing storm.

Adam stared down at the man who had been his father for twenty years, the man who had betrayed him—and yet, there had been good times. And love. In the end, love had won out, he thought as he took Salvatore into his arms and held him.

Grief poured through him. For the time he had lost with his parents. For the sacrifice Salvatore had made on his behalf.

"Kikin," his mother said, and laid her hand over his as he held Salvatore. With gentle pressure, she urged Adam's hand upward to a spot directly above Salvatore's chest and the marks from the electrical blast.

"Focus," she said. "Another attack could be imminent. We must act accordingly."

Bobbie sat back on her haunches, still feeling weak, watching as mother and son leaned close together, and at a spot beneath their hands a silver-red glow emerged.

"Focus," she heard Selina repeat, and Adam screwed his eyes shut and gritted his teeth, engaged by the command in his mother's voice.

His mother, Bobbie thought again, and looked up, searching for Adam's father. His real father. He was slogging through the surf, where one of his fellow Hunters emerged from the waters, carrying his partner. The man was limp weight in the man's arms. Adam's father helped him haul the man to shore, where they laid him down gently on the wet sand, heads bowed over their fallen comrade.

Another death, she thought, and looked up the beach toward the spot where their attackers had stood, but the space was empty. As the beacon flashed over the spot, the sand where they had stood glistened like ice.

Weird, she thought, but then a vibration pulled at her core, dragging her attention back to Adam and his mother. The light emanating from beneath their hands was ever stronger, almost blinding, but then came a flash and Salvatore's body jumped. Another pulse erupted, almost as strong. A new spasm followed, only this time there was movement as Salvatore's foot wiggled, and the sound of a sharply drawn breath filled the night. Selina shifted away then, her face looking ashen beneath the light of the beacon as it swept over them.

Bobbie reached out a hand to her and Selina clutched it, locked her gaze with Bobbie's.

"Why?" Bobbie asked.

Selina glanced back at where Adam held Salvatore. The other man weakly lifted his hand. He patted Adam's head in a fatherly gesture before his hand fell back limply to lie across his stomach. When Selina looked back, she said, "Sometimes love isn't easy to understand."

As if that statement roused some previously unconnected thought, Selina peered over Bobbie's shoulder, searching for her husband. Shadows crept into her gaze as she turned it to where her husband and the fellow Hunter knelt beside the body on the sand.

"I must go," she said, but took a moment to pass her hand tenderly over Bobbie's cheek.

Bobbie came to her feet, wobbly at first, but resolve stiffened her spine and kept her upright. She took the step or two necessary to kneel by Adam and did so, circling his shoulders with her arm and kissing the side of his face as he held Salvatore.

He raised his head then and offered up a ghost of a smile, but then looked around, searching for his parents, fear in his eyes once more, as if he were that lost young child again.

Bobbie lifted her hand and pointed in the direction of the shoreline, where his parents knelt beside the body of their injured friend.

"Would you watch him?" Adam said, inclining his head toward Salvatore.

Bobbie nodded and shifted to hold Salvatore's head in her lap. He was a sickly green color and bathed with sweat, but alert.

Adam surged to his feet and approached his parents, guilt and worry driving him. When he stood beside them, he could see the weakness of the man's aura and the faint spidery lines of silver and red, like hairline cracks in an eggshell.

"He's too far gone," his mother said, and her head sagged sadly.

His father embraced her as the other man knelt beside them, his features hard as granite, glaring at Adam, his gaze almost accusatory.

Adam dropped to his knees beside them. "There must be something we can do. Something like what you did with—"

"Nothing, except salvage his energy," his father said brusquely, and looked at him. It was like staring into a mirror and seeing an older version of himself, Adam thought.

"Quinchu, we must act before it is all gone. We cannot waste even a drop of his life force," the man beside him cautioned.

"Mother?" Adam questioned, and she raised her tear-stained face to him.

"They are right, son. There is nothing to be done for Eduardo."

The three laid their hands upon the man, and then his mother reached for Adam, took hold of his hand, and guided it to the man's body. The buzz began in his head, and as his fingers brushed along the man's aura, he sensed its weakness and how his power feebly flowed through his body.

A faint flash of lightning came near as the tail end of the storm fled quickly above them. Adam lifted one hand to the sky and focused on the eddies of power swirling through the clouds directly overhead even as the three beside him concentrated on their nearly dead friend. Reaching deep within himself, he tapped the core of power gathered there, visualized it summoning the similar energy high up in the turbulent clouds.

Bobbie experienced the profound pull of Adam's energy within her center, and a glimmer of light slowly coalesced into a ball in Adam's hand. Before her eyes, the light from his palm reached upward like a searchlight, illuminating the heavens.

Suddenly a zigzag bolt of lightning traveled along that path, straight into Adam's hand. Before her eyes a blood-red light burst forth from the five Hunters and grew ever stronger as the heavens continued pumping bolt after bolt through Adam.

The thunder began a millisecond later, loud and disturbing, making her jump at its unexpected violence, shaking the ground beneath them with its force as it rolled over and over across them, thrashing the space along the beachfront until Adam closed his hand and dropped his arm.

The lightning stopped as easily as if he had flipped a light switch. A final rumble, like the ringing vibrations of cymbals, followed before the night grew preternaturally silent.

"Adam," Salvatore said weakly and patted her arm, his movements frail and uncoordinated.

She peered across the distance and the haze that had grown thicker with each blast of energy. She made out the outlines of Adam, his parents, and the one man. One by one they rose, and then suddenly a fifth body joined them from the mist covering the ground near the shoreline.

Adam turned and marched toward her, his face grim, but softening as it fell on Salvatore. Once again he knelt by Salvatore and took hold of his hand. "We have to get you to a hospital."

"Home. Take me home, Adam," Salvatore insisted, his voice faltering. His gaze grew unfocused for a moment until it settled on Selina as she approached.

"I'm sorry," he said.

"As am I. Thank you for saving my son," she replied, and glanced at Adam. "We will wait for you, Kikin. Bobbie knows where to find us. Be safe. This is only the beginning."

With that Selina motioned to the men with her and they quickly returned to the sea, wading deeper and deeper until their bodies changed color. Arms disappeared and heads tapered to sleek lines as the Hunters morphed back into dolphins and sank beneath the wind-whipped waves.

Bobbie stroked a sweat-soaked strand of hair from Salvatore's face. She wanted to hate him, but she couldn't. He had saved not only Adam, but possibly her, by jumping in front of the blast from the Shadow Hunters.

"He needs medical attention," she said, but as father and son exchanged a look, she knew her plea would go unheeded.

"I'll take him home."

"*We'll* take him home," she said, and helped Adam lift Salvatore into his arms.

At the Bentley, Adam eased him gently into the passenger seat and buckled him up, leaving no room for Bobbie. Salvatore reached into his jacket pocket and pulled out a set of keys.

"Blue CTS. Across the street."

Bobbie snagged the keys and turned. Just a few cars away was the Cadillac. "I'll follow."

Adam nodded, hugged her hard, and dropped a kiss on her cheek. "Be careful."

"You, too," she said, fearing that the two Shadows who had appeared on the beachfront were just the start of even bigger problems.

CHAPTER
33

Adam tucked Salvatore into bed, mimicking the many times Salvatore had done the same for him, tucking the sheets tight to his body and making sure a glass of water sat on the nightstand.

"You really need to see a doctor," he said, worried that Salvatore seemed as weak as a newborn. His skin had a pasty-white look and the chill sweat refused to leave his body.

"Not until you talk to them. Find out who attacked you on the beachfront," Salvatore urged, his voice slightly stronger.

Adam risked a glance at Bobbie, who stood at the end of the bed, battle-ready, as if she, too, believed that they were still not safe. And maybe they weren't. Maybe he was deluding himself in thinking that tonight had been an aberration. Which meant that while they might have won tonight's battle, he could still lose Bobbie, who had little taste for being in another war.

With a paternal pat on Salvatore's hand, he said, "We'll be back later."

"I'll be fine," Salvatore said, nodding, and closed his eyes, drifting off.

Adam rose from the bedside and approached Bobbie. He wrapped her in his arms and laid his forehead on hers. "Are you okay?"

She shrugged and returned his embrace. "Feeling a little wired, but okay. I think Salvatore took the brunt of the blast."

He lifted his hands to her shoulders, tenderly moving them to run this thumbs along the set line of her jaw. "I died a little when I saw you were hit."

"Believe me when I say your lightning act scared the bejesus out of me. I thought you might be nothing but toast when it was all over," she said, and swept a kiss across his lips.

"I wish I knew the how and why of it, but I don't. I'm hoping my parents will have some answers for us," he said, and deepened the kiss, wanting to taste her and savor the warmth of her breath, needing to celebrate the life that still pulsed through their bodies.

"Me, too," she said, and grabbed his hand, pressing him to leave.

Salvatore listened to their footsteps on the wooden steps. Heard the creak of the front door opening and then the snick of the lock as Adam secured it. He had little time. His heart beat a frantic rhythm in his chest, and the icy grip of death in his body refused to go away. He had to act now or forever risk his son's life.

Luckily he always kept the file within reach.

Gingerly he got to his feet, using the bedpost to steady himself as he walked around the edge of the bed.

His desk was just a short distance away. Shuffling from the bed like a centenarian rather than the robust fifty-year-old he had been before the orb of energy smacked into him, he somehow made it to his desk.

Plopping into the chair, sweat oozing from every cell in his body, he unlocked the side drawers and pulled out the paperwork for the Genesis project and his Texas Ranger file on the murders. From beneath the desk he removed a heavy-duty shredder and, hands shaking, fed each and every sheet from the files through its angry teeth. When he was done with the papers, he carefully destroyed the file jackets.

But even with that he didn't feel it was safe.

Tossing aside the shredding unit, he lifted the receptacle with the heavy paper shreds and tottered back toward his bed and the fireplace opposite it.

The remnants of an earlier fire were still there, scattered ashes and bits of charcoal from the wood. The smell of it drifted to him as he opened the glass fireplace doors and covered the grate with the paper strips until the waste receptacle was empty. Then he opened the flue, lit a match, and flicked it onto the papers.

Flames flared immediately, bright and hot. As he stood there, watching twenty years of his life disappear, the warmth from the fire filled him. Or maybe it was the realization that he was finally doing the right thing giving him that warm fuzzy feeling inside.

As the last bit of paper crinkled into a red-white ember, Salvatore smiled. Although Sombrosa had been able to get the dummy NSA file that had been entered into their electronic systems, the real file and all the related investigations had solely been on paper since Salvatore had little confidence in safeguarding anything electronic. Satisfied that it would take Sombrosa a lot more effort to find Adam, Salvatore trudged back to the bed.

It was done.

In the morning he would confide to Adam about Alexander Sombrosa. Perhaps with that knowledge, Adam would be able to safeguard himself, he thought. He closed his eyes and finally rested.

Adam sat across the table from his parents. It was almost too much for him to believe that after so long they were really there. It was even harder to imagine the kind of life he might have had with them as he listened to their detailed explanation about the Hunters, their clans, and the two men who had attacked them that night.

"You say they were Shadows? People like us?" he asked, just to make sure he was understanding the history of his people.

"No, not like us. At least, not anymore," his father replied, and then continued.

"When the human smallpox brought by the conquistadores touched us, it forever changed our people." Motioning to his two cadre members who stood by the door, he continued. "Hunters like Eduardo and Andres cannot absorb power on their own any longer. They rely mostly on the Quinchus to sustain them."

"You and Mom," he said, and glanced across the way at his mother. She was beautiful, although sadness had taken its toll. Besides the streaks of gray in her hair, lines of sorrow were etched along the edges of her beautiful almond-shaped gray eyes.

"And you," she chimed in. "At all costs the power of

the Quinchus had to be preserved for the good of our people. It is why you were promised to the daughter of the Ocean clan Quinchus."

Adam risked a glance at Bobbie. There had been tension within her during the entire ride to the large oceanfront mansion his family had leased for their entourage. The tension ratcheted upward at his mother's words, and to allay her discomfort, he reached over and placed his hands over hers where they were laced together on the tabletop.

Selina watched the loving movement. A warrior like Bobbie would have been a good addition to the clan, but not for her son, because of her limitations. The Hunters needed their Quinchus to procreate for the good of the group.

"As you near the end of your first triad, the power in you will grow stronger. It will require a mate who can balance you by joining her power with yours. It's called the Equinox," Selina explained.

"I will not marry someone I do not love," he said, only half-glancing at his mother, his attention fixed on the woman beside him. Bobbie gazed up at him then, her eyes traveling over Kikin's features as if to memorize them.

"I love you, Adam. I know how important family is. I can't deny you yours—your family, your people, your fate," Bobbie said, and rose from the table. She walked to the far side of the room and stared out the large windows facing the beach. In the distance behind her, the hint of rosy light warned that the sun would soon rise to start another day.

Selina realized then that they had been up for hours since the attack, filling in Kikin on the missing pieces of his life and the history of the Hunters. Kikin rose, intent on following his woman, but Selina held up her hand to stop him. She wanted to speak to Bobbie herself, to try to make the woman see reason, so that the decision would be simpler for Kikin.

She strode from the table to where Bobbie stood. Even at a distance the strength of her aura was apparent, only now it was blue-violet with the churning of her emotions. But within that hue was something else. Something Selina had not expected or noticed before when she had stabilized her after the energy blast from the Shadows.

Just to confirm it, Selina laid her hand on Bobbie's shoulder, releasing seeking energy that explored Bobbie's body, returning to Selina with confirmation just before Bobbie shrugged off her touch.

Selina stood close and wrapped an arm around Bobbie's waist. This time she sensed the strong push of power similar to Kikin's, along with a tiny pulse of nascent power.

His Equinox had already come and Bobbie had been the receptacle that had balanced his power. That exchange had also worked what some might consider a miracle. In time, Bobbie and Kikin would realize it as well, she thought with a smile. But she would leave that for them to discover on their own.

Leaning toward Bobbie, she said, "Do you love him, child?"

"With all my heart and soul," Bobbie replied in a whisper choked with emotion.

"That is all that matters," she said, and turned to the two men, who had risen from the table to watch the exchange.

As they stood side by side, the resemblance was undeniable. Father and son, although Kikin had a bit of her in the mouth and chin, she thought, and wondered whether his child would as well. Urging Bobbie to turn, Selina said, "We will deal with our promise to the Ocean clan. I suspect the Quinchu daughter will be relieved that we are not forcing the issue of the arranged marriage."

Surprise flared across her husband's features and rippled to Kikin before they both contained it. She pressed forward.

"There is a spare bedroom we've been keeping in anticipation of your return. You and Bobbie should go get some rest," she said, and motioned to Andres.

"Please show them to their room."

With a salute, Andres immediately went into action, leaving Bobbie and Adam with little choice.

Adam tenderly grasped Bobbie's hand as they walked down the long hall to a room at the far end. When they reached the door, Andres opened it and first checked the interior before assuming a position at the door.

"If there is anything you require, Quinchu," he said with a deferential nod.

"No, thank you," Adam replied, and quickly closed the door, wanting some privacy.

Everything in the room was luxurious, from the antiques to the expensive linens on the large four-poster bed in the center of the room. At one end of the chamber was a liquor cabinet with an assortment of top-shelf beverages, while on the other side French doors led to a balcony. Oceanfront, he assumed, but couldn't quite care as he noted the tired droop of Bobbie's shoulders.

He stood before her, reached up, and brushed back a wayward lock of her soft brown hair. "Are you okay?"

"Tired," she admitted, and glanced lovingly at the bed.

He cupped her shoulders and gently caressed them. "Get undressed. I'll be there in a second."

He was tired as well, but thirsty. He walked to the liquor cabinet and poured some wine, his hands shaking as he did so. Bracing his hands on the edge of the mahogany bar, he inhaled deeply to quell the aftereffects of all that had happened.

He'd almost lost her. Almost lost Salvatore.

For sure he'd lost one thing—the life he had known before. With the arrival of his parents and their clan, he suspected nothing would ever be the same. And he once again feared what that would mean for him and Bobbie.

Grabbing the two wineglasses, he returned to the bed and handed one to her. She was bare, the sheets pulled up to just above the swell of her breasts. There was a bruise on one shoulder and it came to him that that was where the Shadow's power shot had struck her after deflecting off Salvatore.

He skipped his fingers across the purpling mark. "Does it hurt?"

She shook her head. "No. I just feel weird."

He placed his glass on a nightstand, eased off his polo shirt, and tossed it aside. Then he did the same with his pants and boxers, toeing off his shoes along the way in his eagerness to be beside her, because he couldn't get enough of her. He rested against the massive headboard and pulled her into his lap. She tucked her head beneath his and lazily traced the whorls of hair on his chest with her index finger before raising that hand to take a sip of the wine from the glass she held.

He reached out and picked up his own glass, took a bigger mouthful of the wine before asking, "Why do you think Selina...my mother changed her mind so quickly about the commitment to the Ocean clan?"

Bobbie shrugged. "I don't know."

Adam rested his head back on the headboard, considering that answer. "Did she say anything to you?"

"She asked if I loved you."

His heart caught on a beat, expectant, waiting for her to continue, and when she didn't, he pressed forward. "So what did you say?"

Bobbie smiled and leaned over, placing her glass on the nightstand. She straddled his legs and faced him. Raising her hands, she laid them on his shoulders and caressed them before moving upward to hold his face between them. She covered his mouth with a kiss, determined to leave no doubt about her feelings for him. When they broke apart, they were both breathing heavily and passion rose quickly.

"Things may be very different now, Bobbie. If tonight was any hint of what's to come—"

"More reason for us to be together. I will always watch your back," she reminded him, and gently urged him to lie down, after which she proceeded to blanket his body with hers. Chuckling, she teased, "And whatever other part you want to share."

Adam grinned, more enamored of her than ever. Seasoned warrior. Sexy woman. Unquestioned soulmate. Rolling her beneath him, he quickly sheathed himself in her, drawing a long, satisfied breath from her.

"How about we start with that?" he teased. He bent his head and kissed the side of her neck before playfully biting it.

"That's a good start," she said, and gave herself over to his loving.

EPILOGUE

Christopher and Ryan stood just beyond the police line, watching the law enforcement personnel traipsing along the sand, back and forth from the red-brick lighthouse to a spot at the far shoreline. Murmurs came from the crowd around them but he and Ryan remained silent, vigilant for any signs that might clue them to what had happened here.

They had spent the night combing the area they had identified as the origin of the power, only to find nothing. It had been in the late hours as they headed home that the traces of a strong source of energy had called them to this spot. Of course by then there was a swarm of humans in and around the lighthouse, clearly excited about something.

As they stood there, listening to the crowd, it became apparent that a rather unusual lightning storm had caught the attention of the humans. Person after person gathered there spoke of sheets of lightning, both horizontal and vertical, that had struck along the beach, as well as thunder so powerful it had knocked pictures off walls.

But Christopher knew it had been no ordinary storm.

Even now, after hours of watching and waiting, the wisps of great power lingered, wafting throughout the people crowding behind the barricades the police had set up just beyond the lighthouse.

A sudden surge of the crowd ahead of them alerted him that something was finally occurring. With a look from the corner of his eye at Ryan, he and his captain pushed forward, weaving through the crowd until they could see what had prompted its reaction.

From their height head and shoulders above the crowd, Christopher easily saw the two big blobs being pushed along on gurneys by the EMTs. As the sunlight touched them, they glittered, and he realized then that he was staring at two large bits of irregular glass.

"I've heard about lighting strikes in sand making glass . . ." one person ahead of them began.

"Fulgurites," Ryan said from beside him.

Christopher nodded, though these were nothing like the hollow tubes caused by a lightning strike superheating sand. The kind of power needed to create such large pools of glass had to have been extreme. And it had to have been concentrated outward, along the surface, rather than traveling deep into the sand the way the power of a bolt would normally descend.

These fulgurites spoke of immense energy and control. But why two of them? he wondered, until something occurred to him.

"Have we heard from William and his friend?" he said, and with a final stare at the glass being loaded into the back of an ambulance, presumably for further examination down at the local coroner's, he pivoted and walked away from the crowd.

Ryan chased after him, but not before craning his head for another look at the unusual fulgurites. "We haven't. Why do you—"

Christopher stopped and raised his hands, turning in a circle as he picked his head up like a dog chasing a scent. "Do you not feel it? They were here—Light Hunters. And the Quinchu we seek as well. The traces of his power linger."

"You think William found them here?" Ryan asked, mimicking Christopher, his eyes opening wider as the remnants of power finally registered. "I feel it, Añaru. The Light Hunters were here."

"And so were my father's men, before someone turned them into those blobs you saw back there." Christopher jerked his thumb in the direction of the ambulance and then charged forward toward his car.

It had been a late night and he needed to rest.

His captain chased after him once more, like a puppy after its master. "What do we do now?"

Christopher smiled patiently. "We wait. Power that strong can only hide for so long."

On that Christopher would stake not only his life, but the continued existence of his people. For that reason, he could not fail in his quest. He would find the Quinchu and once he had discovered the secret of that power, there would be nothing to keep him from seizing control of his Shadow clan.

Look for the second sinfully
sexy novel in the
Sin Hunters series!

Please turn this page
for a preview of
The Claimed
Available in May 2012

CHAPTER
1

The flares of energy shooting off Alexander's aura were Christopher's first clue that his father could be defeated.

The second clue was the way his father rubbed at a spot on his chest. The action left dirty streaks on the pristine white fabric from the pustules beneath that ruptured with each angry stroke of his father's hand. Clearly his father was too weak to control the pox.

"What happened to my men?" Alexander repeated, agitation apparent in every jerky movement and the emerging red rash along the edges of his collar. Soon the rash would blossom into even more angry sores.

"I suggest you call the Monmouth County Coroner's Office. I hear they have some unusual objects in their possession," Christopher replied drolly, and walked to the bar tucked along one side of his father's office. He picked up the cut crystal decanter and waved it toward his father.

"Would you care for a drink, Alexander?" Christopher

asked as if his future and the very fate of his people weren't at risk. Inside, however, his gut churned with the possibility that since his father's control was so diminished, he wouldn't hesitate to attack to replenish his energy.

The sly glance that Alexander shot the other occupants of the room—Christopher's cadre captain, Ryan, and Christopher's fiancée, Maya—hinted that some part of Alexander's twisted mind was, in fact, considering a strike. That his intentions were obvious to the others was evident as Ryan dipped his head in deference and said, "Añaru. We only live to serve. We believe William and his man were killed by the Light Hunters."

"And I can guarantee it was not the same death that my man Andrew suffered," Christopher added, still angered by the fact that his father had drained his cadre member's life force.

Alexander shrugged, but shot a sly glance at Maya. For some time Christopher had believed that his fiancée had known the truth about Andrew's murder. The look confirmed his suspicion and reinforced another: Maya could not be trusted.

With a dismissive flip of his hand, Alexander said, "Andrew betrayed you, Christopher. He came here with tales—"

"Not tales, but you know that, don't you? You tasted the power the Light Hunter infused in Andrew when you fed from him," Christopher said as he uncapped the decanter and poured brandy into three matching snifters.

"Amazing power. Have you discovered the source of it?" Alexander asked, wringing his hands before him like a hungry man staring at a feast.

Christopher strolled to his father's desk and placed the glass on its surface. "Possibly."

Not wanting to get too close to Alexander in his unstable state, he continued across the room toward Maya, glancing at Ryan, who stood at ease a few feet away. Ryan's hands were held before him loosely, but Christopher could tell from his stance that he was ready to take action if necessary.

Maya lounged in a leather wing chair, her legs crossed, displaying their elegant lines. Her skin was a flawless creamy expanse, a testament to the fact that she had recently fed to abate the pox in her body. Her demeanor was seemingly relaxed, but Christopher knew her well enough to recognize the changes in her aura that signaled her unease. Small tendrils of silver and blue shivered in the dirty red of her visible life force.

Christopher balanced on the arm of the wing chair and handed her a snifter. This close to her, he could feel the pulse of her sexual energy, awakening need in him. Too bad it was empty need, he thought, and took a sip of the aged brandy.

His father continued with his plea. "You cannot be so selfish, Christopher. The clan needs such power."

"You mean you need it, father." He glanced at Alexander over the rim of his snifter as he took another pull on the liquor.

"You ungrateful bastard," his father growled as he charged around the edge of his desk, all vestiges of control gone.

With practiced ease, both Christopher and Ryan jumped to action and raised their hands, discharging waves of power that stopped Christopher's father in his tracks.

Alexander lifted his hand and pushed against their combined energy fields. "You dare defy your Añaru?" With a determined push, he dug his fingers into the wall of energy.

Tiny tendrils erupted from his fingers and slowly wove a web across the surface of the field. Like the spiders for which the Añaru were named, Alexander spun a web to capture the men's energy and drink it in along the rapacious tendrils.

"Break off, Ryan," Christopher called out.

Christopher experienced a ripple through his body as Ryan pulled back his life force, leaving only him and his father connected. As the Añaru, his father's power should have been devastating, rendering Christopher weak and listless in a matter of minutes. Instead, Christopher sensed only a negligible draw.

"You are weak, Father," he said as he took a step closer and pushed his father backward with the strength of his energy.

"I am your Añaru. You will obey me," Alexander replied, but there was little conviction in his words. He, too, recognized that the son had become greater.

If Christopher had been like Alexander, he would have issued the challenge for leadership of the clan now, the way Alexander had done to his father. But Christopher had no desire for the fight to the death that was demanded by the traditions of his people.

Christopher was not his father.

He took another step forward, and Alexander stumbled back again until he was pinned to the edge of his desk. "You are weak because you continue to feed on the humans and Hunters. That only strengthens the pox that blights us."

"You are wrong," Alexander replied, wild-eyed from the euphoria of his feeding and fear of the power imprisoning him against his desk.

"You forget the ways of our people. We were stronger when we worked to gather energy," Christopher chastised.

Shaking his head in denial, his father increased the size of the web ensnaring Christopher's field of power.

"You see. I am stronger," Alexander said, and as Christopher watched, the red rash along his father's neck slowly faded.

With a sharp mental command, Christopher jerked away his power, severing the connection with his father, who slumped against his desk, obviously weakened by the disruption.

"The problem with your way, Alexander, is that eventually either you run out of people to drain or they revolt."

With a sidelong glance at Ryan and then at Maya, Christopher gestured with a flick of his hand to the door. "I will not challenge you, Father. But I cannot allow my people to follow this path to ruin."

He strode to the door, Ryan at his back, protecting him. When Christopher reached the entrance, he paused to look toward his father and Maya, who stood hesitantly in the middle of the room, glancing from his father to him, as if trying to decide with whom to cast her fate.

"Maya?" he questioned, having no delusions that his fiancée would make her choice out of love. She was his mate solely because she was the most powerful female in their clan and nearly at her Equinox, as was he. When that peak came, a mating between them would heighten their power and bring forth even more powerful children to ensure the continuation of their Shadow Hunter clan.

He had no need to wait for Maya to make a choice. He walked out of the room with Ryan. In the hall outside his father's office, the remaining members of their respective cadres waited.

Christopher inspected his men and women, aware that he would be asking them to make a difficult choice. Go with him and they would likely be banished from the clan. To a people who often relied on their collective energies to sustain them, exile was almost like death.

And yet Christopher had no doubt that continuing down the path on which his father was leading the clan would be their downfall. Those who chose to follow Christopher would return to the old ways of their people. He was certain that would not only make each of them more powerful in his or her own right, but lift the prospects of all within the clan.

"Do you go with me?" he asked his people after his father's cadre members had stepped back into Alexander's office and closed the door.

One by one the members of his cadre lined up before him. Almost in unison they dipped their heads and raised their right hands to their chests. In a chorus of powerful and united voices, they said, "We live to serve, Añaru."

Christopher glanced at Ryan and Maya, who left his side and came to stand before him. As the others had done before, they saluted him and repeated the vow.

Christopher walked from one Hunter to another, shaking hands and clapping their backs, acknowledging the trust they had placed in him and the sacrifice they had made. When he was done, he stepped before them once again. With a regal nod, he said, "Let us leave the past. Our future awaits."

Christopher's one hope was that the future would be peaceful, but knowing his father, that was unlikely.

THE DISH

Where authors give you the inside scoop!

♥ ♥ ♥ ♥ ♥ ♥ ♥ ♥ ♥ ♥ ♥ ♥ ♥ ♥ ♥

From the desk of Caridad Piñeiro

Dear Readers,

I want to thank all of you who have been writing to tell me how much you've been loving the Carrera family, as well as enjoying the towns along the Jersey Shore where the series is set.

With THE LOST, I'm introducing a much darker paranormal series I'm calling *Sin Hunters*. The stories are still set along the Jersey Shore and you'll have the beloved Carreras, but now you'll also get to meet an exciting new race of people: The Light and Shadow Hunters.

Why the change? There was something about Bobbie Carrera, the heroine in THE LOST, that needed something different and something very special. Some*one* very special. Bobbie is an Iraq war veteran and she's home from battle, but wounded both physically and emotionally. She's busy trying to put her world back together and the last thing she needs is more conflict in her life.

But I'm a bad girl, you know. I love to challenge my characters into facing their most extreme hurts because doing so only makes their happiness that much sweeter. I think readers love that as well because there is nothing more uplifting than seeing how love can truly conquer all.

Bobbie's challenge comes in the form of sexy millionaire Adam Bruno. Adam is different from any man she has ever met and Bobbie feels an immediate connection to him. There's just one problem: Adam has no idea who he really is and why he possesses the ability to gather energy. That ability allows him to do a myriad of things; from shape-shifting to traveling at super speed, to wielding energy and light like weapons. But these powers are challenging for Adam: as his abilities grow stronger, they also become deadly and increasingly difficult to control.

Enter Bobbie Carrera. Bobbie brings peace to Adam's soul. Adam feels lost in the human world, but in Bobbie's arms he finds love, acceptance, and the possibility for a future he had never imagined.

But before he can reach that future, he must deal with the present, and that means battling the evil Shadow Hunters and facing the shocking truth about his real identity.

I hope you will enjoy the *Sin Hunters* series. Look for THE CLAIMED in May 2012, which will feature someone you meet in THE LOST. Not going to spill who it is just yet, but keep in mind I just love stories of redemption. . . .

Thank you all for your continued support. Also, many thanks to our military men and women, and their families for safeguarding our liberty and our country. THE LOST is dedicated to you for all the sacrifices you make on our behalf. God bless you and keep you safe.

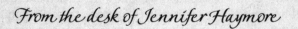

From the desk of Jennifer Haymore

Dear Reader,

When Serena Donovan, the heroine of CONFESSIONS OF AN IMPROPER BRIDE (on sale now), entered my office to ask me to write her story, I realized right away that

I was in trouble. Obviously, there was something pretty heavy resting on this woman's shoulders.

After I'd offered her a chair and a stiff drink (which she eyed warily—as if she's never seen a martini before!), I asked her why she had come.

"I have a problem," she said.

I tried not to chuckle. It was obvious from the permanent look of panic in her eyes that she had a very big problem indeed. "Okay," I said, "what's the problem?"

"Well—" She swallowed hard. "I'm going to get married."

I raised a brow. "Usually that's reason for celebration."

"Not for me." Her voice was dour.

I took a deep breath. "Look, Miss Donovan. I'm a romance writer. I write about love, blissful marriages, and happy endings. Maybe you've come to the wrong place." I rose from my chair and gestured toward the door. "Thanks for stopping by. Feel free to take the martini."

Her eyes flared wide with alarm. "No! Please . . . let me explain."

I hesitated, staring down at her. She seemed so . . . desperate. I guess I have a bleeding heart after all. Sighing, I resumed my seat. "Go ahead."

"I do respect and admire my future husband. Greatly. He's a wonderful man."

"Uh-huh."

"But, you see, he—" She winced, swallowed, and took a deep breath. "Well, he thinks I'm someone else."

I frowned. "You mean, you told him you were someone you're not?"

"Well, it's not that simple. You see, he fell in love with my sister."

"O . . . kay."

Her eyes went glassy. "But, you see, my sister died. Only he doesn't know that. He thinks I'm my sister!"

"He can't tell that you're not her?"

"I don't know . . ." Her voice was brimming with despair.

"You see, we're identical twins, so on the outside we're alike, but we are such different people . . ."

Oh, man. This chick was in big trouble. "And you want to fashion a happy ending out of this, how?" I asked.

"But I haven't told you the whole problem," she said.

I thought she'd given me a pretty darned enormous problem already. Still, I waved my hand for her to elaborate.

"Jonathan," she said simply.

"Jonathan?"

"The Earl of Stratford. He's a friend of my fiancé and the best man," she explained. She looked away. "And also, he's the only man I've ever—"

"That's okay," I said quickly, raising my hand, "I get it."

She released a relieved breath as I studied her. I really, really wanted to help her. She needed help, that was for sure. But how to forge a happy ending out of such a mess?

"Look," I said, flipping up my laptop and opening a new document, "you need to tell me everything, okay? From the beginning."

And that was how it began. By the time Miss Donovan finished telling me her story, I was so hooked, I had to go into my writing cave and write the entire, wild tale. The hardest part was getting to that happy ending, but it was so happy and so romantic that it was worth every drop of blood and sweat that it took to get there.

I truly hope you enjoy reading Serena Donovan's story! Please come visit me at my website, www.jenniferhaymore.com, where you can share your thoughts about my books, sign up for some fun freebies, and read more about the characters from CONFESSIONS OF AN IMPROPER BRIDE.

Sincerely,

Jenny Haymore

♥ ♥ ♥ ♥ ♥ ♥ ♥ ♥ ♥ ♥ ♥ ♥ ♥ ♥ ♥ ♥

From the desk of Sue-Ellen Welfonder

Dear Reader,

Does a landscape of savage grandeur make your heart beat faster? Do jagged peaks, cold-glittering boulders, and cauldrons of boiling mist speak to your soul? Are you exhilarated by the rush of chill wind, the power of ancient places made of stone and legend?

I love such places.

TEMPTATION OF A HIGHLAND SCOUNDREL, second book in my Highland Warriors trilogy, has a truly grand setting. Nought is my favorite corner of the Glen of Many Legends, home to the series' three warring clans. These proud Highlanders prove "where you live is who you are."

Kendrew Mackintosh and Isobel Cameron love wild places as much as I do. Kendrew boasts that he's hewn of Nought's soaring granite peaks and that he was weaned on cold wind and blowing mist. He's proud of his Norse heritage. Isobel shares his appreciation for Viking culture, rough terrain, and long, dark nights. She stirs his passion, igniting desires that brand them both.

But Isobel is a lady.

And Kendrew has sworn not to touch a woman of gentle birth. Isobel is also the sister of a bitter foe.

They're a perfect match despite the barriers separating them: centuries of clan feuds, hostility, and rivalries. Bad blood isn't easily forgotten in the Highlands and grudges last forever. Kendrew refuses to acknowledge his attraction to Isobel. She won't ignore the passion between them. As only a woman in love can, she employs all her seductive wiles to win his heart.

The temptation of Kendrew Mackintosh begins deep in his rugged Nought territory. In the shadows of mysterious cairns known as dreagan stones and on the night of his clan's raucous Midsummer Eve revels, Isobel pitches a battle Kendrew can only lose. Yet surrender will bring greater rewards than he's ever claimed.

Kendrew does open his heart to Isobel, but they soon find themselves caught in a dangerous maelstrom that threatens their love and could cost their lives. The entire glen is at peril and a brutal foe will stop at nothing to crush the brave men of the Glen of Many Legends.

Turning Kendrew loose on his enemy—a worthy villain—gave me many enjoyable writing hours. He's a fierce fighter and a sight to behold when riled. But beneath his ferocity is a great-hearted man who lives by honor.

Writing Isobel was an equal joy. Like me, she feels most alive in wild, windswept places. I know Nought approved of her.

Places do have feelings.

Highlanders know that. In wild places, the pulse beat of the land is strong. I can't imagine a better setting for Kendrew and Isobel.

I hope you'll enjoy watching Isobel prove to Kendrew that the hardest warrior can't win against a woman wielding the most powerful weapon of all: a heart that loves.

With all good wishes,

Sue-Ellen Welfonder

www.welfonder.com

❤ ❤ ❤ ❤ ❤ ❤ ❤ ❤ ❤ ❤ ❤ ❤ ❤ ❤ ❤ ❤

From the desk of Sophie Gunn

Dear Reader,

Some small-town romances feature knitting clubs, some cookie clubs, and some quilting clubs. But my new series has something else entirely.

Welcome to Galton, New York, home of the Enemy Club.

The Enemy Club is made up of four women who had been the worst of enemies back in high school. They were the class brainiac, the bad girl, the princess, and the outcast. Now, all grown up, they've managed to become the best of friends. But they're friends with a difference. They've promised to tell one another the truth, the whole truth, and nothing but the truth so help them Gracie (the baker of the pies at the Last Chance Diner). Because they see things from their very (very!) different points of view, this causes all sorts of conflicts and a nuanced story, where no one has a lock on what's right or wrong.

In *Sweet Kiss of Summer*, Nina Stokes is the woman with the problem, and she's going to need everyone's help to solve it. Her brother lost his life in the war. On his deathbed, he asked a nurse to write Nina a letter, instructing her to give his house back in Galton to his war buddy, Mick Rivers.

Or did he?

How can Nina know if the letter is real or a con? And even if it's real, where has Mick been for the past two years, during which Nina tried everything to contact him to no avail? How long should she be expected to keep up the house in this limbo, waiting for a man who obviously takes her brother's last wish lightly?

So when a beautiful man claiming to be Mick roars up Nina's driveway one summer afternoon in a flashy red car, demanding the house that he feels is rightfully his, every member of the Enemy Club thinks that she knows best what Nina should do. Naturally, none of them agree. The themes of friendship, duty, and honor run deep in Galton, and in *Sweet Kiss of Summer*, they are all tested. To whom do we owe our first duty: our family, our friends, our country—or ourselves?

What I loved most about writing *Sweet Kiss of Summer* was that there was no easy solution for anyone. As I wrote, I had no idea what Nina would do about her dilemma. Mick struggled with an even thornier problem, as his secrets were bigger than anyone in the Enemy Club could imagine. I could understand everyone's point of view. There is just so much to consider when you're not only out for yourself, but for your country, your community, your family, and ultimately, something even bigger.

I hope you'll enjoy reading about these characters as much as I've enjoyed writing about them. Come visit me at SophieGunn.com to learn more about the small town of Galton and the Enemy Club, to see pictures of my kitties, and to keep in touch. I'd love to hear from you!

Sophie Gunn

www.sophiegunn.com

Find out more about Forever Romance!

Visit us at
www.hachettebookgroup.com/publishing_forever.aspx

Find us on Facebook
http://www.facebook.com/ForeverRomance

Follow us on Twitter
http://twitter.com/ForeverRomance

NEW AND UPCOMING TITLES

Each month we feature our new titles
and reader favorites.

CONTESTS AND GIVEAWAYS

We give away galleys, autographed copies,
and all kinds of exclusive items.

AUTHOR INFO

You'll find bios, articles, and links to personal websites
for all your favorite authors—and so much more.

GET SOCIAL

Connect with your favorite authors, editors, and
other Forever fans, and share what's important to you.

THE BUZZ

Sign up for our monthly romance newsletter,
and be the first to read all about it.